I was alone in a narrow space between tall shipping containers. I heard a shoe scraping along the pavement. Was there a person in the next aisle over? *You're being foolish*, I told myself. *There are hundreds of people here. Why shouldn't someone else be walking among the production trucks?*

Still, the uncomfortable feeling persisted. My mind began to visualize ugly scenarios. The countryside surrounding the airport was deceiving. It was not just a pretty rural airfield. It was the site of a recent homicide. The people who worked on the film were not just friendly visitors who happened to be production professionals. There was a murderer among them. Perhaps Vera wasn't the only one to provoke violence. Could this person suspect I was seeking information to flush him or her out? My association with the sheriff surely would not have gone unnoticed. Although I had to assume that the people from Hollywood were, for the most part, unaware of my previous involvement with investigating murders, an exception was certainly possible. Someone in town could have spread a rumor that Jessica Fletcher was at it again. It wouldn't have been a rumor, though. It was the truth. Seth always warned me I would get myself in trouble.

Close-up on Murder

A *Murder, She Wrote* Mystery

A NOVEL BY

JESSICA FLETCHER & DONALD BAIN

**Based on the Universal Television series created by
Peter S. Fischer, Richard Levinson & William Link**

AN OBSIDIAN MYSTERY

OBSIDIAN
Published by the Penguin Group
Penguin Group (USA) LLC, 375 Hudson Street,
New York, New York 10014

USA | Canada | UK | Ireland | Australia | New Zealand | India | South Africa | China
penguin.com
A Penguin Random House Company

Published by Obsidian, an imprint of New American Library, a division of Penguin Group (USA) LLC. Previously published in an Obsidian hardcover edition.

First Obsidian Mass Market Printing, September 2014

ISBN 978-0-451-46525-2

Printed in the United States of America
10   9   8   7   6   5   4   3   2

With gratitude and appreciation to literary agent Bob Diforio. We look forward to a long and fruitful relationship.

ACKNOWLEDGMENTS

No book exists in a vacuum, and there are always those to thank. Since we are avid Internet researchers, we are grateful to all those who have so generously posted information online on practically any topic in the world. Credit also goes to the *New York Times*, our daily accompaniment to coffee and breakfast, and within the pages of which we always find ideas. We are indebted to a dear friend, who shall remain nameless, who shared his astrological charts with us. And often unstated but never forgotten, we are grateful to the crack editorial team at Obsidian, Sandra Harding, Talia Platz, and Kerry Donovan. Thank you all.

Chapter One

Hollywood, California

"You should be flattered that she chose to play the character from your book," the executive producer, Terrence Chattergee, told me. "Vera Stockdale has been offered many plum parts over the years." His eyes roamed the room even as he addressed his comments to me. "But none of them were up to her standards." Chattergee was a handsome man with a dusky complexion and thick black hair going gray at the temples. He had made a name for himself as a producer in what was then Bombay, and had brought his Bollywood sensibility to California with great success.

"For some reason she took a liking to your story," Chattergee continued, sending a smile and raised eyebrows to the director, who'd just entered the room. "Vera is very particular."

I was in Hollywood to attend a read-through of a

screenplay Chattergee was producing. It was based upon one of my mystery novels, *A Deadly Decision*. I had developed the story using a real-life incident that had taken place in Cabot Cove about half a dozen years ago. A local judge, Ruth Harris, had ruled against a husband in a custody case. The husband, a man with a hair-trigger temper, had denounced Judge Harris in the courtroom and warned of retribution. A week later, while the judge was out walking her dog, she was shot in the back by an assailant. There were no apparent witnesses other than the dog, but the spotlight of investigation shone brightly on the angry husband and his threats against the judge's life. When it was determined that the man had a solid alibi, the focus shifted to the judge's husband, Neil Corday, a shady attorney with a string of lawsuits against him. He had been playing footsie with a waitress at a local café, among other women. Although I'd been skeptical, evidence piled up against the waitress, Jenny Kipp, who'd reacted with fury when the marriage proposal she'd expected from the judge's husband never materialized. She confronted Corday—and his new lover, Tiffany Parker—with a gun, the very weapon, it turned out, that had been used to shoot his wife, the judge. Jenny Kipp was convicted and sent away for life.

Vera Stockdale, who was playing the judge, had been a big star decades earlier and had come out of retirement to take this role.

"She wouldn't accept just any part," Chattergee said. "She wanted one with gravitas and a chance to show her dramatic range."

The lady under discussion sat halfway down a long

rectangular table. Her platinum mane was styled in a smooth pageboy, not a hair out of place, and she wore a pink cashmere sweater set and rhinestone-adorned black-framed eyeglasses attached to a gold chain, which rattled against the table as she leaned over to peer at her lines in the open script in front of her. In one arm she held her Chihuahua; the other rested on a book, *Famous Actors' Famous Monologues*, that she'd been hugging to her chest when she arrived. It should have warned me of what was to come.

"So, here we are, Jessica Fletcher," Chattergee said, "about to make a movie of your book."

"I'm delighted to be here," I said. "Thank you for inviting me. I look forward to seeing Ms. Stockdale in the role."

Without bothering to respond to me beyond a grunt, he turned abruptly, walked along the table, and placed himself in a chair opposite the star and next to the director.

Frankly, I didn't see how the role of the judge served as an especially good opportunity for the actress's triumphant return to the silver screen—after all, she gets murdered in the first half of the story—but I knew enough from past experience with movie productions not to question the opinion of the executive producer, at least not to his face.

The case had been prosecuted in Cabot Cove, and the state of Maine offered production companies financial incentives to film there, so the Hollywood types were going to shoot "on location" and make our town a giant set. But before the production moved to the East Coast, the cast and principal production executives had gathered in Hollywood for a preliminary review of the script, and I was among them.

"Not exactly the hail-fellow-well-met type, is he?" said Hamilton Twomby, the screenwriter, who had introduced me to Chattergee. "But as an executive producer, he's done okay. We should be in good hands."

Twomby and I had worked on the script long-distance, mostly by e-mail, occasionally by phone. More precisely, he'd written the script based upon my book, and I, as "script consultant," was permitted to review it and to make suggestions. Not that many of my suggestions had found their way onto the page. It would be easy to chalk it up to difficult communications. "Ham," as Twomby was called, didn't have a landline telephone, so our conversations often began with "Can you hear me now?"

Twomby smoothed a hand over his mouth and left it there. "Vera, on the other hand, is a diva," he said in a low voice. "At least she was before she retired. Should be interesting to see if the leopardess has changed her spots. If she's really itching to get back in the game, maybe she'll be more accommodating than she was when she had top billing." He waved at a tall woman with a mass of curly hair. "I have to say hello to someone," he said. "I'll be right back."

Vera hadn't spoken to me herself—she'd merely nodded when we were introduced—but her personal astrologer was eager to assure me that the movie was the "perfect property" to relaunch the career of the former star. "I have studied her chart," Estelle Fancy confided as the rest of the cast and production company officials filed into the room and took seats at the table. "She has a close alignment of intellect and self-expression. Her high ability to transmute ideas, inspiration, and artistic potentials into actualities will carry her through."

"That sounds impressive," I said. "Have you told Ms. Stockdale?"

"Oh, yes. She knows I endorse this venture. Venus is approaching retrograde and is slowing down. It's an auspicious time for her to advance her goals, also an incredible chance for major healing and forgiveness. I advised her to go forward, and I'm to accompany her on location. I doubt she would have done it without my approval or, for that matter, at another time in the universe." Before I could come up with an appropriate response, she drifted away like some ghostly apparition and took one of the chairs lined up along the wall for those not invited to sit at the table.

"Don't you just love that baloney?" a deep voice murmured in my ear.

I turned sharply to face the smile of actor Walter Benson, the male lead in the film, who was playing the judge's husband.

"Vera's astrologer has been trying to get her a part for years," he said, winking at me. "No one was interested."

"I wasn't aware that finding roles for clients was the responsibility of an astrologer," I said.

"It is if you want to get paid. Ms. Fancy, Vera's resident stargazer, finally hit the jackpot with Chattergee. Rumor has it that our esteemed producer owes Vera a fortune in back child support, and paid Ms. Fancy a handsome sum to persuade our star to accept the role and drop her claim against him as a deadbeat dad. Not that he doesn't have the money. But he knew Vera would be willing to let him off easy for a starring role."

"They've been divorced for years, if I remember correctly," I said. "Aren't their children adults?"

"Child. Yes, she must be by now. Awkward little thing—at least she was before they shipped her off to boarding school. But while the battle is over, the war rages on."

"And how do you know this?"

"Oh, my darling girl," he said, holding out a chair and bowing toward me, "inside knowledge is the coin of the realm in Hollywood."

"I'll keep that in mind in case I'm ever in the market for some ready cash," I said, acknowledging his gesture by sitting down.

Benson took a seat next to Vera, picked up her book on monologues, and began leafing through it. I mulled over what I knew about him. He was a virile leading man who'd spent most of his time on-screen with his shirt off. At least that was my impression from having seen a few of his early films. The screenwriter had made a snide comment about Benson's being typecast as the philandering husband of the judge—"His most bankable asset is a strong jaw and a sculptured set of pectoral muscles, although he's getting rather long in the tooth for bare-chested roles," Twomby had said. The Hollywood business magazine *Variety* had reported that it had taken numerous auditions and screen tests for Benson before he'd won the role. I'd shown the article to Twomby when I arrived.

The screenwriter squeezed himself into the chair next to mine. He was a hefty man with a thin mustache and a narrow beard that ran along his jawline, leaving his cheeks clean-shaven. "Benson should be grateful he's here," Twomby said, continuing his catty comments about the actor. "His acting abilities were never in question, but his penchant for pursuing every would-be starlet here in La-La-Land almost scuttled his chances for the role."

"I wouldn't think that was so unusual in Hollywood," I said.

"Oh, it isn't at all, if you're subtle about it, or even if you're not. However, on Benson's last film, several production assistants charged him with sexual harassment."

"Oh, dear, that's certainly not good."

"There's nothing quite like a lawsuit to cast an actor in a poor light with producers who want to keep a tight fist on the budget—and that's all of them."

"How did Benson get into their better graces?"

"That's the good part," Twomby said, lowering his voice again, although it was doubtful anyone could overhear us above the buzz of conversation filling the room. "His agent maneuvered two glitzy magazines into putting him on their covers. Even bad publicity has a positive effect on an actor, especially when his prowess in private matters translates to profits at the box office."

Chattergee tapped his coffee mug to attract the group's attention and to start the meeting. I decided on the spot that the gossip shared by Benson and Twomby, while grist for the tabloids, was not an area in which I was especially interested or even comfortable, and I resolved to do everything in my power not to contribute to the movie business rumor mill.

Not an easy resolution to stick to when "surrounded" by Hollywood.

"I have a complaint," Vera said, once the room had quieted.

"Yes, Ms. Stockdale," the producer said, addressing his ex-wife.

"I don't like this scene on page fifteen."

There was a rustle of papers as everyone turned to that page.

"What's wrong with the scene?" The question came from Mitchell Elovitz, the director.

Vera shifted her dog from her right hand to her left so she could point at the page. "Frankly, this dialogue feels insipid and unfinished. You're talking about a sitting judge. Wouldn't someone in her position have more to say when the district attorney is making his case?"

"Want to give us an example of what you mean, Vera?" Elovitz said.

"I know this is only your second—is it?—film, Mr. Elovitz," she replied, "but even you should be able to see that the judge should be expressing her dismay at the husband's behavior, lecturing him on what it means to be a good father and how he should conduct himself." The actress pulled her glasses down her nose and sent a withering glance in Chattergee's direction. "In addition, we need an internal monologue here to fill out her character," she said, her right hand now resting on her book. "Something meaty and with meaning. I will not portray someone who is wishy-washy, and that's what I see on the page."

"I think the scene is fine as it is," Chattergee said. He

looked around the room for confirmation, but avoided Vera's gaze.

"Let's let the screenwriter comment," Elovitz said. "Ham? What do you have to say?"

Twomby shifted in his seat. "I . . . I don't know," he replied. "That's not what the scene calls for." He frowned as he ran his index finger down the page, scanning the lines. "Ah," I heard him say and his face brightened. "Actually this dialogue came straight from the book. I didn't change a word here." He sat back with a smile.

All eyes in the room focused on me. *Oh, boy!* I thought, mentally calculating how the scene had played out in real life and whether I had missed something in my dramatization of it.

"Mrs. Fletcher, would you like to add anything?" Elovitz asked.

"I would," I said. "Some of the dialogue in my novel, as in this case, was lifted from the actual trial transcript. But in general, a judge doesn't make a lot of comments while a trial is ongoing. She rules on objections and may clarify a point of law, but she is supposed to be *listening* to both parties so she can make a fair judgment at the appropriate time."

"I have to do more than just *listen*," Vera said. "I'm not coming out of retirement just to listen." A low growl came from her dog, as if echoing her annoyance.

"I understand," I said, "but the judge usually reserves her comments until she delivers her decision. I think you'll find she shares her opinions quite eloquently later on in the script."

"I don't care what she *usually* does. I want her to be

eloquent right from the beginning," Vera said, glaring at me. "I don't see her personality coming through here." She closed the script. "If I'm to play this role, I need to have more background on this woman, her likes, dislikes, the way she thinks about her position and its importance in the courtroom. I expect that to be added here." She thumped her palm on the script, and switched her gaze to Chattergee. "It's ridiculous to expect me to play this part as it's written. Brannigan has more lines in this movie than I do, for crying out loud. And she's just the tart who's cheating with the judge's husband."

"I don't have more lines than you," said Lois Brannigan, who was playing the mistress, and who sat three seats down from Vera. "But I'd be delighted to switch roles if you're not happy."

"Don't think I wasn't informed that you coveted my part, dearie," Vera said acidly. "But you don't have the box office value I do. And you never will. The role of the judge was written for me, and I'm keeping it. But I want Twomby and Fletcher to bulk it up."

"We'll work on strengthening the part, Ms. Stockdale," Twomby said, frantically scribbling notes to himself in the margin of the script.

"See that you do. I'll expect a better version by the end of the day." She rose, taking her dog and her book with her, and left the script on the table.

Chapter Two

Mort Metzger stuck his head in the door and called to me. "Mrs. F., you've got to do something. This is a disaster!"

"I'll be right with you, Mort," I shouted over the racket of pounding sledgehammers and splintering wood. I turned back to Loretta Spiegel, who clutched my hand tightly.

"I tell you, Jessica, it's very exciting, but I'm not sure about the changes they want," she said. "What if I don't like it in the end?" Loretta looked around as a crew of carpenters dismantled the powder-pink room divider in her beauty salon and shouldered the pieces outside—nearly whacking Mort with a curlicue plank of lumber—then tossed them into a Dumpster. I heard our sheriff dressing down the offending parties in his best former New York City police officer language, which I will not repeat here.

"Didn't the set designer tell you they would put it back exactly the way it was if you didn't like their work?" I asked Loretta.

"Yes, but they're never going to be able to duplicate my fancy openwork panels."

"Why not?" I asked.

"The man who carved them retired years ago. I'm not even certain he's still alive."

"Now, Loretta, I'm sure you'll love the new design. You've been saying for years that you wanted to update the decor in the shop. Here's your opportunity. Not only won't it cost you anything, but they're *paying* you to let them use the shop as a set."

"But it's costing me business, Jessica, not to mention wear and tear on my car. Since this place is being torn apart I've had to run all over town to do customers' hair in their homes. You try washing Ideal Malloy's hair in her kitchen sink. She dripped all over the floor. I nearly threw my back out getting her into a chair."

"Mrs. F.! Please," Mort said, stepping into the construction zone.

"Yes, Mort. Just give me a minute."

"I don't have a minute. And there won't be a hair left on my head if you don't corral these movie people. They're causing more traffic jams than the Macy's Thanksgiving Day parade and the president's visit to the UN combined."

"Looking to get yourself a manicure and pedicure, Sheriff?" a carpenter quipped as he manhandled one of Loretta's hair dryers out the door.

"Oh, for the love of . . ." Mort said. "I'll be outside."

"Loretta, try to be patient just a little longer," I said. "I'm sure the shop will be spectacular when they're done."

"But they're making everything black and white," she said. "I was thinking of something more along the line of aqua, you know, to give the shop a spa vibe. All the elegant beauty salons on TV use this stunning color. It's somewhere between Seafoam and Tropical Paradise. Those are the paint colors I had picked out at the hardware store."

"Why don't you talk to the set designer the next time she comes in and tell her how you'd like it to look when they're finished filming?"

Loretta contemplated that idea as her eyes scanned the interior of her shop. "All right," she said. "I guess I can do that."

I could practically hear the wheels turning as she pictured the changes she wanted made. "If they were going to put it back the way it was," she murmured more to herself than to me, "I'll just have to convince them to put it back the way I want it."

"Exactly! And I'm sure you'll succeed," I said, patting her arm. "You're very persuasive. Now, I'd better go before Mort arrests the whole carpentry crew."

I stepped outside Loretta's salon into the bright sunshine to find Mort nervously combing his hair with his fingers and fanning his face with his Stetson. "I'm sorry, Mort," I said. "Loretta needed a bit of hand-holding. She and the set designer have different opinions on how a small-town beauty shop should look. I thought it looked fine just the way it was, but they have other ideas."

"I'm not surprised," he said, escorting me to his patrol car, where the passenger door stood open.

I climbed in.

Mort shut the door, circled around the back of the car, and took his seat behind the wheel, tamping down his hat so that it sat low over his eyes.

"Have you spoken to the director yet?" I asked.

"These movie people don't have the slightest idea what goes on in a small town, and they don't care," Mort said, ignoring my question. "They have me closing streets left and right so they can film and then they don't show up for hours, if at all. The merchants are screaming that their customers can't get into their shops. The mayor won't talk to the big shots at the film company because he says they're bringing lots of business to town. I'd like to see where. They have a caterer, so they don't much use the local restaurants. They brought their own woodworkers. They should've brought their own police. I had to hire on two more deputies just to direct traffic. Not to mention the fact that most of them aren't even staying in town. They're living in trailers out at the airport. How does *that* benefit Cabot Cove?"

"But, Mort, we don't really have any hotels apart from the Blueberry Hill Inn and a few bed-and-breakfast places. Lots of people in town are renting rooms to the crew, including me. I have a young lady staying in my spare bedroom."

"That may be, but the shopkeepers keep dialing nine-one-one when they can't get their cars out at lunchtime, and your director is never available when I call to find out when they'll be finished for the day."

"*My* director? I don't know what you expect me to

do. I don't have any influence. I barely know these people."

"You know them better than I do." He reached into his pocket and popped an antacid into his mouth.

"Are you okay?" I asked.

"My stomach has been doing somersaults ever since they rolled into town," he replied, "and this time it isn't Maureen's cooking."

Maureen was Mort's second wife, a bubbly redhead who was the love of his life. She was an enthusiastic chef and avid fan of the food channels, and loved nothing more than trying out exotic combinations in her cooking. The results were mixed, however. Sometimes the dish she came up with was a winner, but just as often her experiment was more suited to a laboratory than a kitchen. I'd been on the tasting end of both kinds of meals. Nevertheless, Mort, ever the gentleman, almost always praised his wife's efforts.

Mort made a U-turn and took the road leading out to the airport. It was the only place for miles around large enough to accommodate the film company's employees and equipment. If you've been in a movie theater in the past ten years, you know how fast the credits roll at the end of a picture in order to fit in the names of all the people who made a contribution, large or small, to the creation of the final product. That should give you an idea of how many people had arrived in Cabot Cove, swelling our population by a considerable number.

Mort was right about the trailers. The production company must have commandeered every recreational vehicle they could get their hands on in the state of Maine. With all the RVs, the land surrounding the airport resembled the campground at Acadia National Park on Memorial Day weekend.

In addition to separate vehicles for props and for wardrobe, hair, and makeup, the director and the cinematographer each had his own trailer, not to mention those shared by the location manager, assistant location manager, location scout, and assistant. Add another for the executive producer for his occasional visits to the set, and more for the line producer, unit manager, first assistant director, second assistant director, screenwriter, script supervisor, and the casting director, who'd been given the unenviable task of hiring extras for the crowd scenes. It seemed that half of Cabot Cove had sent in a résumé and a head shot. And of course there were mobile homes for the principal actors, Vera Stockdale and Walter Benson, and their respective entourages.

Mort pulled up in front of one of the hangars just as Jed Richardson strolled out, swinging the lanyard that held the key to his Cessna 310.

"Whoa, Jed, where are you off to?" Mort called out, turning off his engine.

Jed ambled over to the car. "Gotta take a run over to Bangor to pick up some electrical thingamajig for Zee over there." He pointed behind him at a muscular, dark-haired man in his thirties wearing shorts and pushing a black case on wheels toward the twin-engine plane. He was followed by a young woman in a cowboy hat and jeans, trying to catch up to him.

"What did you say that guy's name was?" Mort asked.

"Never learned his first name; everyone calls him

Zee. It's short for his last name, some hard to pronounce Spanish name. He's the key grip, the head of the technicians who rig lighting or camera mounts or some other equipment they use in making a movie. Don't ask me. All I know about is plane engines. Anyway, something is malfunctioning and we're going to Bangor to find a replacement part." Jed leaned down to peer into the car. "Well, hello, Jessica," he said. "Didn't see you behind this big guy. Are you planning to go up again?"

"Not today, Jed, but soon, I hope."

He tapped Mort on the shoulder. "Anything I can do for you before I leave?"

"Would you happen to know where we can find Elovitz, the director?" Mort asked.

Jed shook his head. "Maybe Zee knows." He trotted over to where the young couple waited and returned a moment later. "He says try the production office. It's parked near the back door."

"Great! That's a help." Mort caught the young man's attention and called out his thanks. The young woman turned to look our way.

"I think it's Sunny," I said.

"Yeah, the weather's pretty nice," Mort replied.

"No. I mean she's Sunny, Sunny Cee, who's staying in my guest bedroom."

"Cee, Zee," Mort said. "Are all these people named after the alphabet?"

"Sunny!" I called from the car, and waved. She squinted at me from under the brim of her hat. Recognition blossomed on her face. She returned my wave, said something to Zee, and loped over to Mort's car.

"Hi, Mrs. Fletcher. I didn't recognize you at first."

"And I almost didn't recognize you wearing that cowboy hat."

"Oh, this," she said, grinning and taking it off. She ran a hand through her dark shoulder-length hair, fluffing it out. "I stole it from the director. Mitch was wearing it this morning and I took off with it."

"Perhaps you shouldn't admit to that in front of our sheriff," I teased, introducing Mort to Sunny. "Sunny is a production assistant on the film, a PA for short."

"Nice to meet you," Mort said, tipping his own Stetson at her. "What's a PA do?"

"All the things that no one else wants to do," she said, laughing.

"And that includes stealing hats?" he said lightly.

"I didn't really steal it," she said. "I just borrowed it for a while. Mitch and I are friends, at least as much as you can be friends with your boss. I worked on his last film. He was just a nervous newbie then, not the big shot he is now." She giggled.

"Then I take it the film was a big success," Mort said. "Was it his first?"

"Not really—just his first winner. I think his very first film was a bomb, but don't tell him I told you."

"My lips are sealed," Mort said. "So what was his big hit? Would I have seen it?" He turned to me. "Did you see it, Mrs. F.?"

"I'm sure I didn't," I said, shaking my head and laughing.

"You two are not exactly the target audience," Sunny said, winking at me.

"What? I go to the movies," Mort said, affronted.

"I'm sure I've seen it, or at least I've heard of it. What was the name of it?"

"I may be wrong, but I can't imagine you would have seen *Vampire Zombies from Jupiter*."

Mort shook his head. "Never heard of it."

"It did very well," Sunny said.

"Really?" Mort said, his face reflecting his skepticism.

"Enough to get him this picture, although I hear he's getting paid scale. Still, it's a step up."

"Anything would be a step up from vampires and zombies," Mort said.

"You'd be surprised," Sunny told him. "The audience for vampires and zombies and monsters and aliens is very loyal. They'll see a movie they like over and over again. That's why those movies get made. The audience makes up in multiple visits what they lack in numbers."

"Speaking of your boss," I said, "Zee said we could find him in the production office. Do you happen to know which trailer that is?"

"Sure. I can point it out to you."

"Hop in," Mort said.

Sunny climbed into the backseat of the patrol car and Mort started the engine.

We waited while Jed taxied in front of us to the end of the runway.

"I didn't think he was going to be able to fit that big box in that small plane," Mort said, "but it looks like he did."

"The weight may make it unbalanced on takeoff," I said, "but Jed can handle it."

I'd spent a lot of time with Jed Richardson learning

how to fly. Some people think it's funny that I can fly a plane when I can't drive a car, but I've never felt comfortable at the wheel of an automobile the few times I've had that experience. Sitting at the controls of a single-engine airplane, however, is the most natural feeling in the world for me. I love the sense of freedom when the wheels leave the ground and the nose of the plane points up toward the sky. I love to see the countryside spread out below with its beautiful patchwork quilt of farms and towns, rivers and roads. Best of all, I love flying high in the air with nothing nearby that I can possibly crash into.

Jed had been an excellent instructor. A former airline pilot, he'd escaped the pressure-cooker bureaucracy of a major airline and taken early retirement, settling back in Cabot Cove to establish Jed's Flying Service, giving flying lessons and ferrying townspeople to larger cities in his "fleet" of three planes, two single-engine and one twin-engine craft.

"I wish I could have gone with them," Sunny said, as we watched Jed's plane lift into the air. "Zee said there wasn't enough room inside for both me *and* the camera-mount case, and the camera-mount case is more important."

"Couldn't get *me* up in one of those," Mort commented as he swung the squad car around and drove to the back of the hangar. "I like to have a lot of steel between me and the thin air up there, like in a big commercial jet, the bigger the better."

"I don't know, Mort," I said. "I imagine it's the difference between sitting behind the wheel of a truck and driving a motorcycle. You like motorcycles. I think you'd enjoy flying in a small plane."

"Yeah? Well, maybe I'll give it a whirl one of these days, but don't hold your breath."

Sunny directed us to park next to a line of golf carts the movie company used for local transportation around the airfield.

"There's the production office," she said, indicating a green trailer. She exited the car and donned her—or rather Elovitz's—hat. "Nice to meet you, Sheriff. See you later, Mrs. Fletcher."

"Cute kid," Mort said as she sauntered off.

"She's been a delight," I said. "I've never had a more cheerful houseguest."

"Maybe that's why she's called Sunny."

The production office was a windowless trailer the size of a moving van, with several narrow sets of metal steps leading up to doors. Mort knocked at the first one and turned the knob when a voice called, "Enter."

The director, Mitchell Elovitz, was wearing a telephone headset and holding an unlit cigar. He was seated at a small square table across from two other members of the production team, Nicole Domash, the script supervisor, a lady with thick curly brown hair caught back with a headband, and the cameraman, Jason Griffin, whose official title was director of photography. They were huddled over a storyboard, a large placard on which Elovitz had outlined a scene to be filmed the next day. It looked like a page from a giant comic book with comments under each panel, and arrows indicating the camera angle and POV ("point of view" to us novices). In one panel, a photograph of the star, Vera Stockdale, replaced the black-and-white sketches that were typically shown elsewhere on the board.

"With you in a minute," Elovitz said, glancing up briefly.

"That seems to be the song of the day," Mort muttered as he leaned against a wall.

Beyond the small table was a television set on a rolling cart, with a black hood draped on three sides to block the glare. Behind the TV were two long desks with what looked like computer monitors arrayed in a row on top of elaborate consoles with as many buttons and toggles as the cockpit of a 747. The desk closest to us also held an open cooler of sodas and beer, and a large platter of food covered in pink cellophane.

"Help yourself to a snack," Elovitz said, raising a can of Coke in our direction. "There are drinks, sandwiches—tuna wrap and roast beef, I think—and side salads."

"No, thank you," I replied. "I've had my lunch."

"I might try something," Mort said, using his index finger to nudge aside the cellophane. He lifted out a half sandwich and took a bite. "Definitely turkey," he said around a mouthful.

Elovitz shrugged and turned back to his colleagues, pointing to a panel with his cigar and telling the cameraman, "Jase, I want the camera on the crane to start from a bird's-eye view of the scene and then close in on the dog on the floor, move up the judge's robes to her face, nice and slow so you don't know what you're going to see."

"I hope the wrangler brings the right dog," Jase replied, "not the yappy one. It can't hold a pose for more than five seconds."

"Get Sunny to call him."

"You may have to move the lamp on the judge's desk to get the right angle," said Domash, the script supervisor, making a quick sketch on her pad in red marker to show the men where the lamp was located. "I'm afraid that wide shade will get in the way."

Loud rock music sounded from Elovitz's pocket and he yelled into his headset, "Answer phone." Conversation ceased while the director took his call. "Who? What? I don't care about that. Tell Sunny to call Butch. We need the white dog for tomorrow, the one that's laid-back. No, not the Chihuahua. That's Vera's dog. I don't care if it's back home already. Tell him to get it."

"We've barely started the scene yet, Nic," the cameraman said in a low voice. "Why can't we get props to put in a different lamp, one that's narrower?"

"The production designer said he wanted the set to be an exact duplicate of the judge's office, Jase. Besides, I'm not sure we can get a substitute lamp by tomorrow," Domash whispered back.

"I think we can cheat on a lamp, if props can find the right one," Elovitz said, stroking what looked like a three-day-old beard.

Domash looked up with surprise. "Sorry, Mitch," she said. "I didn't realize you were off the phone."

"Go see what you can do so I can talk to these people," Elovitz said, cocking his head at Mort and me. He pushed up the sleeve of his bush jacket to check the time, glancing down at a heavy gold watch with a green dial and a black bezel. "Meet me back here after the dinner break and we'll finish up."

His colleagues gathered up their notes and left. Elovitz set his storyboard on the floor in front of a stack of others, tucked his cigar into his breast pocket, and stood. He wore a pair of brown tooled cowboy boots that matched the hat Sunny had pinched, and tan cargo shorts, an unusual combination even for Hollywood, and certainly for Maine. Holding up a finger to keep us from talking, he pulled his cell phone from the pocket of his shorts, checked for messages, and returned a call. Eventually, he tucked the phone back into his pocket, then gave us a friendly smile.

"Mrs. Fletcher, Sheriff Metzger," he said, lifting a booted foot onto his chair and resting his arm on his knee. "How can I help you?"

"I don't want you to think we're trying to put a Popsicle stick in your gears," Mort began. He's fond of coming up with sayings like that; I hadn't heard that particular one before. "We want to cooperate. But my men had to close off three streets this morning." He looked at Elovitz for a reaction.

"Good. That was good."

"Good for you, maybe," Mort continued, building up steam as he vented his irritation. "The traffic downtown was snarled for hours, the schools had to start an hour late because the bus routes had changed, the merchants are about to string me up on the nearest lamppost because their customers can't get to the stores, and then, to top it off, no one showed up to do any filming. It was all for nothing."

Elovitz put his hands up as if warding off an attack. "I can understand your frustration, Sheriff, but I can promise you that everything we do is done for a reason."

"Well, I'd like to know the reason the streets had to be closed for so many hours when you didn't even use them."

"We used them the night before last. We were downtown shooting until one in the morning."

"I'm talking about today," Mort said.

"My crew has to sleep sometime," Elovitz said. "Just kidding," he added when Mort's expression said he was not amused. "Look, it's really simple." Elovitz smiled sweetly, as if explaining his rationale to a child. "We were set up on Main Street this morning, but the sun was at the wrong angle, causing a glare in the camera. We had to delay filming. I can move jet planes and freight trains, and even mountains when necessary, but even I can't move the clouds and the sun."

I wondered why the director didn't decide simply to change the position of the camera, but I kept quiet. It was pointless to debate "creative" decisions.

Elovitz continued. "When it comes to weather, we just have to wait for the right time."

"And the right time never came?" Mort said, tossing his hat from one hand to the other, a clear sign of aggravation.

"We had some problems," Elovitz conceded, taking his foot off the chair. "We try to be efficient with our crew, so we started filming a different scene. There were wardrobe malfunctions."

"Wardrobe malfunctions?" Mort said, his brows rising to his hairline. "I thought those only happened on TV during football games."

"Everything had to be put on hold while the wardrobe mistress found a pair of pants to match the ones that got stains on them when the actor spilled a bowl of cereal and milk all over himself." Elovitz shrugged and held out his hands, palms up. "These things will happen. It's annoying but not tragic. You understand, I'm sure. We'll be back on Main Street tomorrow at two, providing it doesn't rain, of course."

"Oh, that's not so bad," Mort said, relaxing. "The weather report calls for another clear day. And at least I can have my men let the traffic through in the morning so the school buses can make their pickups."

"I'm afraid not, Sheriff. Once the location has been roped off, we can't let anyone in. If we do, we'll have problems of continuity. And not only that—we had a devil of a time getting your citizens to vacate the property. That's why we had to work so late. My production assistants were forced to do a sweep of the area. They rousted some old nut trying to stop the shoot, ranting about how we were ruining everything. One lady stuck her head in the scene just as the clapper clapped the sticks. That costs us time and money. No, we have to have the area cleared well in advance."

"There's nothing you can do to make this a little easier on the sheriff's department?" I asked. "He's been a model of cooperation with you. He just wants a little consideration."

Elovitz stuck out his hand. "Sheriff, if I can do anything to help you, I promise I'll make my best effort."

Mort took his hand and shook it. "I appreciate that,

but I'm sorry to have to tell you, I think the mayor is going to have a conniption. This whole movie deal is interrupting the smooth running of the town. I really think he's going to have something to say about it." He tipped his head to the side and smiled. "Just letting you know."

"Mayor Shevlin?" Elovitz said, barely resisting a smirk. "Met with him this morning. He loves us. We promised to put him front and center in one of the crowd scenes."

Chapter Three

Like a Las Vegas gambler, Mort Metzger knew when to fold his cards. He thanked the young director for his time, asking only that Elovitz try to limit the inconveniences he was causing.

In response, the director turned on the charm, offering to give Mort and me a tour of the "soundstage" in the hangar that was the scene of the next day's shoot. "Give me a minute and I'll meet you there."

We left him in the production office yelling into his headset, "Call Nicole."

"Bet you a stack of pancakes at Mara's that that's a Rolex he's got up his sleeve," Mort said as we walked toward the hangar.

"I won't take that bet," I said, "but I'll treat you to pancakes anytime you like."

"Yeah? How come?"

"I think you conducted yourself admirably back there," I said. "You explained the situation, told him the problems he was causing, and you knew when it was futile to fight. There's no use in banging your head against the wall."

"I know."

"You retired from the arena gracefully."

"Yeah, well, at least I got to state my case," he said. "By the way, was that Judge Borden's office that they were talking about back there?"

"I believe so," I replied.

Jacob Borden was a local jurist and an old friend. When the production designer had asked me if I knew of any judge's rooms in town where they might be able to film, I'd suggested they get in touch with Jacob. His downtown office occupied an old Victorian house, complete with egg-and-dart crown molding and beautiful wainscoted walls, visible where they weren't covered by floor-to-ceiling bookcases holding matched sets of leather-bound volumes on the law.

The production designer had fallen in love with Jacob's office. He'd marched around the room taking photographs from every angle, and gushed over Jacob's collection of comic figurines of lawyers displayed on his antique mahogany partner's desk. What he hadn't loved, however, were the creaky boards in the floors and the height of the ceilings, which would have restricted the movement of the camera and made it difficult to keep the suspended microphone out of the frame. Jacob had been both disappointed and relieved when his office had been ruled out as a location.

"Lorraine is so excited that they're in town. I think she's starstruck," he said of his wife, when they stopped by my table at Mara's Luncheonette, where I was having breakfast with my good friend Seth Hazlitt, Cabot Cove's favorite physician.

"I love Vera Stockdale," Lorraine said. "I think I've seen every movie she ever made. Aren't the old movies wonderful? I'm not as crazy about the ones they're putting out these days."

"It was fun to contemplate having them shooting in my office, but can you imagine what a mess they would have made?" Jacob said. "It would have set me back three weeks' worth of work. I would've had to study my cases in the kitchen at home."

"Not my kitchen!" Lorraine shot back. "You could have worked in the judge's chambers at the courthouse."

"Only if there wasn't a trial going on," her husband replied. "The trial judge gets first dibs on the chambers."

"You folks want to sit down?" Seth asked, slicing into the blueberry pancakes Mara's was famous for.

"No, thanks. We just had our breakfast," Jacob replied.

"They ruled out my house, too," Seth said, pouring syrup over his neatly sliced stack. "Not that I would have put my practice on hold for them. Too much fuss and bother for a silly moving picture I'm never going to see. No offense, Jessica."

"None taken," I said. Seth hadn't been to the "moving pictures" in at least ten years. But even though he denied it, I knew he would make an exception and go see this one because of his fondness for me.

With his pancakes properly soaked in syrup, Seth

shoveled a forkful into his mouth, closed his eyes, and hummed his pleasure.

"Actually, I kind of liked the idea of their using Jacob's office," Lorraine told us. "I put a lot of time into making that space just so. It would have been nice to see it up on the big screen."

"But your work is going to be on display anyway," her husband reminded her.

"Well, sort of," she said, smiling at him.

It turned out that the production designer had been so charmed by Jacob's workplace that he stated his intention to reproduce it on the soundstage. According to an article in the *Cabot Cove Gazette*, our local newspaper, the result was an exact replica of Jacob's office down to the framed Honoré Daumier caricature on the wall and the double candlestick lamp with the wide shade that the script supervisor and cameraman had been discussing today. I hadn't had a chance to see it yet and was eager to view the final result to decide for myself if it really did look like the original.

Mort and I were lingering outside the back door of the hangar waiting for the director when I heard my name being called.

"Jessica, thank goodness you're here." Hamilton Twomby waved as he lumbered toward me. "We have work to do, milady."

"Hello, Ham," I said. "Have you met Mort Metzger, our sheriff? Mort, this is Hamilton Twomby, the screenwriter."

"Pleasure to meet you, Sheriff," Twomby said, his hand engulfing Mort's.

"Same here."

"How soon can you come to my trailer?" Twomby asked me.

"Actually, I didn't come out to the airport to work with you," I replied. "I'm afraid I'm busy this afternoon."

"You really must make some time for me, Jessica. These people are driving me crazy."

"They're good at that, aren't they?" Mort said.

Twomby looked at Mort. "You, too, huh?"

"What's the problem, Ham?" I asked. "I understood that our most recent changes to the script were supposed to be the last ones."

"So did I. So did I. In fact, I even made arrangements to fly back to L.A. the day after tomorrow. But that plan has been scrapped."

"What happened now?" I asked.

"Can't you guess? Vera, that paragon of stage and screen, who hasn't set eyes on a screenplay in umpteen years, has been counting lines again. We have to cut Lois Brannigan's part so her on-screen time is three minutes less than Ms. Stockdale's."

"That's a lot of dialogue," I said. "It will change the whole second half of the story."

"It's either that or give Vera her own version of Hamlet's soliloquy. 'I want the audience to feel the conflict in my soul,'" he said, imitating Vera's throaty voice. "I'll bet she's been comparing her lines to the monologues in that stupid book she's always carrying around. She's the *star*, you know," Twomby said. "She wants a star's piece of the cake."

"That's ridiculous! The judge is a pivotal role of

course, but it isn't the largest one. She knew that the judge would be murdered early on."

"You mean she would have known had she read the entire script," Twomby said, rolling his eyes. "Chattergee told her it was a starring vehicle; that's what she expected, and now we've got to make it one. What Vera wants, Vera gets."

"Oh, dear."

"'Oh, dear' is right," he said. He turned to Mort. "I've worked with some of the finest actresses in Hollywood and they never argued over my scripts."

"No kidding," said Mort, clearly at a loss as to how to respond.

Twomby poked Mort in the shoulder with his index finger. "These people have large egos, but small minds. They don't recognize talent when it's all but dancing in front of them."

"Gee, that's too bad."

"But, Ham, can't you get the director to talk to Vera?" I asked.

"Elovitz?" Twomby roared. "That rookie is too wimpy to challenge her." He took a calming breath, raised the back of his hand to his brow, then said dramatically, "I could kill that woman, but I won't. I'll make the changes and go collect my check. But"—he dropped his hand and looked me in the eye—"I'm going to think seriously of having my name removed from the credits. I don't want anyone to think I actually wrote this mess. You might consider doing the same."

I was pretty certain Twomby wouldn't do that. Ham had his own sizable ego. Besides, he tended to exaggerate. The script was far from a mess, even if, in my opinion, it was no longer as compelling a story as when it had started out. We agreed to meet the next day to see how we could juggle the dialogue to give Vera more screen time and Lois less.

"Your colleague is not a happy camper," Mort commented as Twomby trudged away.

"I don't blame him," I said. "I'm not thrilled myself. This movie is making a lot more work for me than I anticipated."

"I know the feeling," Mort said. "But it's no use banging your head against the wall." He winked.

I laughed. "Good advice," I said.

As soon as Twomby disappeared, the director emerged from the production office trailer wearing a pair of dark sunglasses and a Red Sox baseball cap set backward on his head. I wondered if he'd been hiding inside to avoid having to face the screenwriter's wrath. But that was silly of me. There were no windows in the production trailer. How could he have known Twomby was outside?

"You're still here?" Elovitz said. "You didn't need to wait. I could've caught up to you."

"That's okay," Mort said. "You're our official tour guide."

Mort pulled open the door to the hangar and held it for me. I stepped inside and was immediately confronted by a wall of fabric. Heavy black curtains were suspended from the ceiling, shielding the soundstage from daylight and making it difficult for me to find the way in. I poked my hand into the material, feeling around for a break in the drapery.

"To the left," Elovitz said, coming through the door after Mort. He grabbed a handful of curtain and tugged it aside.

We ducked under the cloth and found ourselves "backstage," facing a long row of wooden flats and scaffolding. Inside it was cool and dark and quiet. Dull red lights, the only illumination, glowed from the walls every ten feet.

"This is creepy," Mort said, squinting to accustom himself to the dim light. "Reminds me of the fun house we used to go to every Halloween when I was a kid. I half expect to see one of those mirrors that make you look wavy with a big head."

"This is the back of the scenery," Elovitz explained, leading us along the wooden panels. "We'll circle around so you can see the full set from the camera's POV."

We heard footsteps behind us and a woman's voice called out, "Mr. Elovitz? Mr. Elovitz? Are you here?"

The director stopped in his tracks and turned toward the voice. "What now?" he muttered. He excused himself to us and backtracked toward the gap in the curtains.

"Oh, Mr. Elovitz, thank goodness I've found you. I've been looking all over."

"Until five minutes ago I was in the production office, Estelle. Surely you know where that is."

"Yes, of course, but that's not what I meant."

"Who's that?" Mort whispered as the pair came into view.

"Vera Stockdale's astrologer," I whispered back.

Estelle Fancy was dressed in a diaphanous skirt that fell to her ankles and a blouse, belted at the waist. She wore several strings of beads around her neck, at least three rings on each hand, and a pair of dangling earrings that tinkled when she moved her head. A long scarf, close to the color of her gray hair, was wrapped around her shoulders like a shawl.

"You misunderstand me, Mr. Elovitz," she said, shaking her head and setting the earrings to jangling. "I meant I was looking all over for Ms. Stockdale. I'm almost certain Vera was supposed to have a costume fitting at twelve thirty. I was to meet her there, but she didn't show up. I must say, the wardrobe mistress was very rude to me, but I told her I am not Ms. Stockdale's keeper. Even so, I went to Vera's trailer to wake her. I assumed she was taking her afternoon nap and just hadn't set the alarm clock, but she wasn't there. And then I . . ."

"Get to the point, Miss Fancy," Elovitz said. "I don't have all day."

"The point is I can't find her, and you know she's a Gemini and they have a duality of personality. It's not a propitious time for her; I checked her chart this morning and—"

"Vera Stockdale is an independent woman who doesn't need to report to you," Elovitz said, interrupting her. "She's not scheduled to be on set until tomorrow's eight o'clock call. Maybe she went into town."

Fancy shook her head. "She would have told me. Anyway, she doesn't have a car here."

"So, maybe she got a ride, or decided to take a walk."

"There's really nowhere to walk out here. I've tried. We're in the middle of the woods, except for the runways. And those are dangerous. A man yelled at me yesterday when I was making a circuit of the airport."

I could imagine the fit Jed Richardson must have had upon seeing someone taking a stroll around his airfield while his students were practicing takeoffs and landings.

"Besides," Fancy continued, "Vera has been complaining about an ingrown toenail lately and it hurts her to walk."

"Too much information, Estelle," Elovitz said, his patience wearing thin. "I don't know or care where Vera is at the moment, as long as you make sure she shows up tomorrow morning. Now, if you'll please excuse me, I'm in the middle of giving these people a tour."

"But—are you certain she isn't here?"

"Would you like to join us, Miss Fancy, and see for yourself?" I asked.

"Oh, no. I don't think so. I'll just look around a little bit more if you don't mind."

"No one is in the building but us," Elovitz said.

"She might have come here to soak up the atmosphere before her scene tomorrow."

"I doubt that," Elovitz said.

"She's very conscientious, you know."

"I *don't* know." He glared at the astrologer to stop her from talking. "You may look around. Just don't bother us again, and don't touch anything. It's a hot set. Understand?"

"Of course, Mr. Elovitz," she replied, straightening her shoulders. "It isn't as if I haven't been on a movie lot before. I know the rules."

"Then abide by them. You aren't supposed to be in here."

I thought that Elovitz was being a little harsh with Estelle Fancy. After all, the astrologer was simply looking out for the director's leading lady. Movie stars often have personal assistants who travel with them. Perhaps Miss Fancy doubled as Vera's personal aide. Or if not, maybe her presence was part of the deal to secure Vera's cooperation in the first place. I wondered briefly if the actress was paying the way for her astrologer. Someone surely was.

"What's a 'hot set'?" Mort asked Elovitz, who frowned as he watched Miss Fancy float ahead of us into the gloom.

"I beg your pardon?"

"You told Miss Fancy not to touch anything because it was a 'hot set.'"

"That's the location we're already filming in or going to film in next," Elovitz explained. "Come on. I'll show you." He escorted us to the last part of the panels, where the red lights ended and a sign on a metal stand had been positioned. I could just make out the words HOT SET. Beyond it was the dark, cavernous space of the hangar.

"Let me get the lights and you'll see," Elovitz said. He walked to an electrical panel and we heard the clicks as he flipped the breakers. One by one, the lights came on—first the overhead spotlights, then the klieg lights on stands, then smaller lights on metal beams above us—not only illuminating the interior of the set but also revealing the cameras, cranes, dollies, and other filmmaking equipment arrayed around the hangar. The lights reflected off the windows of several internal offices on the far side of the huge space. The last switch Elovitz hit turned on the double candlestick lamp with the wide shade that sat on the desk of a room that was eerily familiar.

"Wow!" said Mort, his eyes scanning the set. "That looks just like Judge Borden's office."

"It certainly does," I added, marveling that the production designer had been able to find an Oriental rug exactly like Jacob's—or was it?—and his tall leather wing chair. At least I thought it was a wing chair; I could only see the back of it—but wasn't his chair maroon, not red? And there was the little blue-patterned settee Lorraine had found at a tag sale—only the pattern on this one was not exactly the same. The overall impression was that this was Judge Jacob Borden's office, but I realized that while it had been duplicated in spirit, it was not identical to the original.

"The only part missing is the ceiling," Mort commented.

"We have a small portion of the ceiling in case we need to include it in a shot," Elovitz said, walking to Mort's side and pointing to where five feet of ceiling jutted out from above the bookcase on the back wall. "This is a hot set. All the furniture and props have been positioned. Nothing can be moved, even an inch, or it will break the continuity."

"What is this continuity thing?" Mort asked. "I

heard you talk about continuity in the trailer—I mean, your office."

Elovitz smiled. "Continuity is simply keeping everything the same. Let's say the script calls for an actor to put a book on the desk in one scene, and then we break for lunch. That book must be in the exact same position when we come back to resume filming. Otherwise it might confuse the actor—or worse, if we don't catch it, it could distract the viewer."

"Oh, I get it now," Mort said.

"Continuity is what Nicole is responsible for. You saw her in my office."

"Yeah. The lady with the curly hair."

"Right. She's the script supervisor and I rely on her to make sure the continuity is maintained so . . ." He trailed off, scowling into the scene before him. "But I don't remember the desk chair being turned around." Elovitz twisted his head from side to side. "Estelle," he yelled at the top of his voice. "Where are you?"

"Over here, Mr. Elovitz," the astrologer said, coming from the opposite side of the set.

"I thought I told you not to touch anything in this room."

"But I haven't, Mr. Elovitz."

"That chair did not have its back to the camera yesterday when I left this soundstage."

"I didn't turn it," the astrologer said. "Maybe someone else did."

"No one else has been in this building except you."

"But I only peeked into the set to see if Vera was here. I didn't touch anything."

"You better be telling the truth, or I'll have you on the next plane out of here."

"I am telling the truth. Besides, Ms. Stockdale would be very upset if you sent me home."

"Vera will just have to manage without another reading of the stars. Now, go turn that chair back to the exact position it was in before you stepped into this set."

Estelle wrung her hands and looked to me and Mort. "I didn't move anything, I swear," she whispered to us.

"Go!" Elovitz roared, and she tiptoed onto the set, looking back at us nervously.

Elovitz paced. "Nicole is going to have a fit. She'd better have photos of the set as we left it. I'm going to have to look at the rushes to make certain everything is exactly the same."

"Yeah, your continuity is important," Mort said.

"I'm sure you'll be able to put it back the way it was," I said to Elovitz, just as a scream cut through the air.

"What the h—" Elovitz stopped pacing.

Mort and I whirled around.

Estelle Fancy was standing with her hands over her mouth, eyes wide, staring at the chair.

Mort and I rushed to see what had frightened her.

"Don't touch anything!" Elovitz bellowed, racing after us.

Estelle reached out with trembling fingers and pushed the corner of the chair. It slowly swiveled around to reveal Vera Stockdale, dressed in a brocade caftan, her platinum hair concealed under a floral turban, slumped in the seat. Her head leaned crookedly against the wing of the chair, a length of thirty-five-millimeter film tightly wrapped around her neck. Her face was gray.

"Is she—?" Elovitz asked.

Mort put two fingers on Vera's wrist and shook his head.

Estelle wailed.

Elovitz cursed.

But I'd known the moment she'd come into view.

The movie star was dead.

Chapter Four

"What happened to her?" Elovitz asked.

"Looks like she's been strangled," Mort said. He gently touched Vera's eyes, checking for a response. A low growl and then a sharp bark startled him. "What the heck is that?"

"Ooh, it's Cecil, Vera's dog," Estelle Fancy said, switching her attention from her employer's body to the sound. She squatted down to peer under the desk. "Come here, Cecil, sweetheart. You poor thing." She extended a hand toward the dog, but he growled and snapped at her. "Oh, he's never done that before," she said, pulling her hand away and standing. "You'll have to get him, Sheriff."

"He's not my first priority," Mort said, taking a cell phone from his pocket.

"I can't believe it," Elovitz said, fists on his hips. "We were all set to shoot her big scene. How could this have happened to me?"

"Everyone out," Mort instructed, waving us away. "This hot set is now a crime scene."

The three of us retreated to the edge of the set and listened as Mort made his call. "We have an apparent homicide," he said. "White female, approximate age mid-fifties, about five foot seven. No idea of the weight. She's wearing one of those flowy robes. Possible strangulation. Body discovered at"—he looked at his watch—"fourteen hundred hours at Cabot Cove airfield, hangar one. Send an ambulance to the rear door of the hangar—I'll meet you there. We'll ship her to the hospital morgue. I want a crime scene squad and photographer. Alert the medical examiner. We'll need an autopsy. He's away? Again? Then get Doc Hazlitt. I'll call you later."

Tears streaming down her face, the astrologer knelt on the floor and called softly, "Here, Cecil. Come here, boy. Sweetie pie, Cecil. Poor puppy." She sniffled and crept forward on her knees, tapping the floor with her palm, and using a baby voice to entice Vera's dog from his hiding place.

Elovitz took out his phone and pushed his finger up the screen, scanning for a number.

"Who do you think you're calling?" Mort asked.

"Rhonda Chen, my casting director. I've got to get her going on a replacement. If we don't stick to the shooting schedule, our backers will fade away and this film will never get made."

"Put your phone away," Mort said sternly. "You can't make any calls now."

"Don't be silly, Metzger. Didn't you ever hear that the show must go on?"

Mort spaced out his words. "Put . . . the . . . phone . . . away."

"This is not the time to play Dirty Harry, Sheriff. I've got a movie to make and this . . . um"—he cast around before finding the right words—"unfortunate development isn't going to stop me."

"Put it away or I'll take it away, and toss you in jail to boot. You're not in charge here anymore."

"Please listen to the sheriff," I said. "You can make your call later. Waiting a few hours won't make a difference."

"A few hours? I can't believe it," Elovitz said with disgust, but he put the phone in his pocket.

Mort's phone rang and he turned his back on us.

"I knew she was going to be trouble," Elovitz said, pacing back and forth in front of the set. "Zee was completely freaked out that we were going to work with her—he was psyched—but I told Chattergee she was all wrong for the part, past her prime, too difficult." He stopped and looked at me. "You know this picture is important to me. It's my chance to go mainstream. The last thing we needed was a prima donna and a condensed shooting schedule. It's a disastrous combination."

"Then why did you cast her?" I asked.

"She was a name. Besides, he wouldn't make the film without her."

"Who?"

"Chattergee. He owed her. I don't know what their deal was. He can't stand her, but still he insisted she was the only one to play the role." Elovitz threw up his hands. "What am I supposed to do now?"

Mort disconnected his call and turned toward us. "They should be here any minute," he said. "They got tied up directing traffic around the streets that are blocked off." He scowled at the director. "You realize when my men get here, your continuity is going to be shot to hell," he said.

"It doesn't matter," Elovitz said, flapping his arms. "We'll have to reshoot her scenes anyway when we get a new actress for her role. What a mess!"

Mort pulled a pad from his hip pocket. "While we're waiting, let's get some of the facts down for my report." He looked around. "Where's the other one?"

"Estelle Fancy?" I said.

"Yeah, the lady astrologer. Where is she?"

"She was here a moment ago, trying to coax the dog out from under the desk," I said.

Mort strode onto the set and ducked his head under the desk. "Gone," he said. "The dog and the lady."

"Estelle?" Elovitz shouted. We waited a few seconds, but there was no answer.

"She can't have gone far," I said, embarrassed that I hadn't noticed the astrologer leave with the dog. "Would you like me to go look for her?"

"No! You two wait here." Mort pointed at Elovitz. "No phone calls. Understood?"

"Understood."

"Mrs. F., I'm holding you responsible."

"He won't make any calls, Mort." I looked at Elovitz. "Please don't make me a liar."

Mort jogged around to the back of the scenery and we heard the hangar door open and close.

Elovitz walked behind a camera and sank into his

director's chair with a big sigh. He pulled out his phone. "I'm not making any calls," he assured me. "I'm just checking my schedule."

"No text messages either, please," I said.

"You have my word."

I stood at the edge of the set and examined the scene from a distance, a million questions swarming in my mind. There was a slight tang in the air that I found familiar, but I couldn't place it. "How recently was this set painted?" I called out to Elovitz.

"Last week," he replied, strolling over to stand next to me. "But they probably did touch-ups a few days ago. Why?"

"Just wondering."

Vera's head leaned against the wing of the chair, the film cutting into her neck, but I didn't see any blood. Odd. I would expect the edges of a strip of film to be sharp enough to cut. But her chin angled down toward her chest. Perhaps there was blood but it was hidden by her clothing. The caftan she wore was made of a heavy material in a riot of colors. It was difficult to see if there were stains on it.

I looked at her hands. I didn't see any defensive marks on them. That was odd, too. If someone had sneaked up on her from behind and thrown the film around her neck, surely she would have put her hands up to fight against the pressure of the celluloid on her throat. And was film strong enough to cut off her air supply without tearing? I didn't know. Could someone have approached her from behind without her being aware of it? It seemed unlikely. Perhaps she'd been sleeping in the chair and was caught unawares by the killer. If not, if she'd meant to meet this person, why would she have chosen the set for an assignation? As always in these situations, the mysteries piled up, one upon the other.

The real question was why would someone want to kill Vera Stockdale to begin with? To be sure, she was an unpleasant woman. She was selfish and rude and egotistical. I'd felt the brunt of her temper myself. But there are many disagreeable people in the world and most of them are still walking this earth. A person's being nasty is not usually enough of a reason to inspire someone to do away with her, although it is not unknown for a killer to have a flimsy motivation. How people respond to insults or humiliations varies widely. Vera had likely cut a wide swath with her venomous tongue. How many enemies had she made? Had someone been so incensed by her spiteful remarks that he or she determined to silence her forever?

I'd been so focused on the murder scene in front of me, I was surprised when Elovitz spoke. "You know what's really strange?" he said, as if he'd been weighing all the same questions that had been occupying my thoughts.

"What?"

"Where did that thirty-five-millimeter film come from?"

"Do you mean what's on it?" I asked.

"Yeah, that, too." He took a step toward the body and I put out an arm to restrain him. "I can't tell from here if it's something that was left on the cutting room floor or if it's just undeveloped film," he said.

"It's not worth putting your fingerprints on it to find

out," I said. "The detectives should be able to determine its origin."

"You're right, but maybe what they don't know is that we don't shoot on film anymore, at least most of us don't. That's the peculiar thing. I don't have any film here. Everything is digital. I haven't seen a film camera on a set since my student days. Where did that piece of film come from?"

"Good question," I said. "Make sure you tell Sheriff Metzger about that."

"How long do you think he's going to keep my set off-limits?" he asked. "I've got work to do."

"I couldn't say," I replied. "This is a crime scene, and he'll need to examine it pretty carefully in case there's evidence here that's not immediately visible. Once you start shooting again, that evidence could be compromised, fingerprints added that weren't there before, items moved. In that case, *his* continuity would be broken."

"Okay, I get it. Maybe we can make a deal," Elovitz said. "I'll help him out with the production stuff, and in exchange he speeds up his investigation and lets me get back to shooting on this set."

We heard a commotion at the hangar's back door and looked up to see two of Mort's deputies entering, pushing a body bag on top of a gurney. They were followed by an evidence technician, who set his case on the floor and proceeded to remove items he would need, snapping on a pair of latex gloves and placing a bundle of cellophane bags to the side. A tray he set on the floor contained, among other items, several pairs of tweezers, scissors, a tape measure, and a magnifying glass. He looked up at the spotlights overhead. "Guess we don't need the high-intensity lights today," he said, as he pulled out a separate camera bag and a handful of rulers, directing the deputies to place the rulers next to items and within areas he intended to photograph.

While the deputies strung yellow tape across the front of the set, Elovitz and I watched as the crime scene was examined and photographed. Elements from it were preserved in clear bags, each bag and its contents logged on a sheet in the technician's binder.

Mort returned with Seth Hazlitt, who gave me a quick nod before approaching the victim, still sitting in the wing chair. Despite the fact that she was clearly dead, he listened for a heartbeat, checked her eyes with a small flashlight, felt for a pulse, tested the movement of her jaw and hands, and peered down the front of her robe.

"How many hours do you figure, Doc?" Mort asked him.

"Hard to say, but from her condition, at least twelve, probably more. I'll have a better idea once I examine the body." He waved the evidence technician over. "Did you get photos of her?"

"Yes, sir. From every angle."

"We can remove the body, then?"

"Just need to bag her hands and she's yours. I'll shoot the chair again when she's off it."

"Shoot? That's what it is," I whispered.

"What did you say?" Elovitz asked.

"I remembered what that lingering odor is. It's not paint. It's a little like fireworks, the smell of a gun being fired."

"I don't smell anything," Elovitz said.

"That's probably because you smoke cigars."

"How do you know I smoke cigars?"

"You have one sticking out of your pocket," I said, pointing. "But even if you didn't, I would know. The smell of smoke clings to your clothing."

"You've got some nose."

"So I've been told," I said.

Seth, who'd been eavesdropping, called out, "And it often goes where it doesn't belong." He smiled and winked at me.

The tech slipped plastic bags over Vera's hands and secured them with tape. Mort's deputies positioned the gurney next to the wing chair and attempted to lift Vera up and into the body bag. It was not an easy task. The chair kept swinging as they maneuvered her body, prompting Mort to lean against the side of it, trying to keep it motionless.

"I'll want to look at her again when she's lying prone," Seth said.

Vera was a tall woman, and the voluminous folds of her caftan blocked the deputies' view of the body bag, causing them to place her off-center on the gurney. She almost slipped off the side of it, but they caught her in time and adjusted her position.

"Well, look at this," Seth said, eyeing the chair.

"What is it?" Mort said.

"Your official report will probably say it's 'a liquid substance, brownish red in color,' but it looks like blood to me," Seth said.

"What? Why? Wasn't she strangled?"

"Don't believe so," Seth said. He leaned over the body and found the zipper of Vera's robe. A moment later, he looked up at Mort and shook his head. "Thought film was a strange item to use to strangle someone, but most likely it's not the murder weapon at all," he said, tucking the tail end of the film into the body bag. "The lady has been shot," he announced.

I knew that scent in the air was familiar, I told myself. It was gunpowder. So she hadn't been strangled at all. I might have guessed, but I couldn't see the blood on the chair until the body was moved.

Seth straightened and stripped off the gloves he'd worn to examine Vera's body. "Should be able to tell if that's what killed her after I conduct the autopsy."

"Oh, wow!" Elovitz whispered to me. "This is not good."

"Was it better when you thought she was strangled?" I asked.

"I was hoping that she might've died of a heart attack."

"With a piece of film tied around her neck?" I said, incredulous.

He shrugged. "Who knows? She was a real drama queen. It wouldn't have surprised me if she'd flung a piece of film around her neck to remind the rest of us how important she was—you know, to make the point that she was part of Hollywood royalty. I wouldn't put it past her."

"Was she prone to such bizarre behavior?" I asked.

"Chattergee would know better than me," he said. "I only met her a few weeks ago, but these old actresses are strange. You saw Gloria Swanson in *Sunset Boulevard*, didn't you? Delusional. Nutty as a fruitcake."

"That was a role she was playing, not the way Swanson herself behaved," I said, becoming exasperated with this young director.

"Yeah, well, you know old people sometimes, um, present company excepted, of course . . ."

"Of course," I said, and waited for him to shove his foot even further into his mouth. But he had realized his error and was backpedaling.

"I didn't mean any offense," he said. "She was a little screwy, that's all. You know, a card short of a deck, as they say, not the sharpest knife in the drawer. Look at her carrying around that dumb dog like a twenty-year-old starlet. I mean, she's not exactly Paris Hilton. And she insisted on quoting from that dumb book like it was a sacred tome. And then she had to have her astrologer . . ."

I shook my head and rolled my eyes.

"Before you bury yourself even further, young man," Seth said, "I'll have you know Mrs. Fletcher here *is* the sharpest knife in the drawer, so you'd best be careful what you say to her."

"Apologies! Apologies all around," Elovitz said, holding up his hands as if we were pointing a gun in his direction. "I'm just shooting off my mouth because I'm nervous. I've never seen a dead body before. I . . . I've never even known anyone who died."

"Well, you're a lucky fellow," Seth said.

And I silently agreed.

Chapter Five

Mort's first order of business after Vera's body had been removed, accompanied by Seth, was to find Estelle Fancy to get her official statement for the record. Leaving the investigative team in place to finish its work, Mort posted a deputy at the entrance to the hangar with instructions not to allow anyone inside. He got Elovitz to give him a list of people who needed to be alerted to Vera's death, and made arrangements for the director to stop by the sheriff's office for an in-depth interview. He also cautioned Elovitz not to discuss the discovery of Vera's body with anyone.

Then he asked for my assistance in tracking down the astrologer.

"Mrs. F., I could use your help," he said to me.

"Are you sure, Mort? I don't want to get in the way of police business."

"This is kind of a delicate situation. You know these people. I don't. Besides, she'll probably be more comfortable talking to another woman. Maybe you can get some answers here."

"I'll do my best," I said.

We found Estelle Fancy at her trailer, a modified van with a bed and two chairs. She was trying to coax the growling Chihuahua to eat.

"Didn't you realize you were not supposed to leave the scene of a crime?" Mort asked.

"I'm sorry, Sheriff, but I had to get Cecil out of there," Estelle said, her eyes red from crying. "He's just a little guy, but he's so sensitive. I couldn't let him stay with Vera in that condition. His heart must be broken."

Cecil, who was crouched on a gold velvet pillow, barked and growled as Estelle approached him and set the bowl of food on the bed.

"What are you giving him?" I asked.

"Leftover hamburger. He usually loves that."

"Can he chew it?" I asked. "It doesn't look as if he has many teeth."

"I cut it up into tiny little pieces." She pushed the small bowl closer to Cecil, who bared his gums and looked as intimidating as a miniature dog possibly could.

"Can we get down to the reason for our visit, Miss Fancy?" Mort said, pad out and pen poised. "I'd like to know your whereabouts for the past twenty-four hours, when you last saw Ms. Stockdale alive, and what her mood was."

Estelle looked at me. "You were there when I told Mr. Elovitz why I was looking for her," she said, sprinkling salt on the crumbled hamburger, and peering expectantly at the dog. "She had an appointment for a wardrobe fitting today and she missed it."

"And what time was the appointment?"

"Twelve thirty."

"When did you last see her alive?" Mort asked.

"Yesterday. I brought her fruit and half a plain bagel from craft services, as usual."

Mort frowned. "What is craft services?"

"It's the buffet table that's available all day for the crew," I told him.

"Why don't they just call it catering?"

"I don't know the answer to that," I said.

Mort turned back to Estelle. "So, okay, you brought her breakfast. What kind of mood was Ms. Stockdale in? Was she angry?"

"About the breakfast?"

"No! With someone," Mort said. "Was she angry at anyone or was anyone angry with her?"

"She was always very kind to me."

"Had she argued with anyone recently?" he asked. "Someone who might have held a grudge?"

"Not that I know of."

"Aren't you her personal assistant?"

"Well . . ."

"Wouldn't you know if someone in the production company was angry with her?"

"I'm not with her twenty-four hours a day."

"Let's put this simply," Mort said. "Did Ms. Stockdale have any enemies?"

The question inspired a fresh spate of tears. "Enemies?" Estelle wailed. "Why would she have enemies? She was a movie star."

"It's just a turn of phrase," I said, shooting Mort a look that said he should slow down. "Sheriff Metzger is just trying to determine who might have been angry enough with Ms. Stockdale to kill her."

"I don't know," she said, sniffling and shaking her head, causing her earrings to jingle like tiny wind chimes. "I just can't believe that she's gone."

I pulled a packet of tissues from my shoulder bag and handed it to her. "Here. Sit down for a moment and rest. You've had a terrible blow. We understand. But you probably knew her better than anyone else here, don't you think?"

She nodded as she blew her nose, and sank down on the edge of the bed that took up half her living quarters. Cecil growled.

"How long had you known her?" I asked.

"At least thirty years, maybe more. That's us," she said, pointing to a cluster of photographs that had been taped to the wall.

I leaned over to see the pictures. In one, a young Estelle Fancy and Vera Stockdale playfully posed for the camera. In another, Terrence Chattergee stood between them, his arms around their shoulders. They were both striking young women, Estelle as dark as Vera was blond, a Rose Red to the actress's Snow White, as in the old fairy tale. Vera had retained her beauty—with professional help, I was sure. Estelle's face showed the signs of a harder life, lacking the pampering and perhaps surgical assistance that the movie star had access to.

"How did you meet?" I asked.

Mort sighed and clicked his ballpoint pen closed.

Estelle straightened her back and lifted her chin. "I was working for another actress, one who was very successful, but of course I can't tell you her name."

"That's okay," I said. "Did this other actress introduce you to Ms. Stockdale?"

"Oh, no. They were in competition for the same role. She wouldn't have wanted Vera to get an advantage over her."

"And if Vera knew you, how would that have given her an advantage?"

"Not just knowing me," Estelle said, smoothing her skirt over her knees. "But if I had been consulting for her, she might have learned something she could use that would have helped her get the part." She looked up at me pertly. "And that's just what happened."

"What happened?" Mort asked.

"Ms. Stockdale called me up and asked me to do her chart."

"And that's how you met?" Mort said.

"Yes." Estelle Fancy's lips tipped up in a small smile. "I read her chart, told her she'd have to put the producer off for a few days. Mercury was in retrograde, a bad time to make life-altering decisions, certainly not favorable for signing contracts. But if she met with him on the following Friday, everything would be in the proper alignment. It would be the best time to talk with him, and she would be able to negotiate the best deal for herself, and . . . and . . ."

"And?" Mort said.

"She got the part. There were some complications, but I helped her overcome them. After that, she wanted an exclusive contract with me. I've been with her ever since."

"As her personal astrologer?" I asked.

"Yes."

"Are there a lot of actresses with a personal astrologer?" Mort asked.

"Many in the acting profession—and a lot of other professions, for that matter—will consult with an astrologer from time to time," Estelle replied. "But those who have a personal astrologer are special. You'll find them at the top of their fields."

"But hasn't it been quite a few years since Ms. Stockdale acted in films?" I asked.

"Oh, yes. But until she retired we had quite a run together."

"What prompted her to retire?"

"She was going to have a baby. When she found out about it, she decided to call it a day." Estelle gazed down at the balled-up tissue in her hand. "The roles were drying up anyway," she said softly.

"They were?" I said. "Why do you think that was so?"

"Far be it for me to speak ill of the dead," she said, looking up at me from under her brows. "I don't know if you're aware of this, but Vera could be difficult."

I resisted making a comment, and Estelle continued. "Some of the studio executives had complained to Mr. Chattergee. He knew she was very high-strung, of course. Theirs was a tempestuous marriage. I was surprised when he said he was thrilled about the baby and more surprised that Vera wanted to be there for her child."

"Why were you surprised?" I asked.

Her expression was pensive. "He was never the fatherly type. And she was focused on her career."

"So, when you say you've been with her ever since," I said, "do you mean that even when she was retired she still required your services?"

"I wasn't on salary, if that's what you're asking. I worked for her for a while—she was willing to go back to business if the right role came along—but then they divorced, and after that . . . well, I had to support myself."

"Then you only started working for Vera again recently?" I said.

"When she decided to make a comeback, she called me right away, of course. It's just taken a little time."

"I see," I said.

"I don't," Mort said. "Can we get back to my questions? I don't even remember what we were talking about anymore."

Estelle smiled. "You were asking about the last time I saw Ms. Stockdale. And I told you I'd brought her breakfast yesterday."

"Did you see her again after that?" Mort asked.

Estelle shook her head. "She sent me into town to get a charger for her iPad. There was a film she wanted to watch and she'd forgotten to bring her charger from home."

"Do you know the name of the film?"

"What a strange question," Estelle said. "No. I've no idea what film she wanted to watch."

"Did you find a charger for her?" I asked.

"Yes, at a place called Charles Department Store. You know it?"

"Go on. What happened after that?" Mort said.

"I came back. She wasn't in her trailer, so I left the charger on the counter. But she wasn't there later when I knocked after dinner."

"What time was that?"

"Around nine. I didn't think anything of it. But when she missed her fitting today, I began to fear something was wrong and started to look for her. And you know the rest."

I looked at Mort as he tucked his pad into his breast pocket. "We'd like to talk to you again, Ms. Fancy, so I'll ask you not to leave town."

"We're supposed to be here for the duration of the movie."

"If they don't cancel it," I said. "They've just lost your employer, the leading lady."

"Oh, dear," she said. "I hope they don't cancel. I have a contract."

"I hope so, too," I said.

"Miss Fancy, I'm sorry to ask you this, but it's vitally important that you don't talk about Ms. Stockdale's death with anyone," Mort said. "We want to keep details of the circumstances confidential so we don't tip off the killer about what we know. Understand?"

"Of course."

Estelle rose when Mort put his hand on the doorknob. She glanced over her shoulder at Cecil. "Oh, look, he's eaten all the hamburger," she said.

Cecil barked at her.

"I think he's asking for more."

When we left, Estelle was cooing to Cecil, who was growling again despite having been fed.

"Seems to me," Mort said when we were outside, "that if she was really able to predict the future, she would have seen this coming."

"From what I understand, astrologers don't exactly predict the future," I said. "They simply determine when the alignment of the moon, planets, and stars create a receptive environment for decisions or actions."

"So what does that mean?"

"It means," I said, "that if the stars were in proper alignment, someone had a receptive environment for murder."

Chapter Six

"Dead! What do you mean she's dead? I saw her only . . . I saw her . . ." Terrence Chattergee sputtered to a stop. "When did this happen?"

"We just found her body," Mort said, trying to keep his voice soothing.

"I don't believe it. I want to see her," Chattergee said, reaching for his jacket, which he'd slung over a chair.

"Hold on," Mort said, grabbing his arm. "We will want you to identify the body, but not right now. My team is bringing her to the hospital morgue."

Chattergee collapsed onto a brown leather sofa, his tan face gone ashen. "This is awful," he managed to say, his voice raspy. "She wouldn't talk to me for years. I finally found a role for her, and she was so excited about this film. What am I going to do? What am I going to tell my daughter?"

Mort and I were going down the list he'd gotten

from Elovitz. Mort wanted to be able to inform certain individuals himself to control how the news of the murder was communicated. And also, I suspected, to gauge the reactions of those supposedly first learning of Vera Stockdale's death.

Terrence Chattergee had been on a conference call to the coast when we knocked at the door of his trailer. "Can't you see I'm busy?" he'd shouted, flinging open his door. "I'm talking to California, Mrs. Fletcher. Come back later."

"I'm afraid not," Mort had replied, slapping his hand on the door to keep it open. Perhaps the sheriff's uniform and grim expression tipped off the producer to the seriousness of our visit. He'd ended the call and invited us inside.

Chattergee's trailer was four times as large as the one Estelle Fancy occupied, and in addition to the sofa, had a curved red leather banquette and three matching side chairs—sufficient seating to accommodate a good-sized meeting. In the center was a round table with the speakerphone Chattergee had been using when we'd interrupted him.

"I can't believe it," the producer said, shielding his eyes with his hand and moaning. "How did she die?" he asked. "She was as strong as an ox, exercised every day, ate carefully. Used to drive me crazy with her strict diets. Did she have a heart attack?"

Mort gave me a little nod.

"We're not certain yet," I said, sitting down next to Chattergee and resting my hand on his arm, "but we don't believe she died of natural causes."

Chattergee's head came up sharply. "What are you saying?"

"I know this is hard to hear," I replied, "but someone killed her."

"No!" Chattergee roared. He jumped up, then sat down again. "Who? Why? How? Why would anyone want to kill Vera?" He smacked his forehead with his hand and snorted. "What a question to ask! She was impossible. But still, who would take it this far?"

"That's what we're hoping you can help us with," Mort said. "Ms. Stockdale was found sitting in the wing chair on the set in the hangar. Did she happen to tell you who she was planning to meet there?"

"No! I have no idea," he said, clearly trying to get his emotions under control. He coughed and took a hand-kerchief from his pocket and pressed it to his lips. "On the set, did you say?" He cleared his throat. "That was a hot set. No one is supposed to go on that set until the call. When can I see her?"

"Probably later this afternoon," Mort said. "There's going to be an autopsy to determine the cause of death."

Chattergee's expression changed from dismay to anger. "But if you don't know how she died, how can you say someone killed her?"

"There was a bullet hole in her chest," Mort said.

Chattergee suddenly sat back, his hand over his heart, as if he'd been the one who'd been shot. "Oh! Dear God! Poor Vera."

"Are you all right?" I asked. "Would you like us to call a doctor for you?"

"No. No. I'll be okay. Just a glass of water, if you wouldn't mind." He gestured at the maple kitchen built into the space across from the conference table.

I opened several cabinets before finding the glasses. The full-sized stainless-steel refrigerator held a dozen bottles of water. I poured some into a glass.

"Thank you," he said when I handed him the tumbler. "This is such a shock."

"May I ask when you saw Ms. Stockdale last?"

"I'm not supposed to be here," Chattergee said, sipping the water. "I only came east to make sure everything was going well. When did I see her? Last night, when I got in."

"And what kind of mood was she in?" Mort asked.

"She was a bit tense, but that's normal for her."

"Where did you see her?" I asked.

"Right here."

"Here in this trailer?"

"Yes, of course."

"She came to see you here?" Mort said.

"Yes. She was waiting for me."

"What time was that?"

"I don't know, nine o'clock maybe. She was upset about"—he waved his hand to the side—"who knows?"

"You don't recall what upset her?" I asked.

"Something was always bugging her. That's Vera."

"Did she ever complain that someone was stalking her?" Mort asked. "Like a deranged fan?"

"No, but she hadn't been in a film in some years. We were hoping to develop a new fan base—not a crazy one, of course."

"It would be helpful if you could remember something specific she may have said to you," I said. "Did she have an argument with someone?"

"No."

"Was she annoyed with someone or something?"

Chattergee raised one eyebrow as he looked at me. "She was *always* annoyed. She was a complainer, never satisfied. That's hardly news."

"Try to remember what she said," Mort urged.

Chattergee raised a hand to stop the questions. "Give me a second." He scratched his forehead and frowned. "I think it was the note she found in her trailer, something cryptic."

"What do you mean 'cryptic'?" I asked.

"Yeah, what does 'cryptic' mean?" Mort echoed.

"It was a reference to something from the past. I didn't read it, but it disturbed her."

"Did she have the note with her when she came to your trailer?" Mort asked.

Chattergee shook his head and sighed. "I don't know. I was getting ready to go out again. Now I wish I'd paid more attention. I dismissed it, told her she was always making mountains out of molehills, that some idiot probably wanted to spook her and that if she allowed that to happen, the idiot would probably do it again."

"You say you were getting ready to go out. Where did you go?" Mort asked.

"Elovitz hosted a poker game," Chattergee said.

"That's easy enough to check," Mort said. "I'll ask him about that."

"Ask him?" He glared at Mort. "Go ahead, ask him. You think *I* had anything to do with Vera's murder? That's ridiculous! I'm the grieving husband."

Ex-husband, I silently amended. But I could see Chattergee working himself into a froth and tried to distract him.

"Do you play poker often?" I asked. "Is that something people routinely do on a movie lot?"

"Well, not so often at the studio," Chattergee replied, "although it's not unheard of." A small smile crossed his lips. "But we're on location. In the boonies. No offense, but this isn't exactly Hollywood and Vine. There's not a lot of entertainment available. So, sure, we entertain ourselves playing poker."

"Did you win?" I asked.

Chattergee chuckled. "Took home a bit of cash. They're novices, those boys."

"Who else was with you at the poker game?" I asked. Off to my right, I could see Mort taking notes.

"Elovitz—he's the director—Walt Benson, the actor, and Jason Griffin, the DP, the director of photography, a few others. I don't know all their names."

"What time did you get back from the poker game?" Mort put in.

"Must've been around two." He looked at Mort.

"And Ms. Stockdale wasn't here?"

"No. She'd gone back to her trailer. At least I assume that's where she went."

"And you didn't see her after that?" Mort asked.

Chattergee shook his head.

"The men you played cards with, were they with you the whole time?" I asked.

"I guess. I mean, someone might've taken a break, gone out for a smoke or something, you know what I mean. I was focusing on the cards, not on them." He looked from me to Mort. "Anything else?"

Mort closed his notepad and put it back in his pocket. "Not for the moment. Mrs. F., you got any more questions?"

"Would you mind showing us her trailer?" I asked.

"Vera's trailer? Sure."

He rose slowly from the sofa and stopped at the kitchen to place his glass in the sink. "Can't believe it," he muttered.

Vera's trailer was next to the one her ex-husband used on his visits. It wasn't locked, and I wondered if that was typical. Certainly it's not unusual to find doors unlocked in Cabot Cove. People in small towns tend to be careless about their security. But for an actress from Los Angeles, it seemed strange.

"Did Vera always leave her trailer open?" I asked.

"She did. She was careless, kept losing her keys, so she stopped carrying them. She said it wasn't a problem. There are always a lot of the crew walking around. She tended to trust them."

Vera's trailer was the same size as Chattergee's and similarly kitted out, except for the fabrics. In his, the upholstery was leather; in Vera's it was velvet with silk throw pillows. His quarters had been pristine; hers looked more lived-in. There was a bottle of dishwashing soap next to the empty sink and a tray of medicine bottles on the counter, mostly vitamin supplements. A saucer held a pair of earrings. On the floor were two bowls for the dog.

Chattergee picked up a sweater that had been left on her sofa, held it to his nose, and closed his eyes. Then he folded it and replaced it on the seat. "As you can see, there isn't much here," he said, "but then, I don't know what you're looking for."

"The note, if she left it here," Mort said.

"May we see her bedroom?" I asked.

Chattergee walked down the hall, opened the door to Vera's bedroom, and stepped back to allow us to enter. It was a tight space but lavishly furnished, with a green silk coverlet on the bed over a pleated jacquard bed skirt in green and white. A stool upholstered in the same fabric stood in front of a dressing table, which held a pair of open boxes of makeup and creams, a woman's wig on a stand, and a hair dryer, the cord plugged in. Above the dressing table was a mirror framed with lights. A chiffon robe with feathered collar and cuffs had been draped over a chair piled with throw pillows. Several photographs of Vera during different times in her career were taped to the sides of the mirror. I studied them. One showed a younger Vera holding a dog, either a young Cecil or his predecessor. A little girl with dark hair leaned into Vera's leg, a shy expression on her face.

Chattergee pointed to the photo. "I took that one," he said. "Happier times."

"I'm so sorry," I said. "This must be very difficult for you."

"Difficult on many levels, and sad." He walked out of the room.

Mort and I gave the room a fast once-over, but we didn't find a note. "I'll have the team come through and do a more thorough search," he said.

We found Chattergee sitting on Vera's couch, holding her sweater. "Is there anything else you need from me? I have to call California again."

"We'll leave you alone in a few minutes," I said.

"We need to know about the guns," Mort said.

"What guns?"

"Exactly," Mort said. "Are there any people in the production who carry guns, whether they're licensed or not?"

Chattergee shifted in his seat and looked uncomfortable. "I'm not sure, but there could be some people who are armed," he said.

Mort and I glanced at each other briefly. His expression was as surprised as I was sure mine was. "Why would people working on a movie carry guns?" Mort asked.

"The studio doesn't provide us with security. It's a matter of cost, extra personnel, extra expenses. I don't work it into the budget, either. But occasionally there are incidents. There are a lot of nuts in the world." He shook his head. "I told Vera she should carry one, too."

"Maybe you should have told her to lock her door instead," Mort said.

"Do you have a gun?" I asked.

"I do." Chattergee leaned over and tugged up the cuff of his pants to reveal an ankle holster.

"Can I see that?" Mort said. There was only one answer to his question.

Chattergee unsnapped the holster and handed Mort his silver-and-black palm-sized gun. "It's a Beretta Bobcat," he said. "Small, lightweight. I'm licensed to carry."

Mort sniffed the barrel. "Did you fire it recently?"

"Only at the range."

"When was that?"

"Probably the day before I left California."

"How do you load it?" Mort asked, holding the barrel and giving him back the pistol, butt end first.

"It's a little tricky," Chattergee said, demonstrating as he spoke. "It has this tip-up feature on the barrel so you can load the chamber without having to move the slide. But the thing is, instead of ejecting the casing to the side like most semiautomatics, the spent casing shoots up over your head. It's a bit awkward." He slipped out a bullet and showed it to Mort.

"May I have that?" Mort asked, taking out a handkerchief.

"Sure. Figured you'd want one. I didn't shoot my wife, Sheriff. But you go ahead and compare bullets."

"Is there any way we can get a list of everyone who has a gun?" Mort asked, tucking the handkerchief with the bullet into his breast pocket.

"I doubt if one exists, but I can ask around."

"Would appreciate it if you'd do just that."

"What about prop guns?" I asked. "The judge in the movie is shot. Doesn't the props department have a gun?"

"More than one," Chattergee said, returning his weapon to its holster, "but they use blanks, not real bullets."

Errors can be made, I thought, but said instead, "Who should we see there?"

"I'll get the first AD to take you around," Chattergee said.

"AD?" Mort said. "You got to spell out these initials for me."

"Assistant director," Chattergee said. "That'll be Eric Barry. I'll call him and have him escort you where you want to go."

Mort and I spent another two hours at the airport, visiting production departments and interviewing people. We were accompanied by the first assistant director, a tall man with sandy brown hair and fingernails bitten to the quick. The prop guns were all accounted for, with no telltale odor of recent firing—if there is any identifiable smell when you're using blanks. But of course that's a moot point; the gun that killed Vera hadn't been loaded with blanks.

Everyone we spoke with demonstrated the proper amount of shock at the news of Vera's murder, although I was pretty sure that for most of them, the news was secondhand by the time we got around to delivering it. Mort took names and told people that his department would follow up, and then he drove me home. It was almost time for supper.

"Isn't it amazing how everyone has an alibi for the last twenty-four hours?" I said when he pulled up in front of my house.

"Yeah. Especially since we don't even know her time of death."

"We know it was sometime after nine, since Chattergee saw her when he arrived," I said. "What I find hard to believe is that no one can remember overhearing Vera Stockdale having an argument. Her exhusband implied that she fought with everyone."

"Makes me think they must all be hard of hearing, or they're walking on eggshells for some reason."

"Or they're afraid of offending someone. Perhaps

the person who oversees their job," I said. "Even Estelle Fancy danced away from the question when you asked her if the actress had any enemies. But one thing's for certain."

"What's that?"

"Vera Stockdale had at least *one* enemy."

Chapter Seven

Sunny Cee was sitting on the sofa in my living room when I walked in, her rolling suitcase on the floor by her feet. She looked up at me with a watery smile and I saw that she'd been crying.

"I guess you've heard," I said.

She nodded, tears silently coursing down her cheeks.

I sat down next to her. "It's a tragedy when anyone dies unexpectedly," I said, "but it's made much worse when it's in this manner."

"Oh, Mrs. Fletcher. It's so awful. How could anyone do this? I know she was difficult, but still . . ." She curled over and buried her face in her hands.

"I can see you're very upset," I said, patting her back. "It's getting late. Are you hungry?"

She shook her head. "I couldn't eat."

"Why don't I make us some tea, and we can talk. Would you like that?"

"Sure," she said, pulling a tissue from her pocket. "Thank you."

I left her to compose herself and went to the kitchen, filled my kettle with water, and set it on the stove.

Sunny had been living with me for two weeks. She hadn't come in with the principal production people from California, who had flown in earlier, but rather had arrived with the rest of the crew members, some of whom had been hired locally, though the majority were called up from Boston or New York. She was one of seven production assistants; most of them were film students and all of them were renting rooms from Cabot Cove residents. A van came around early each morning to pick them up, and delivered them back to their respective temporary homes after the workday, often late at night. In lieu of having to wait up for her on those evenings, I'd given Sunny her own key to my front door, although I confess to listening for her return like a worried parent.

Sunny was a charming houseguest, as I'd told Mort, cheerful, helpful, and full of enthusiasm for her new job. A graduate of a boarding school in Switzerland, she had been accepted by New York University into its film production program, and was in the last year of her studies there. Sunny's job as a PA on *A Deadly Decision* necessitated her taking off a semester from school. She'd told me it was "a no-brainer"—her words. Having the chance to work on another movie was an opportunity she couldn't possibly pass up. I only hoped the glamour of working in the movies didn't keep her from completing her studies and earning a degree.

Sunny trailed me into the kitchen. Her eyes were

swollen, but dry. "Can I do anything to help?" she asked.

"You can take down the mugs for us from the cupboard," I said. "I'm sure we have milk in the refrigerator, and you know where the sugar bowl is."

We settled at my kitchen table with two mugs of English breakfast tea and a plate of butter cookies from Charlene Sassi's bakery. Sunny had poured milk into a small pitcher and had smoothed the sugar in my bowl with the back of a spoon before placing those items on the table. She'd also carefully folded two napkins for us.

"When I was in boarding school, afternoon tea was practically a course in itself," she said with a soft smile. "We were divided into small groups and took turns at serving each other. Woe to the girl who even thought about taking a shortcut. Everything had to be just so."

"We're not quite so formal here," I said. "I hope you don't miss the silver service."

"Not a bit," she said. "My first act of defiance when I moved into the dormitory at NYU was to serve myself a 'cuppa' tea with the milk carton on the table." She chuckled. "Some rebel, huh?"

"I think you're a lovely young lady," I said. "Whatever they taught you in boarding school has stood you in good stead."

"Thank you, Mrs. Fletcher." She took a sip from her mug and put it down. "And thank you for not grilling me as to why my parents sent me off to boarding school instead of educating me at home."

"It's not my business why decisions are made in anyone's family," I said.

"But you'd be amazed at how many people here in

the States just come right up to you and ask the most personal questions. I have to admit it took me aback when I first got home."

"Just because people ask doesn't mean you have to answer," I said. "I'm always curious about people; I hope I haven't intruded on your privacy in the time you've spent here."

"Oh, not at all," she said, looking at me earnestly. "Just the opposite. You've been so welcoming and accepting. It's because you've never asked that I'd like to tell you why I went to boarding school. I don't want you to think badly of my parents."

"It would certainly be presumptuous of me to criticize your parents for any decision they made," I said. "I can hardly be called an expert in child rearing since I've never had children of my own—although my nephew, Grady, did live with us for a long while." I smiled at the memory. Grady was now a grown man with a family of his own, and I was delighted to play "Grandma" with his son, Frank. "You don't need to explain anything to me," I told Sunny, "but I'm happy to listen if you want to talk."

"It's not such a big secret," she said. "Both my parents were professionals and they felt I would be better taken care of in a boarding school than having a series of nannies coming and going."

"Are you an only child?" I asked.

"Yes, and before you ask if I ever wanted siblings, I'll tell you that when I was five I told my mother I wanted an older brother, but if she couldn't arrange that, I didn't want them to give me anyone younger." She smiled at the memory. "She practically spit her coffee across the room."

"So where did you go to school?"

"Geneva. My father attended a British boarding school, but he thought the best finishing schools for girls were in Switzerland. I was upset at first, but I managed to fit in well, and I really enjoyed it after a time. Living abroad allowed me to travel around Europe on my school breaks, and that was an education in itself."

We talked for a while about the differences between American schools and those overseas—Sunny was fluent in French and Italian, a legacy of her boarding school education—before circling back to the death of Vera Stockdale and the reason Sunny had packed her bags.

"Do you know a lot about how she died?" Sunny asked.

I hesitated. "I know more than I'm free to talk about with you," I said. I'd decided it was better not to discuss Vera's death beyond the simple fact that she had been killed. I was conscious that Mort's investigation was only in its early stages and that he wanted to hold back information that might affect the case. Sunny was young and impressionable. I didn't want to fuel her nightmares. In addition, it seemed to me that whoever killed Vera had achieved his or her goal. Unless the perpetrator turned out to have more victims in mind, it was better to err on the side of discretion than to raise fears about a killer still at liberty.

"I have great confidence in our sheriff," I told her.

"He's a dedicated lawman and I'm sure he's working hard to solve this case as quickly as possible."

"This case," she echoed, nodding slowly.

"I have a question for *you* now."

Sunny took in a deep breath and met my gaze.

"I saw your suitcase," I said. "Why are you leaving? Are you frightened for your safety here? I don't think you need to be. Are you planning to go home?"

She shook her head. "No, not home. Well, maybe I am going home, in a way. You've been wonderful, Mrs. Fletcher. I appreciate all you've done for me. But . . ." She stopped, gathering her thoughts. "Please don't be offended," she said. "I'm not running away. I just feel . . . I just need to be out at the airport. We're a community, all of us on the crew. I need my friends, my family, around me at this time."

"I understand," I said. "Is there room for you in someone's trailer?"

"Oh, yes. I'll be fine," she said, dabbing at tears that had started again. "Movie people are happy to help you out when there's a . . ." She swallowed. "When you're feeling down or alone."

"Do you have a ride out to the airport?" I asked. "I can call a cab for you if you need one."

"That's okay. I'm being picked up." She checked her watch. "He should be here any minute." She took her mug to the sink, washed it out, and had picked up the kitchen towel to dry it when my doorbell rang.

"Don't bother with the mug," I said. "I'll finish up."

"I don't want to leave you with a mess."

"You aren't leaving me with a mess."

"At least let me take care of the milk and sugar," she

said, replacing the top on the sugar bowl. "I'll put them away."

"All right," I said. I left her in the kitchen and went to open the front door.

Terrence Chattergee stood on my front step. His black hair was mussed and he had deep circles under his eyes. Behind him, a car waited at the curb with one of Sunny's fellow PAs behind the wheel.

"Good evening, Mrs. Fletcher," he said. "I've come for Sunita."

Before I could wonder at why the executive producer of the movie had arrived to pick up a lowly production assistant, Sunny came up behind me, and he reached for her suitcase. She gave me a fast hug and whispered, "Thank you." Then she turned to look at Chattergee, who was studying her face.

"Hello, Daddy," she said.

Chapter Eight

Sunny had told everyone her last name was Cee. It wasn't exactly a lie; that was the first initial of her last name, after all. I suspected she hadn't divulged that she was the daughter of people involved with the production because nepotism, while common in Hollywood, as it is in many businesses, is not something that's usually greeted warmly. If everyone had known that Sunny was the child not only of the star but also of the executive producer, it would have made it difficult, if not impossible, for her to fit in.

I alerted Mort about their relationship right after Chattergee and Sunny left my house, and I confided in Seth, too, when I spoke with him the next day.

Mort was too busy to follow up with father and child right away. He had instructed everyone we'd interviewed at the airport not to discuss the crime until he'd had the opportunity to inform people and question them first, but word got out anyway, to no one's surprise. I later learned that only a short time after we'd left, he was deluged with calls from the production staff, from studio people in Hollywood, and, naturally, from the press. Cabot Cove had experienced other odd deaths over the years, and the town was abuzz with the news of Vera's dramatic demise. Reporters were on their way from the movie industry's trade papers, the *Hollywood Reporter* and *Variety* among others, as were correspondents from the major news outlets. TV crews from New York and Boston, as well as local ones from Bangor and Portland, descended on our village the next day, keeping Mort busy making official comments about the murder and hindering his investigation.

Evelyn Phillips, editor of the *Cabot Cove Gazette*, had been one of the first local experts consulted by the press, and enjoyed advising big-name journalists on the best places to eat lobster and where to find a late-night cocktail. But she fumed to me about their being able to obtain exclusive interviews with the celebrities whom she'd been denied.

Before the press packed up their equipment and took off to cover more-urgent stories (leaving only a few persistent reporters behind), Mort mounted a hastily called press conference in the high school's combination auditorium-gym to handle the reporters in one large batch.

"Vera would have been delighted with all this attention," Lois Brannigan told me as she regarded the press corps. "Too bad she's not here to see the lineup of cameras and microphones."

Lois wasn't as strikingly beautiful a woman as Vera had been, but she had the kind of soft, pretty features that could be made up to appear appropriate for a variety of characters. Never an ingenue—she was too buxom for those roles—she'd lasted in Hollywood as an adaptable actress, taking the parts of best friend, older sister, wife, faithful secretary, schoolteacher, storekeeper, whatever secondary woman a movie required.

"Will the film still get made?" I asked her.

"Well, I, for one, certainly hope so," she said. "Just between us girls, I already put in my bid with the casting director for Vera's part. Not that the role of the mistress isn't a juicy one; I was looking forward to playing a floozy for a change." She struck a playful pose, thrusting out her hip and cupping the back of her head with a hand. "I'd get to express my inner party girl." She glanced around to see if anyone was watching, then dropped her hand. "Truth to tell, it's actually a better part than the judge. There's more meat for an actress to work with."

"Then why would you want to play the judge?" I asked, amused.

"I have to look out for my career, don't I? Vera got top billing and whoever replaces her will, too. That's what I want. I haven't said anything yet to Chattergee and Elovitz. I don't want to appear too eager. They make the final decision. I only hope they don't do something drastic like canceling the production. I'd hate it if this whole exercise was a waste of time. Besides, I need the work."

"Do you think a decision will be made soon?" I asked.

"Not too soon. It wouldn't be seemly," she replied. "But since they've spent a large fortune on trekking the cast and key crew members across the country, I think the powers that be will give it a few days' grace before they announce that"—Lois raised her hands in mock prayer and gazed upward—" 'Vera would want us to go on without her.' "

"Would she?" I asked, egging her on.

"Never! She'd want us in mourning for at least a year. But we may as well make a movie. We can't leave yet anyway. Your sheriff has ordered all of us to stay put."

Our sheriff approached the podium, a music stand that had been commandeered from the band room, and made a statement to the press as close to "no comment" as he could get away with. He gave the date, time, and location of the discovery of Vera Stockdale's body, and revealed, "She was killed with one shot. However, we do not have information on the ballistics for you at this time." He left out the telling detail of the film looped around the deceased's neck and insisted that he wasn't at liberty to disclose more information while the investigation was ongoing. Wisely, however, he'd arranged a lineup of people from the movie company to provide comments to the bottomless pit that was the news-gathering machine.

Terrence Chattergee, Vera's former husband and the current producer of the film, stepped up to the make-shift podium and took the microphone after Mort. He held his notes in a hand that trembled. "My family and I are very grateful for the outpouring of love and affection from Vera's fans around the world," he said. "Even though Vera and I were separated for many years, we were still valued colleagues. I held her in great esteem, as she did me. We never let our personal disagreements spill over into work. Vera was the consummate professional, always prepared. She demanded the best from others as she gave her best to them. I was fortunate to have had her in my life and my films. She was a great lady and a great actress."

"Just not a great wife and mother," Lois muttered under her breath. "They only had one child and even she was too much for Vera to handle."

"Is that so?" I said, wondering if Lois knew that Vera's child had been working on the film.

"They waited until she was old enough for school, then shipped her off to some academy overseas, about as far away from Hollywood as you can get," she offered. "The marriage didn't last much longer after that. I always wondered if Chattergee had wanted Vera to stay home and become the happy housewife. That's one role she never wanted to play."

I looked around the auditorium for Vera Stockdale and Terrence Chattergee's daughter, but if she was there, she was staying out of sight.

"No, funeral arrangements have not been made yet," Chattergee said in answer to a reporter's question. "We will be taking Vera back to Hollywood as soon as we possibly can." He shot a glance at Mort, who was keeping Vera's body in the hospital morgue until all the tests could be completed. "Interment is expected to be at Forest Lawn," Chattergee continued. "There's nothing more I can add at this point. However, on behalf of the company, cast, and crew, we ask that you allow our family, both relatives and professional associates, to grieve in private. I'd like to introduce our director, Mitchell Elovitz, who has asked to say a word."

"More likely he was ordered to say something," Lois confided to me. "Talk about a command performance."

Chattergee cocked his head to indicate it was the director's turn to speak.

Several reporters called out their questions as Elovitz replaced Chattergee at the microphone.

"First, I'd like to extend my most heartfelt condolences to Mr. Chattergee and his family. It was my very great honor and privilege to have had the opportunity to work with the celebrated Vera Stockdale, a monster of an actress whom I had admired my whole life." In deference to the occasion, Elovitz was wearing jeans instead of cargo shorts, and a clean white T-shirt under a navy blue linen jacket. He held a Boston Celtics cap in his hand.

"I'm up after Benson," Lois said, giving me a grim smile. She shouldered her way through the crowd and moved into the on-deck position near the music stand where the actor Walter Benson was smiling into the eyes of a young woman with a microphone. Over her shoulder, a man in a wrinkled suit was taking a picture of Benson with his cell phone. His face was vaguely familiar, but I couldn't place him. His gray hair was in need of trimming and it looked as if he hadn't shaved for a few days. That's not so unusual among young men trying to look macho, but is less common with those from an older generation.

Benson stepped to the microphone and tried not to look pleased at the whir of camera shutters set off by his presence. I looked for the man who had been photographing him, but he'd disappeared into the crowd. Where had I seen him before?

I listened to a few more statements by members of the cast and crew before I slipped out the side door and rode my trusty bicycle downtown to Peppino's Restaurant, where I joined Seth Hazlitt for lunch.

"I'm guessin' you're not going to want to discuss the autopsy over steamed mussels in red sauce," he'd said earlier that morning when we'd arranged to meet.

"Don't be so sure," I'd replied. "But if it offends your delicate sensibilities, I can put off my questions until dessert."

Peppino's was down to half its usual lunchtime crowd. Clearly the bigger attraction was in the gymnasium, and in front of the high school, where rented limousines waited to drive the VIPs back to the airport campground.

"Did they ask for me?" Seth said, holding the back of my chair as I took a seat at the linen-covered table.

"Not by name," I replied. "Mort said the autopsy was pending and reminded them that it may be several weeks before he gets the results of toxicological tests. There was a groan at that. Are those test results important?"

"Just standard procedure," he replied. "We already know the contents of her stomach, blood was negative for alcohol, and I don't expect the tox tests to hold any great surprises, but you never know."

"True. So what is your conclusion, Dr. Hazlitt? Care to spill the beans?" I asked just as Marie, our waitress, came over to take our order.

"Actually, I didn't plan on having the cannellini beans," Seth said, opening the menu. He looked up at Marie. "How are the mussels today?"

"We have them in white sauce with wine and garlic, or you can have red sauce," she said.

"Better make it red sauce. I have to see patients this afternoon. Don't want to offend them with garlic breath," he said, handing her his menu.

"For you, Jessica?"

"I'll have the same."

"Spaghetti on the side, folks?"

Seth glanced over at me before saying, "Just a smidge, Marie."

"Not for me, Marie, but I'd like some garlic bread, and some water when you have a moment."

"You're going to wave that garlic bread under my nose just for spite, aren't you?" Seth said, picking up the corner of his folded napkin, shaking it loose, and draping it across his lap.

"You could have had bread, too," I said, "if you hadn't already ordered spaghetti."

Marie brought us two glasses of water and a basket of garlic bread before she left to place our order.

"Let's get back to the guest in the hospital morgue," I said. "What was your verdict?"

Seth picked up a large piece of garlic bread and took a thoughtful bite. "By my best estimate, whoever killed her did it more than twelve hours before you found the body. Rigor mortis had already set in."

"We found her at two in the afternoon, so that would mean she was killed earlier than two in the morning, and after nine, the last time she was seen alive."

"And I'm figuring that she died from the gunshot wound, if that's what it was. The hole went clear through her heart."

'What do you mean 'if that's what it was'?"

"The damage was consistent with a bullet, but no bullet was found in the body. There was an entrance wound and an exit wound, and they appear very similar. I sent photos of them off to a colleague for his expert opinion. Unless we know for certain what made those holes, it's still conjecture."

"Mort's team didn't find the bullet in the chair?"

"I wouldn't know," Seth said stiffly. "But I'm not a detective. I'm just the doctor doing the postmortem. I'm not deserving of having all the facts."

"Didn't you ask?"

"I did. I left a message at the sheriff's office, and he never called me back." He sounded irritated that Mort had withheld information from him.

"He's been so busy with the press," I said. "I'm sure he'll get back to you soon."

It didn't add up that Mort would deny Seth information about the case, but I decided to drop the subject for the moment.

"Is that why there wasn't a lot of blood?" I said. "With a bullet through the heart, wouldn't it have stopped pumping right away?"

"That's the theory," he replied.

"Do you think the body was moved?" I asked.

"Not unless someone had a wheelbarrow handy or was an Olympic weight lifter," Seth said. "You saw how difficult it was just to place her body on the gurney. There's a reason they say it's hard to lift 'dead-weight.' It is."

"It would've been possible, of course, if the killer had an accomplice," I said.

"Ayuh. Any evidence of that?"

"Not that I know of. But someone went to a lot of trouble to create a dramatic picture with the body."

"True."

"What did you do with the piece of film?" I asked.

"Believe the sheriff took it for the evidence locker."

"Did you look at it at all?" I asked. "The director said he couldn't tell from a distance if it was a clip from a motion picture or simply undeveloped film."

"It was from some movie, all right," Seth said. "But I wouldn't know any more than that. Held it up to the light and you could see these square images between the sprocket holes."

"Mort will have to find out what movie the film was from. It could be a message from the killer."

"And how's he going to do that?" Seth asked, taking another piece of garlic bread. "He likes to watch cartoons. His favorite film star is probably Yosemite Sam." Seth looked over my shoulder. "Isn't that right, Sheriff?"

"I see you're saying nice things about me again," Mort said, pulling out an empty chair and sitting down.

"I take it the news conference is over," I said to him.

"Must be," he replied, waving at our waitress. "Saw you sneaking out the side door," he continued. "Figured while the movie stars were drawing their attention, it was a good time to make my exit." He took the menu from Marie, gave it a quick once-over, and ordered a small sausage pizza. "And tell the chef I like my crust thin and crispy."

"I'll tell him," Marie replied, "but he'll make it the way he always does."

"Just give him the message, please," Mort said, grinning. He waited until Marie disappeared into the kitchen. "Actually, it's not bad for not–New York pizza," he told us.

"So how is the case going, Sheriff?" Seth asked. "Locate the bullet yet?"

"No! Can't find the darn thing. And I had my guys comb that set." Mort tore off two pieces of the garlic bread and stuffed them into his mouth, leaving the hard heel in the basket.

I waited, giving him time to chew, then asked, "How do you explain it?"

He shrugged. "The killer must have moved her from somewhere else," he said, swallowing, "but the evidence techs didn't find any blood smears on the carpet or carpet fibers on her robe or whatever you call that thing she was wearing. There was nothing to show the body had been dragged."

Marie brought Mort a napkin, plate, silverware, and a glass of water, and replaced our bread basket with a full one. I grabbed a piece before all the bread disappeared again.

"So where do you go from here?" Seth asked.

"Back to square one, I guess," Mort answered. "I'm planning to drive out to the airport tomorrow to question some more people—that is, if I can get away with it without having some reporter dogging my steps." He looked at me. "I especially want to interview your former houseguest, Mrs. F. She might have some insights into who disliked her mother, and I'd like to know where she was when Ms. Stockdale was killed. Will you give me a hand with that?"

"Be happy to," I said.

"Here's your mussels," Marie said, deftly balancing two heaping bowls of the bivalves and placing one in front of me and the other before Seth. "Your pizza will be out in a minute, Sheriff, and I'll be right back with a basin for the shells and with Dr. Hazlitt's spaghetti."

"She's a wonderful waitress," I said. "Do you mind if we start without you?" I asked Mort.

"Go ahead."

As I picked up my fork, Mort leaned over to inhale the spicy scent rising from my dish. "May I?" he asked me.

"Help yourself," I said.

He plucked out a mussel and tipped his head back to allow the plump meat to slide into his mouth along with a bit of the sauce. He made a fist. "Mmm! *Delizioso*. Reminds me of home."

"Your mother was Italian?" Seth asked.

"Nope, but we had a great Italian restaurant right around the corner. This was my favorite dish."

"Then why didn't you order it for yourself just now?" Seth asked.

Mort shrugged. "I don't know. I was in the mood for pizza."

"And here it is," Marie said, sliding a metal stand on the table with Mort's pizza atop it, and placing a side dish of spaghetti next to Seth. *"Bon appétit!"*

"That's French," I said.

"Sorry," she replied. "I've been watching Julia Child reruns. *Buon appetito!*"

I waited until Marie turned to another table before saying to Mort in a low voice, "What are you going to do with that piece of film we found?"

While the tables at Peppino's are not on top of each other, and the sound level is pretty high, I was nevertheless being careful not to be overheard. Many a rumor had begun as an innocent statement plucked at Peppino's, then nurtured at Sassi's Bakery, until it burst into full bloom at Mara's Luncheonette. It was like a grown-up version of Telephone, a game I'd played as a child. The first player whispers a secret phrase into the ear of the one sitting next to her, something like "I'll call for you." The second whispers the message into the ear of the third, and so on down the line until the last child to receive the message announces what she heard: "cauliflower." We didn't want any "cauliflowers" grown in the gossip garden.

"Do you have any idea what movie it might have been from?" I asked.

"I didn't recognize anything on it, but frankly it was hard to see the pictures," Mort said. "They were so tiny. I didn't have my reading glasses with me."

"Maybe you should see if someone can run it slowly through a projector for you," Seth put in. "Let you look at a bigger image."

"Great idea, Doc!"

"The problem with that," I said, "is that the light from a regular movie projector is so strong, it could burn a hole in the film."

"It went through a projector at the movies, didn't it?" Mort asked.

"Yes, it did, but very quickly, before the film had time to burn," I replied. "But maybe we can blow up the images and take photographs of them using an overhead projector. They have one at the high school."

"A neighbor of mine is a science teacher there," Mort said. "I'll give him a call."

"Well, that problem's solved," Seth said, adding his last empty mussel shell to the pile in the basin. "What's next?" He patted his mouth with his napkin.

"We dusted the film strip for prints," Mort said, "but it was pretty well wiped clean—some smudges, but nothing I could send to AFIS."

Also known as IAFIS, but not as easy to pronounce as *ay-fiss*. Mort was referring to the Integrated Automated Fingerprint Identification System maintained by the FBI that serves police departments across the country. IAFIS is a central record of fingerprints, as well as criminal history, mug shots, scar and tattoo descriptions, and other pertinent details, and has aided in the solving of many a crime.

"It's a shame there were no prints, but I keep coming back to the strip of film. It must have significance, given where we found it. And if we can learn what movie it's from, that may lead us to the killer."

"I watch a lot of old movies on TV," Mort said, "but it didn't ring a bell."

"If you didn't have your reading glasses," Seth said, looking askance at Mort, "you couldn't see anything to begin with, never mind recognizing what motion picture that truncated bit of celluloid came from."

"Yeah. I guess so."

"Mitchell Elovitz said he would be happy to help you with any production questions," I said to Mort.

"Who's he?" Seth asked.

"The director," I replied. "You met him at the scene."

"You mean that child is the director?"

"He is," I said. "Mort, maybe if you show him the images your friend gets from the overhead projector, he might recognize what movie it's part of. It's worth asking him, don't you think?"

"Yeah, I bet a lot of those kids out at the airport are film buffs. We could show the images to all of them. We might just get a hit. I'll talk to my neighbor tonight."

"Looks like you've got it all worked out," Seth said. "There's just the one little matter left to tie up."

"What's that?" Mort asked.

"Who pulled the trigger and where did that bullet end up?"

Chapter Nine

"So I told Eve that if she wanted to play a role in the movie, she'd need to change her hairstyle," Loretta Spiegel said as she ran a comb through my wet hair. "It's about time. I've been pushing her for years to get her to try something new."

Loretta was talking about Eve Simpson, Cabot Cove's crack real estate agent, who with little encouragement can make a mud hut sound like a mansion. Eve is a friend of long standing, although we have been known to see things differently when she occasionally stretches the truth.

I was sitting on my back porch with a towel around my shoulders and a plastic garbage bag spread out on the floor under my chair while Loretta caught me up on the latest gossip and gave me what she called "a wash, curl, and dry." With her salon still under construction, she was making the rounds of her regular customers' homes to ensure that they didn't miss their weekly appointments.

"And what did Eve say to that?" I asked.

"She said she'd 'take it under consideration.' But Ideal Malloy said Eve's had the same hairstyle for twenty years, and since the movie is set in the past, she should be just right for the role."

"It's not that far in the past," I said. "And what role is that?"

"I'm not sure," Loretta said, as she wound a lock of my hair around a foam roller and secured it to my head. "Eve said she was convinced they wouldn't let her play the judge even though she'd be perfect for the part, but she bought a legal phrase book just in case. She said she was flexible as long as she had some lines to say. I think she's going to audition for the casting lady today."

"Oh, dear," I said. "Does the casting lady know she's coming?"

"I don't know. Does she need an appointment?"

"I doubt if they're holding auditions," I said. "At least no one's mentioned them to me. They haven't even announced if they're planning to go forward with the film."

"Ideal said she saw Elsie Fricket down at the Merry Mart and *she* said she heard from her nephew Albert, who drives the bakery truck for Charlene Sassi, who told him that one of the catering people told her that they're going to start filming again soon."

"Then it must be so," I said, thinking about the game of Telephone and trying to keep a straight face.

"Oh, you," Loretta said, tapping her comb on my shoulder. "Well, if they give Eve Simpson a speaking part, then I'm going to ask for one, too."

"You are?"

"I know exactly what the styles looked like when the judge was murdered. I could raid my sister's closet. They wouldn't even have to bother the wardrobe people for my costume."

"I didn't know you were interested in being an actress," I said.

"I played Persephone in our high school production of the Greek myths," Loretta said, holding up the hand mirror she ordinarily used to show me the back of my hair. She patted her own curls, and checked her teeth for lipstick. "I beat out Eve Simpson for the role."

"Anything more recent?" I asked.

"Who'm I kidding?" Loretta said, putting the mirror down. "Eve will never get any lines. She'll just be an extra like the rest of us."

When Loretta finished up, I was washed, curled, and dried to perfection. I waited until she left the house to run upstairs and brush out my hair, hoping the tight ringlets she'd arranged would loosen up a bit.

"Going for the Shirley Temple look?" Mort said when he came to pick me up.

"Loretta doesn't have access to all her usual supplies," I replied. "It'll look better tomorrow. It always does the next day."

"Heard anything new about the movie folks?" he asked, turning the patrol car toward the airport.

"According to the Cabot Cove grapevine," I said, "the production company is going to start filming again."

"That's good news if it's true."

"Why do you say that?"

"Gives us more time to interview these people and figure out who had a grudge against Ms. Stockdale."

"From the way her former husband put it, it could be just about everyone. Vera Stockdale was not one to stand on formalities. She spoke her mind whether you liked it or not."

"Yeah. She doesn't sound like the nicest person around."

"Yet her daughter is. Sunny couldn't be, well, sunnier. I'm curious about their relationship. Mother and daughter."

"Here's a case where the apple fell pretty far from the tree, don't you think, Mrs. F.?"

"I do. But if Vera's child was in school in Europe while she was in Hollywood making movies, they might not have had much of a relationship at all."

Our first stop was the hangar, where Mort consulted with the deputy at the door and was assured that no one had been allowed inside. I knew there were several alternative ways to get into the hangar apart from the back door, and mentioned it.

"Had my guy check it out. They're all locked," Mort said.

We went inside and groped our way around the back of the scenery flats until we saw the lights focused on the make-believe judge's office. While the set was illuminated, the vast space of the rest of the hangar lay in shadows. One end of the yellow crime scene tape had come free and was draped around the base of the metal stand to which it had been affixed. We stepped over it and stood at the edge of the set, gazing out over the scene of the crime. It was easy to spot evidence of the investigation squad's presence. In addition to the white residue left behind when they dusted for fingerprints, someone had forgotten to pack up a ruler that sat on the judge's desk, and a cellophane envelope had been discarded on the floor near the bookcase.

"Where's the chair?" I asked, noting that the seat in which Vera had been found was missing.

"Had it sent to the State Bureau of Identification crime lab," Mort said. "It had one of those tufted backs. I figure it was possible the bullet was lodged in one of the folds. If it is, those guys will be able to dig it out."

A noise from the front of the hangar caught our attention, and we turned to peer into the darkness. It sounded like something was being wheeled across the concrete floor. Mort pulled a flashlight from his belt and pointed it away from the set and toward the cavernous area in which the outlines of cameras and equipment could barely be seen. "Who's there?" he yelled.

A black case tied to a hand truck with a bungee cord came into view.

"Stop right there," Mort called out.

Whoever was wheeling the case let the hand truck tip forward until the case was upright. Then a large figure dressed in a black T-shirt and shorts stepped out from behind the case.

"You're Zee, right?" Mort said, switching off his flashlight. "How did you get in here?"

"Came through the front door," Zee said, sticking up a thumb and jerking it back over his shoulder. "Jed unlocked it for me, said it would be okay. We just got in from Bangor. Went to pick up my camera mount. I need to leave the case in place before the next shoot."

"Have you been gone for days?" Mort asked.

"Nah. Just went back this morning to pick it up."

"So you know what happened here?"

"I heard what was found here," he said, "but I don't know exactly what happened."

Either Zee was naturally precise, I thought, or else he'd had experience with the authorities before.

"Did any of my men interview you about the incident?" Mort asked.

"No, sir."

"Then I'd like a little of your time. When would be convenient?"

"Now is convenient," Zee said.

"Okay," Mort said, pulling out his pad. "Let's see if we can find some chairs."

"What happened to the one that was on the set?"

"Sent it out for testing."

"Oh." Zee cast his eyes around the hangar. "We can use the director's chair here and the script supervisor's stool over there. I have a couple of apple boxes I can stack for myself."

"Okay. Let's set them up," Mort said. He grabbed the director's chair for himself. It had the name MITCH-ELL ELOVITZ stenciled on the canvas back. "Do you mind if I use this chair, Mrs. F.? That way I can lean on the arm."

"Go ahead," I said.

Mort picked up Nicole Domash's stool—her name wasn't on it—and set it next to the chair for me to use.

"Can you put on any more lights in here?" he asked Zee. "I'm not a cat; I can't see in the dark."

Zee flipped a switch on a wall panel and the lights in the rest of the hangar came to life. They weren't as bright as those illuminating the set, but at least we weren't squinting into the gloom. He reached into a canvas cart with a big z painted on the side and the words KEEP HANDS OFF! and pulled out two wooden crates that he stacked on top of each other before settling his solid body on it. He tipped his head to the side and ran a hand through his thick black hair.

Mort licked the point of his pencil. "Let me have your full name," he said.

"Ernest Zalagarda," he said, spelling his last name, "but everyone knows me as 'Zee.'"

"Age?"

"Thirty-four."

"And where are you from?"

"Currently, I live in Los Angeles." He recited his address and telephone number without Mort's asking.

"What's your occupation?"

"Key grip on this film. Me and my crew rig the lights, operate the dollies and cranes, work with the gaffer—that's the electrician."

Mort looked up from his pad. "U.S. citizen?"

"Yes. Want to see my driver's license? Union card?"

Mort shook his head. "That's okay. Do you own a gun?"

"No, sir."

"Where were you when the murder took place?"

"I have no idea," Zee said, a small smile on his face. "When did the murder take place?"

Mort gave him the date. "We figure she was killed somewhere between ten at night and two in the morning. Where were you at that time?"

"We weren't shooting that night, but I had been here earlier setting up equipment. That's when I learned we had a malfunctioning camera mount."

"Weren't you invited to the poker game?" I asked.

Zee smirked. "I was invited, but I like to keep my money in my pocket." He patted the side of his pants.

"Was anyone here with you?" Mort asked.

"I didn't see anyone, but I heard a couple of the carpenters when I came in. They were building something back there, in one of the offices. There was a lot of banging." He cocked his head toward the front of the hangar.

"So what happened next? You found a problem with your equipment, and . . ."

"I took it back to my trailer to see if I could fix it."

"You took that whole big case back to your trailer?" I asked.

"It's not *that* heavy," Zee said, chuckling. "Anyway, I can handle it, but, no, I didn't take back the whole thing. I thought the problem was in the head, and if it was, maybe I could fix it. But it turned out I couldn't. Had to bring it to Bangor for repair."

"What time did you go back to your trailer?" Mort asked.

"Around nine thirty."

"Anyone see you?"

"Not that I know of."

"Do you live in the trailer by yourself?" I asked.

"I should," he replied, combing his thick hair with

his fingers. "The union says I'm supposed to have a single room if available. But we're a little squeezed for space here, so I agreed to share with Eric Barry."

"The first AD?" Mort said, writing down "assistant director."

"Yeah," Zee said. "You're getting the lingo, Sheriff."

"Do movie companies always bring crew members all the way across the country for a job?" I asked.

"Depends," Zee replied. "Most of the time, crew is pulled locally or from the nearest city with union members. But some directors like to have their peeps around them, and they specify who's to travel with them."

"Are you one of those *peeps*?" Mort asked.

Zee nodded. "I worked with Mitch on his first big film."

"*Vampire Zombies from Jupiter*?"

"Wow, Sheriff. I'm impressed."

Mort blushed. "So? Go on."

"I worked with Elovitz on *Zombies* and he wanted me on this picture, too. It's kind of a good luck thing. You don't want to break the chain."

"Is the same true of Eric Barry?"

"Yup."

"Mitchell Elovitz said you were excited to work with Vera on this picture. True?" I asked.

"Who wouldn't be? She was a big star."

"Did you speak with her at all?"

"Only in the course of business. She didn't really lower herself to talk with the crew."

"Was that a disappointment?"

"You might say that."

"Was she rude to you?"

His expression hardened for a moment. "She wasn't anything to me."

"Where was Eric Barry while you were trying to fix the camera mount?" I asked.

Zee shrugged. "Seeing his girlfriend, I guess, but you'll have to ask him."

"Who's his girlfriend?" Mort asked.

"One of our PAs, Sunny. I don't know if you know her."

I glanced at Mort. "We know Sunny," I said, "assuming she's the only production assistant going by that name."

"She is."

"Okay," Mort said. "So you couldn't fix the camera mount head—or whatever it's called. Did you bring it back here?"

"Not until the next morning."

"The next morning?" I said. "Did you come in here, to the hangar, to get the case?"

"I did."

"And you didn't see the dead body sitting in the chair?"

He pressed his lips together and shook his head. "I wasn't looking at the set. It was a hot set. I just got the case, replaced the mount, and wheeled it out of here."

"Was anyone else with you?" Mort asked.

"Sunny was. She followed me inside."

"Why?" Mort and I asked at the same time.

Zee shrugged his shoulders. "She wanted to talk. Don't tell Eric, but I think she's hot for me."

"What makes you say that?" I asked.

"She's always trailing me around, trying to get me to talk to her."

"Do you encourage her?" I asked.

"She's too young for me, but I don't *dis*courage her. She's a cute chick. It's flattering."

"And neither of you saw the dead body sitting in the chair on the set."

Zee shook his head. "Sunny was looking at me and I was packing the camera mount, and then we left. It's a little weird, now that I think of it."

"You think?" Mort said, pocketing his pencil. "I don't have any more questions. Mrs. F., do you?"

"Not at the moment."

Mort turned back to Zee. "You can take off now, but don't leave town in case I want to talk to you again."

"I'll be here for a while, Sheriff. I understand we're still making the movie."

"Who told you that?" Mort asked.

"Elovitz. He said he was just waiting for you to take down the yellow tape. As soon as he can have the set cleaned up, we'll be good to go."

"I'm still thinking about it," Mort said. "I'll let him know." He waved his hand as if shooing Zee away. "Use the door you came in by, and make sure it locks behind you."

As Zee sauntered to the front of the hangar, Mort said to me, "I have to have a talk with Jed. Hope he didn't unlock the front door for anyone else while I've got a deputy guarding the back one."

I shivered. "It's terrible to think of Zee and Sunny in here with her mother dead in a chair on the set."

"How did they not see her?" Mort said.

"The lights were off and the chair was turned around," I reminded him. "You and I didn't see her even when Elovitz turned on the lights. She was facing the other way."

Mort pursed his lips and blew out a stream of air. "If you don't mind, Mrs. F., I'd like you to ask Sunny about what they were doing in here. She'll be more comfortable talking to you than me. See if her story matches up to his."

"I don't mind," I said. "I'll ask around for her when we leave."

Mort walked to the edge of the set, pulled off the yellow tape, rolled it up into a ball, and flung it to the side. He stood with his fists on his hips, eyes scanning every inch of the imitation office. "Want to take a last look at the set before I clear it for use?"

"Let's do that," I said.

Mort and I had hunted for some evidence—a bullet hole, for instance—that the murder had taken place on the set. I'd even gone through all the drawers in the desk designed to mimic the one in Judge Jacob Borden's office. Oddly, the set decorator had filled them with fake legal files and folders containing sheaves of papers that looked like they'd been taken from the recycle box in the production office. I'd flipped through each page in hopes of discovering the cryptic note sent to Vera, but found nothing. After a half hour, we abandoned the hangar.

"I should be hearing from the SBI soon," Mort said, referring to the Maine State Bureau of Identification. "I'll let you know what they say about the chair."

We agreed to meet later in the day, and I began my search for Sunny. While Mort went off to find Mitchell Elovitz to tell him his set was cleared for use again, I hunted around the trailers to see if I could track down Vera's daughter. I couldn't let go of the image of her playfully flirting with Zee not thirty feet from her mother's body. It made me shudder.

Chapter Ten

"Hi! I'm looking for Sunny," I said to the ladies inside the wardrobe and makeup trailer. "She's a production assistant. Do you know her?"

"Come on in," one called out. "I can't hear you with the water running."

"Thanks," I said, climbing inside the double-length container on wheels, the front section of which was a mini beauty parlor that Loretta Spiegel would have loved. While the color scheme was not the seafoam green she had in mind, the compact salon had a sleek black porcelain sink built into a counter flanked by glass-doored cabinets holding a display of hairbrushes, combs, and scissors together with multiple bottles, cans, and tubes of every variety of hair product. Above the sink was a lighted mirror, and on the side of one cabinet hung a rack for electric appliances—hair dryer, curling iron, straightening press, and a few other gadgets I'd never seen before.

"Nice, huh?" said the lady who'd invited me inside. "Zee put it up for me." She straightened the cord of a hair dryer.

She was a short, middle-aged woman with a strawberry blond beehive hairdo, which I imagine she hoped would make her appear taller. She wore a pink smock that had AUDREY embroidered on the patch pocket, gray slacks, and thick-soled sneakers. Her slightly younger colleague, in a blue smock with KARLA on the pocket, leaned against the makeup station opposite the sink. Clearly the "wardrobe" half of the duo, she had a measuring tape looped around her neck, and circling her wrist was an elastic band that held a big red pincushion. Her half of the vehicle was easily identified by the hanging racks of clothing that lined the walls leading to a sewing machine and a pair of adjustable dressmaker forms.

Audrey wrung out the towel she'd been washing in the sink and turned off the water. "Who did you say you were looking for?" she asked, as she proceeded to wipe down the black leather styling chair and its circular stand.

"Sunny Cee. She's a production assistant, about my height, pretty girl with long dark hair."

Audrey shook her head. "Doesn't sound familiar. Do you know her, Karla?"

"Isn't she the one Walt Benson saw sneaking into Mr. Chattergee's trailer last night?" Karla said. "Can't believe he's preying on the young ones now that his ex is out of the way. You know her, Aud. The girl who was wearing the cowboy hat. You said what nice hair she has."

"Is that who it was?" Audrey said, tsking. "I thought she was a sweet girl. Too bad. Probably trying to use her charm to move up in the world."

"Charm? Is that what you call it these days?" Karla said. "And him, old enough to be her father."

I had to bite my tongue not to tell them that Terrence Chattergee was indeed Sunny Cee's father, but it wasn't the place to reveal family connections.

"He may be old, but he's a handsome devil. Always was a ladies' man," Audrey said, rinsing out her towel again and draping it over the faucet. "I bet Benson had his nose out of joint because she wouldn't fall into *his* arms."

"May as well go for the gold if you're going to give away the goods," Karla said. "Chattergee's gotta be rich. How many times has Benson been married?"

"Last I heard he's on his fourth."

Karla counted on her fingers, "So that's three alimony payments not counting the palimony suit he lost. The man's gotta be broke."

"Probably why he took this role. There's no sex appeal in it that I can see. Did you see him on the cover of *Hollywood Stars*? Now that's what I like a man to look like."

While it appeared as if the wardrobe and makeup trailer could compete with Mara's Luncheonette in Cabot Cove as an epicenter of gossip, I had stopped by for a specific reason. I cleared my throat. "Have you seen her today?" I asked.

They both looked at me. "Who?"

"Sunny Cee."

"Not today, but I've seen *you* around before," Audrey said, giving me the once-over. "I always notice a good head of hair. Are you on the crew?"

"Script consultant," I said, resisting the urge to touch one of the curls Loretta had given me. "I work with Hamilton Twomby. My name is Jessica Fletcher."

Audrey cocked her head at me. "The mystery writer who wrote the book we're making a movie of?"

I nodded.

"Nice to meet you, Jessica." Audrey pointed at her pocket and Karla's. "You can see who we are."

"Do I know Twomby?" Karla asked Audrey.

"He's that big bear with the funny beard, the one who always cuts in the buffet line."

"Oh, yeah. I know who he is." She looked at me. "What do you want the PA for?"

"She's the daughter of a friend. I just wanted to say hello," I said. "Have you heard if the film is starting up again?"

"The latest rumor is that they're resuming filming on Friday. I haven't gotten the official word, yet," Audrey said, "but I want to be ready just in case." She nodded toward Karla. "Don't you have Benson and Brannigan coming in for a fitting?"

"Benson and Brannigan. They sound like a law firm," Karla said. "Only problem is I don't know what costume to have ready for Lois, the one I already fitted her for or the one Ms. Stockdale was wearing."

"Is she taking over Ms. Stockdale's role?" I asked.

Karla shrugged. "They never tell me until the last minute," she said.

"That must be difficult," I said, "having to refashion a costume for another actress."

"Oh, we do it every day," Karla said. "At least Lois is patient. Ms. Stockdale would fidget all the time. Made it hard to get accurate measurements, and I always pricked my finger when I was fitting her."

"I understand she missed an appointment with you," I said, hoping to get her to offer more information about Vera Stockdale.

"Yeah, but I wasn't surprised," Karla said. "I told Estelle she'd never show up. We had to chase her all over the lot for costume fittings."

"She was always on time for me," Audrey said with a grin.

"Because she loved the pampering. You made her beautiful. I just made her stand still, something she was barely capable of doing."

"Did you two know her for a long time?"

"I never worked with her before," Karla said, "but, Aud, weren't you on her first movie?"

"I was a PA then," Audrey said. She pointed at Karla and herself. "We're a lot younger than she was."

Karla burst out laughing. "Right! By what? Five years?"

"It's still younger, isn't it?" Audrey said, drawing herself up and smoothing the hair at the side of her head.

"Nice to be younger than someone," Karla said and chuckled at her own joke.

"What was Ms. Stockdale like when you worked with her then?" I asked.

"Young. Gorgeous and well aware of it. She had Chattergee wrapped around her finger. His wife did not approve."

"So what could she do?" Karla asked. "Throw a fit? A lot of good that would do."

"She did more than that. She got Vera dropped from the picture."

"No kidding. She must've been a powerful woman. What did Vera do then?"

"She laid low for months in Mexico, I heard, at some secluded resort. 'Trying to get over her heartbreak,' the movie magazines said. Next thing you know, she's back in town and he casts her in the film again."

"Didn't his wife have anything to say about that?" Karla asked.

"Not much," Audrey said with a wink. "She was in Reno divorcing him."

"And then, of course, he married Vera," Karla put in. "Happy ending. Up come the credits." She made a circle with her fingers.

"Yeah. But not for long, and not anymore."

They were silent a moment, thinking of the murdered actress.

Audrey shook her head and took up her cloth again, wiping imaginary water off the counter. "Too bad," she said.

"Did Vera have any friends on this film, apart from Estelle Fancy?" I asked her.

"I never saw her with anyone else," she said. "Did you?" She looked at Karla.

"She struck me as a real loner," Karla said. "I kind of felt sorry for her, even though she was supposed to be such a big star. Shame about what happened, though." She shivered. "Kinda gives me the willies."

"Are you concerned for your own safety?" I asked.

"Me? Oh, no. I get along fine with everyone. Besides, I've got a sweet little forty-five in my shoulder bag. Anyone comes at me, I'm ready for them. Right, Aud?"

"Right! I've got mine in here," Audrey said, sliding open a deep drawer next to the sink. She poked around inside, peering under the towels. "Now where the heck did that thing go?"

"Is your gun missing?" Karla asked.

"I hid it right there," Audrey said, a worried look in her eyes.

"When was that?" I asked.

Audrey shrugged. "When we got here. I never bothered to check again. I had no reason to look for it before."

"So it could have been missing for some time," I said.

"We're only here a couple of weeks. It can't be missing that long," Karla put in. "You probably left it in your suitcase."

"What kind of gun was it?" I asked.

"Nine-millimeter Glock nineteen. I could've sworn I put it here."

"I recommend you tell the sheriff your gun is missing," I said. "He'll want to know."

"Sure. Sure. I'll give him a call," Audrey said, closing the drawer.

"I was just thinking," Karla said. "You know who would be perfect for the role, if they don't give it to Lois, that is. Sharon Stone. I worked with her once. She's the right age and even more beautiful than Vera was. And nice to boot."

"I think Melanie Griffith could do it," Audrey replied. "I like her spark."

"Or Andie MacDowell. How about her?"

I left the hair and wardrobe ladies speculating about who might take over the role of the judge. They were so busy debating the relative merits of Vera's potential replacements that I doubt they noticed when I took my leave to continue my search for Sunny.

The field behind the airport resembled a large campground, one I had wandered through before, when I'd worked with Hamilton Twomby on our script. Beyond the rows of parked vehicles and what appeared to be repurposed cargo containers, I knew there was a large catering tent. It was coming up on lunchtime, and sure enough, there was a big crowd occupying the round tables and lined up at the buffet, a groaning board of salads and hot dishes, pastries and snacks that ran along two sides of the tent. Many of the tables inside that weren't hosting diners were occupied by cast and crew members playing cards or board games, or reading a book or newspaper; several unoccupied tables were littered with empty coffee containers. One section was cordoned off for smokers, and I was surprised to see so many young people still possessed that unhealthy habit.

I ambled undisturbed among the tables, seeking the daughter of the late movie star, and thinking that keeping this many unoccupied people busy all this time must be very costly for the film company. For some reason, I kept stopping to glance over my shoulder. I had the oddest feeling I was being watched. Was someone following me? I gazed around the tent but saw no familiar face.

I shook off the sensation and backtracked to the parking lot of trailers, looking for the long one that was Chattergee's. Even though Sunny had been working incognito, she had been spotted entering her father's trailer. Considering the circumstances, she'd probably bunked in with him, where she was assured of lodging and a sympathetic shoulder. Whether she would reveal their relationship to others in the crew remained to be seen.

When I passed behind Vera's trailer, I heard Cecil barking inside and breathed a sigh of relief.

I walked around to the front and saw that the door was ajar, with crime scene tape dangling from the handle. Perhaps Sunny had decided to stay in her mother's living quarters instead. She ought to have cleared it with the sheriff first, but I could understand. Being close to the belongings of someone you loved—and who had died—could be comforting. Memories of that person wearing a particular article of clothing, the familiar texture and scent of the fabric, could act as a balm for someone in mourning. I remembered with a pang how, many years ago, I desperately needed sleep after my husband, Frank, had died, and the only way I could close my eyes was if the pillow he'd slept on was under my cheek. Chattergee had clung to Vera's sweater after he'd learned of her death. Perhaps Sunny wanted to sleep in her mother's bed, surround herself with her mother's possessions, breathe in the fragrance of her perfume and makeup.

I knocked softly on the open door and heard Cecil bark again. *He must be in the bedroom with her,* I thought. I climbed the short staircase and entered the trailer. Cecil was still barking. I heard a voice say, "Shut up, you stupid dog or I'll lock you in the closet."

That didn't sound like Sunny.

From where I stood, I could see that the bedroom door was open, but I couldn't see who was inside. I tiptoed down the hall and stopped at the entrance to Vera's bedroom. A woman was leaning over Vera's dressing table, the top of her head reflected in the mirror. I noticed there was a cord dangling from the bulging pocket of her jacket. The center drawer was open, and she was pawing through a box of the actress's jewelry, dropping some of the pieces into her pocket. The woman was Estelle Fancy.

Cecil was on the bed, growling, straining at his leash, which was tied around the bedpost. The closet doors stood open and Vera's clothes were strewn across the green silk coverlet, many of the pockets turned inside out. Seeing me, Cecil stopped growling. He lay down on Vera's robe, shoved his nose in one of the feather cuffs, and sneezed.

"May I ask what you're doing?" I said.

Estelle shrieked. She dropped the bracelet she'd been examining, then hastily closed the jewelry box and shoved it back into the drawer. "Oh, my, you startled me."

"I think you may want to return the items in your pocket to the jewelry box before you close the drawer," I said.

Estelle shoved her hand in her pocket and took out a fistful of Vera's jewelry. She lifted the lid on the box and threw the pieces inside, then tucked the dangling cord back in her pocket. "This may not look very nice, but Vera promised to give me her garnet set when she died. It's my birthstone, the stone of love and devotion, passion and courage. I swear she said she'd leave it to me in her will. I wouldn't have touched anything of hers otherwise."

"In that case, I suggest you wait for her will to be read. If she's left something to you, that's when you'll receive it."

"That could be months," Estelle said, wiping her hands on the front of her skirt. "And what if she forgot to tell the lawyer? It would be just like her. She promised them to me right after she got the part in *Danger Comes Calling*. It was her first starring role and I was the one who made it happen. She never would have gotten the part if it hadn't been for me. Never! She said I could have anything of hers except Terry." She snorted. "He wasn't her husband then. In fact, he was married to someone else. Later on, she said I could have him back. So, I told her garnets were my birthstone, and she said, 'Then you shall have my garnet set. It's yours when I die.' There's a necklace, a bracelet, and a pair of drop earrings. They're supposed to be mine."

"If you'd done her such a big favor, why didn't she reward you right away?" I asked.

"Well, that was Vera. People did favors for her all the time. She expected it. She only ever did one favor for me and she never let me forget it." A nasty expression formed on Estelle's face, but she quickly schooled her features. "She was ruled by Mercury. Your best friend one day, your enemy the next. Anyway, I deserve those jewels. They should be mine." She fingered the top of the jewelry box. "She promised."

"If you take them now, I'll report you to the police," I said. "Sheriff Metzger is here at the airport. I don't think you want to explain to him why you were rifling through Vera Stockdale's jewelry box."

"But—"

"If Vera promised something to you, tell Terrence Chattergee. Let him decide when or if you can take what you claim is supposed to be yours."

Estelle drew herself up stiffly. "If you say so."

"I do."

"Then I'll take my leave," she said, closing the drawer slowly and pulling the lapels of her jacket closed.

"Were you searching for the note she received?"

"I don't know what you're talking about. I already told you, I wasn't with her twenty-four hours a day. And contrary to what you may think, I'm not a mind reader. I just study the stars."

I gestured toward Vera's closet. "Then what were you looking for? You took out all of Vera's clothes." When she didn't answer, I asked, "Aren't you going to put her things away?"

"Someone else can do that. They have to be packed up anyway." She turned toward me, her hand still clutching the fabric of her jacket, but I didn't move.

"Are you going to block me from leaving?" she asked coldly.

"No."

She pushed past me roughly and walked down the hall.

"What about the dog?" I called after her. "What about Cecil?"

"You can have him," came the reply.

Chapter Eleven

Before I left the trailer, I untied Cecil's leash and unhooked it from his collar, but he refused to get down from Vera's bed. Rather than fight a stubborn Chihuahua, I refilled his water bowl and went through the kitchen cabinets until I found a canister of dog food, then poured a small amount into his food bowl on the floor.

I taped a note on the locked door of Chattergee's trailer next door, telling him where Cecil was. I planned to check back before I left the airport to make certain *someone* was taking care of Vera's dog. I didn't relish the idea of taking in an orphaned creature, even though I've always been an animal lover.

Whether Estelle Fancy would sneak back into Vera's trailer when I was gone was anybody's guess. The best I could do was let Chattergee know that he should lock Vera's trailer if he wanted to prevent her possessions from being plundered.

I walked back toward the hangar intent on finding Mort to tell him what had occurred. Of course, finding Estelle in Vera's trailer didn't implicate her in the actress's murder, but it certainly cast her in a different light. From what I could see, she was trying to take more than the garnet set from Vera's jewelry box. She had thrown back quite a few other pieces as well. I wondered whether the cord she'd stuffed back into her pocket belonged to Vera's iPad. Had she taken that as well?

And why had she turned Vera's pockets inside out? What was Estelle looking for? Money? More jewelry? Vera had left a pair of earrings in a saucer on the kitchen counter. I kicked myself that I hadn't stopped to see if they were still there. Perhaps she was accustomed to leaving things in her pockets. I had done much the same thing once, when I wore a new pair of earrings to a book signing and they began to pinch. I'd removed them and dropped them in my handbag. A month later when I was dressing for an evening out, I was surprised to discover them at the bottom of the purse.

Could Estelle have been searching for the note Chattergee said had upset Vera so much? Had she been its author? If she had been looking for it, she wouldn't have found it. Mort and I had searched the room, and the crime scene team had followed us and searched the trailer for it as well—with no luck.

If Estelle had lied about looking for the note, was anything she said to be trusted?

These questions occupied my thoughts as I wandered back toward the hangar. Ahead, I noticed a table set up outside one of the trailers with a box on it. A sign taped to the box fluttered in the breeze. Curious, I quickened my pace to see what it was about. The sign read:

DO NOT KNOCK ON THIS DOOR IF YOU WANT TO BE CONSIDERED FOR A PART AS AN EXTRA. LEAVE YOUR RÉSUMÉ AND HEAD SHOT IN THIS BOX. ANYONE VIOLATING THESE INSTRUCTIONS WILL BE AUTOMATICALLY EXCLUDED FROM CONSIDERATION AS AN EXTRA. THANK YOU FOR YOUR COOPERATION. RHONDA CHEN, CASTING DIRECTOR

I knocked on the door.

"Didn't you read the sign?" a woman's voice called from inside the trailer.

"I did," I called out. "May I come in? I'm not here to ask for a part in your movie."

"That's what they all say, and once they're in here, their story changes," the voice said. "You may come in, but I will not be persuaded."

I opened the door to find a small Asian woman hemmed in by cardboard boxes on the table in front of her and filing cabinets behind her along the wall. She wore a Bluetooth headset in one ear and had at least three cell phones and a tablet spread out before her on the flat surface.

"We haven't met before," I said. "I'm Jessica Fletcher, the script consultant on the film." I held out my hand.

"Oh, yes. I know who you are," she said, ignoring my hand. "Your book is the reason we were dragged all the way from California to Maine. Shut the door, please. I don't want anyone else to know I'm in here."

I closed the door behind me and looked around for a place to sit, but there wasn't one.

"I don't keep any chairs in here or I'd never get rid of them," she said. "State your business quickly, Mrs. Fletcher, or your feet will get tired."

I laughed. "I don't want a part in the movie," I said, raising my hand in a salute, "Girl Scouts' honor. And please call me Jessica."

"Well, you're probably the only one, Jessica," she said, sighing. "I'm Rhonda Chen."

"I thought so," I replied. "I know you're very busy. I won't take more than a few minutes of your time. I'd like to talk with you about Vera Stockdale."

"I already spoke with the police."

"I'm sure you have. I would hope that they've interviewed everyone connected with the production."

"Can't imagine that they missed anyone. Unlike me, the rest of them have nothing else to do at the moment."

"But I understand that's about to change," I said.

"You do? Who have you been talking to? That's not supposed to be common knowledge."

I smiled. "I have my sources. If you give me ten minutes, I'll let you know who it is."

She stared at me for a moment and I had the impression I was being weighed and measured for a part. "Okay," she said, drawing the word out.

"Please tell me what you know about Vera Stockdale."

She waved a hand in front of her face. "I barely knew the woman. The major roles are often cast by the producer and director. I didn't even get a chance to suggest someone for the role before. Now it's an emergency;

they want someone yesterday. If they'd asked me then, I could have come up with two or three easily more recognizable actresses for the part of the judge."

"Would one of them have been Lois Brannigan?"

"She's not a bad choice, but she doesn't have a big enough popularity score to rate the starring role. She's a second-banana type. You don't have to raise your eyebrows at me. I've said as much to her. She's angling for the judge's part, but I think she's deceiving herself. The sexy girlfriend would give her a much better opportunity to show what she can do. However, that's Chattergee's decision, not mine. And hers, if she gets offered the part."

"How did Lois get along with Vera?"

"They got along. Lois would have been a fool to take on Stockdale, even if she wasn't the ex-wife of the executive producer. Chattergee handpicked her, and Vera knew how to throw her weight around."

"What do you mean?"

"From what I hear, and this is only secondhand, she was a pill to deal with and people avoided her like the plague."

"Was there anyone with a particular dislike for her?"

She shrugged her shoulders. "I think it was just a general feeling . . . if she was nice to you, watch out. She only smiled if she wanted something."

"Did she have any favorites, people she was friendly with?"

"There's her astrologer, but she gets paid to listen to Vera's rants. Or *got* paid, I should say. I think the production office is going to send her back to L.A. She serves no purpose here anymore."

"Is she aware of that?"

"I don't see how she can't be. Her reason for being here is dead. Sorry to be so blunt, but that's the truth."

"What about anyone else? Who else might have been a friend of Vera's?"

"I'm not the best person to ask. You should try makeup and wardrobe. They saw her the most." She rubbed the back of her neck and said with some impatience, "I'm getting a crick in my neck looking up at you. Do you have any more questions?"

"I'm just trying to get a feeling for relationships on the set. Would you happen to know a production assistant named Sunny?"

"I have nothing to do with the PAs. Is that everything?"

"Not quite."

"All right," she said, as if resigned to my presence. "If you look behind those files over there"—she pointed to a pair of tall file cabinets—"you'll find a folding chair you can use, but you have to put it back when you leave." She rolled her head in a circle, then linked her fingers together behind her neck, giving a little groan.

"Thank you," I said. "I was getting a bit tired standing here." I set my shoulder bag down on her floor and walked to the back of the cabinets, where several folding chairs leaned against the wall. I had just carried one out when the door to Rhonda Chen's trailer flew open and a breathless Eve Simpson climbed inside.

"Oh, Ms. Chen, I'm so relieved to finally meet you," Eve said, her eyes sparkling. "I see you've already met our local celebrity. Hi, Jessica." She waved at me. "You have my résumé, I'm sure," she said, addressing the casting director again. "But just in case, here's another and my latest head shot, taken by Bilberry Studios in Bangor." She placed her papers on top of the array of electronics on the casting director's table. "Jessica can tell you; they photograph all the stars." She tilted her head with a smile and winked at me.

I tried not to look astonished. I'd never heard of Bilberry Studios.

"When I'm not on the stage, I am the queen of local real estate," Eve said, handing Rhonda her business card. "How are your current living arrangements? Not so hot? I can find you a wonderful place to stay while you're here, one with *all* the amenities. Let me introduce myself. I'm Eve Simpson, late of the Little Theatre Players."

Little Theatre Players? That was the name of the Cabot Cove High School theater club. I had directed its members in *Anything Goes* one year during my previous career as a high school English teacher. But that was long after Eve Simpson had graduated.

"You've heard of us, I assume," Eve continued. "I played Persephone, Ophelia, Calpurnia—that's Plutarch, of course. All the great roles. I've been so busy this week, I must have missed your call. But I'm available for a screen test as soon as you can arrange it."

"You may or may not be able to act," Rhonda said, lifting Eve's photo and résumé by the corners, as if they were tainted and would soil her fingers, and dropping them in a box at her feet, "but apparently you can't read. There's a sign outside."

"That's just for the extras," Eve said, undaunted by the

annoyance clearly evident on Rhonda Chen's face. "I'm an accomplished actress. I knew you'd recognize my talent right away. I understand that the part of the judge will be given to a Hollywood favorite, but, *entre nous*, those of us in the theater can act rings around film people. *N'est-ce pas?* We're steeped in the Method. You know, named for Stanley Stanislavski, the great Russian actor and director." She batted her eyelashes and looked achingly at the ceiling.

"Is he the same as Constantin Stanislavski, Eve?" I asked.

Eve squeaked, but recovered quickly. "*Oh mon Dieu*, Jessica. You're so quiet, I almost forgot you were standing there," she said with a flourish. "Is that seat for me? How nice!"

I almost laughed at the look of horror in Rhonda Chen's eyes.

"No, actually," I said, quickly opening the chair and sitting in it. "Unfortunately, you've come at an inconvenient time, Eve. Ms. Chen and I are in the middle of an important meeting. I'm really sorry, but I'm sure you understand."

"Are you discussing the roles in the film?" Eve asked archly. "If so, I'm certain you can find one for me. You know my qualifications, Jessica." She edged closer to my chair. "May I rely on you to persuade Ms. Chen to cast me in a good part?" she said in a stage whisper. "I don't require a large one. A few speaking lines will allow me to add a soupçon of freshness to the film." She twirled around so that her skirt flared out.

"I'm afraid I don't have any influence on casting,

Eve," I said, "but perhaps you can call Ms. Chen later for an appointment."

"Yes, please," Rhonda added drily.

"Of course!" Eve said with enthusiasm. She reached into her handbag and pulled out a thick calendar book and pen, secured with a rubber band. She turned her gaze on Rhonda Chen, pen poised in the air. "If you'll just let me have your personal phone number, I'll be happy to give you a ring later to set up an audition."

I was surprised when Rhonda quickly rattled off a number, which Eve struggled to write down. "I have it!" she said, a note of triumph in her voice. "I shall be in touch. You won't regret this. The film is being made in Maine, after all. You have to make sure it has local color to carry off that Down East *je ne sais quoi*. No one else can supply that flavor as well as I." She dropped her calendar back in her bag. "Speak to you later," she sang as she sailed out of the trailer.

There was a moment of stunned silence. Then Rhonda rose from her seat and hurried to lock the door. She leaned back against it and let out a relieved sigh.

"Whose number did you give her?" I asked.

"Shred Masters outside San Bernardino," she replied. "It's where I send all of these." She kicked the box under her table as she sat down again. "You wouldn't believe how many trees die for head shots and résumés. The least I can do is recycle them."

"I have a bad feeling Eve will think I told you to do that," I said.

"She can't have assumed she'd get a part just by waltzing in here with that ridiculous song and dance, can she?" Rhonda asked. "Besides, she tried to *bribe* me with an apartment."

"Eve is the consummate optimist," I said. "Fortunately one with a thick skin. She's been disappointed before, but she always bounces back."

Rhonda leaned over and plucked Eve's papers from her recycling box. "Maybe I'll hire her as an extra," she said, dropping them into a different box. "We have a crowd scene coming up. I had to put the mayor in it. She can stand next to him."

"That's very nice of you," I said.

"Most likely they'll be edited out of the final cut," she said with a wry smile.

Chapter Twelve

My hunt for Sunny had been unsuccessful, and I was ready to call it a day. Mort had told me to meet him at the production office, and it was toward that green trailer that I directed my feet after leaving the casting office. It rankled that my time at the airport hadn't turned up anything substantial regarding Vera's murder, although the emergence of the true nature of Estelle Fancy had been something of a surprise. This wasn't my first experience with a movie crew, and it was far from my first experience with murder, but Vera's solitary nature made it difficult to track down who might have held a grudge against the actress. From the sound of it, she had kept to herself, using her astrologer as a glorified errand girl, and confining her intimate conversations to the rare visits of her ex-husband, the executive producer.

Chattergee had an alibi for the time when Vera was killed; he was sitting in a poker game. But even without an alibi, what motive could he have had to get rid of his ex-wife when he'd gone to such trouble to find a role for her comeback? The card game also exonerated several others in the production, although I suspected that with the occasional breaks and the rotating in and out of players, it was possible someone had managed to slip away long enough to kill Vera and come back unnoticed. But who? And why?

My reveries were interrupted by a soft sound I recognized, one that jarred me to alertness. Someone was walking nearby, the footsteps matching mine. The sense I'd had earlier of being followed returned in a rush. I spun around to look behind me; no one was there. I was alone in a narrow space between tall shipping containers. I heard a shoe scraping along the pavement. Was the person in the next aisle over? *You're being foolish,* I told myself. *There are hundreds of people here. Why shouldn't someone else be walking among the production trucks?*

Still, the uncomfortable feeling persisted. My mind began to visualize ugly scenarios. The countryside surrounding the airport was deceiving. It was not just a pretty rural airfield. It was the site of a recent homicide. The people who worked on the film were not just friendly visitors who happened to be production professionals. There was a murderer among them. Perhaps Vera wasn't the only one to provoke violence. Could this person suspect I was seeking information to flush him or her out? My association with the sheriff surely would not have gone unnoticed. Although I had to assume that the people from Hollywood were, for the most part, unaware of my previous involvement with murder investigations, there may have been an exception. Someone in town could have spread a rumor that Jessica Fletcher was at it again. It wouldn't have been a rumor, though. It was the truth. Seth always warned me I would get myself in trouble.

I quickened my pace. I had to find Mort. I had to tell him I would talk to Sunny another day. I needed some time away from the airport. I was overthinking the case, imagining things, becoming paranoid.

Stop it! I told myself. I took a deep breath.

Chattergee had said Vera was always making mountains out of molehills. And here I was, doing the same thing. I looked all around. No one was there. I heard the call of a chickadee. A light breeze ruffled the curls Loretta had worked so hard to create. I stretched my arms up and smiled at the blue sky. It was a beautiful day. I shook off the fear and suspicion.

Calm and composed again, I turned the corner at the next break between vehicles—and a man came out of the shadows and shoved me so hard I bounced off a trailer and fell to the ground.

"It's your fault, Jessica Fletcher," my assailant growled as he loomed over me, his fists ready to strike.

It was the man I'd seen at the press conference, the one who'd taken Walter Benson's picture with his cell phone. A strong smell of alcohol surrounded him like a sickly sweet cloud.

"Who are you?" I said angrily and scrambled to my feet. "And what do you think you're doing?"

"You and your stupid book. If it wasn't for your book, they would never be here."

"Who?"

"The movie people. It's going to start all over again now. Things were just starting to go right and now they'll all be looking at me again. And you did it. Butting in where you don't belong. The court convicted her, but your book made people doubt the verdict. I've been . . ." He pulled at his gray hair with both hands.

Recognition dawned. "You're Judge Harris's husband, aren't you?"

"N . . . Neil Corday," he said with a hiccup.

"How dare you attack me like this?" I said, brushing off my clothing and keeping my distance from him to avoid another push.

"Attack you? You're lucky I didn't do more." He dropped his arms and sniffled. "I didn't punch you. I could've, but I didn't." He wiped his nose on his sleeve.

He'd given me quite a start, but instead of fear, I'd reacted with anger. Later on, I might reconsider my response, but at the moment I was fired up, full of adrenaline, and ready to take on the world. He was a pathetic-looking man, disheveled and obviously inebriated. He had trouble standing erect, and I wondered whether he might fall.

"What did you expect to accomplish pushing me to the ground? My book is fiction. The murder of your wife provided the background. If people read into it and come away with a suspicion that the jury might have been wrong in convicting your lady friend, so be it. Besides, I can hardly take back a book that was published years ago."

"You could stop the movie," he whined.

Suddenly I remembered Mitchell Elovitz complaining about "some old nut" downtown trying to interrupt his filming.

"I cannot stop the movie," I said. "It wasn't my decision to make it in the first place. And I have no reason to object to a screenplay of my novel. As I said, my book was a fictionalized account, not a true-crime report of what occurred."

Corday waved his arms around. "But everyone knows that the judge's husband in the book was me. The reviews said it was a . . . was a . . . roaming-something."

"Roman à clef?" I said.

"That's it. I was humiliated, I had to leave town. Everyone was pointing fingers at me. My reputation was in . . . in . . . I lost my good reputation. You forced me to leave my home and my practice."

"You left town because there was a string of lawsuits hanging over your head and you didn't want to take responsibility for your own actions. You were also disbarred. I'm not to blame for that. You are your own worst enemy, Neil Corday."

He looked at me with rheumy eyes. "Jenny used to say that, too."

"Jenny Kipp? Your sometimes girlfriend? She's in jail now, serving a life sentence for killing your wife. Does she deserve to be there?"

Corday's expression changed from pitiful to calculating. "You're trying to get me to admit I killed Ruth, but it's not going to work." He wiped his mouth. "I was ex . . . exoner . . . cleared. Jenny was the one with the gun, not me."

"It was a weapon you gave her, wasn't it?"

"Not my gun," he said, waving his arms around again. "I use these weapons now." He stepped closer, held up a fist, and threatened me with it.

"You'd better stand back and drop your hands," Mort's voice said in a commanding tone.

Mort held his service revolver steady with both hands. It was pointed at Corday.

"Don't shoot!" Corday called, raising his arms in surrender. "Don't shoot! I didn't punch her, Officer. You can ask her. Did I punch you, Mrs. Fletcher? I did not. We were just talking, that's all."

"You all right, Mrs. F.?" Mort asked, keeping an eye on Corday.

"I'm fine," I said, but I walked to Mort's side to increase my distance from the drunken man. "He knocked me down," I said. "But I'm okay. No broken bones."

Mort lowered his revolver. "You're under arrest," he told Corday.

"That's not necessary," I said.

"He knocked you down, didn't he?"

"Yes, but I'm not hurt."

"He's drunk and disorderly."

Corday stood with his head hanging down. He mumbled to himself, sniffling and wiping his eyes and nose on the sleeve of his wrinkled suit.

Despite my protestation, Mort handcuffed the late judge's husband, recited the Miranda warnings, and marched him toward the front of the airport. At the hangar, he turned his prisoner over to a deputy. "Lock him up downtown; keep him till he's sober. If he gives you a hard time, charge him with criminal threatening. While you're at it, check his priors," he said, putting his hand on Corday's head as he placed him in the rear seat of a patrol car. "I'll be in later."

Elovitz, who'd been standing in the doorway of the production trailer watching the scene, stepped down once the deputy drove away. Today he wore a Boston Bruins cap, one of a rotating collection. I imagine that he thought he would ingratiate himself with the Cabot Cove citizenry by showing his affinity for our favorite teams. Maine has no professional sports franchises, but we're big fans of those in Boston. The last time I'd seen Elovitz, he'd been holding a Celtics cap, a nod to our basketball team, even though the season had ended disappointingly. I now wondered if his wardrobe included hats for the New England Patriots and the less well-known Boston Cannons lacrosse team.

"Who was that guy?" Elovitz asked.

"Just an idiot who can't hold his liquor," Mort said.

"I thought for a minute that maybe he was the one who killed Vera."

"Hold your horses," Mort said, shaking his head at the director, "and don't go jumping to stupid conclusions. I don't need more rumors around here."

"So he's not the killer, huh?" Elovitz said through a laugh. "Too bad. I was about to congratulate you."

"I'll let you know when you can do that."

"I'm surprised you didn't recognize him," I said to Elovitz. "I thought he might have been the same man who tried to interrupt your filming the other evening."

"You know, come to think of it, he did look familiar. Yeah, the guy from downtown, the one the PA found hiding in a doorway." Elovitz pulled off his Boston Bruins cap, dislodging the Bluetooth headset in his ear.

He wiped his brow and put the headset back in place. "I told Chattergee we needed a security detail. This is a dangerous situation. Our star is shot and some weirdo is stalking around the production area. Maybe this drunk is the killer, huh? Wouldn't that be great? Case solved, and we can get back to making the film. So, who is the idiot? Just a drunk like the sheriff says?"

"He's the husband of the judge who was shot and killed here in Cabot Cove, the case I based my book on," I said.

"Wow!" Elovitz said. "The real one, huh? The screenplay makes the point that maybe the woman who was convicted for killing the judge was innocent, and maybe her husband did the deed, the way you wrote it in the book. Nice guy."

"He was upset when the book came out," I said. "And he's upset that the movie is being made."

"So there you go," Elovitz said. "He wants to stop production. Isn't that enough? How better to accomplish that than to kill our star?" He looked at Mort, whose expression told him he was far off base.

"Okay! Okay!" Elovitz said, rubbing his hands together. "I'm jumping the gun. I guess I'm just excited because we start shooting again tomorrow. Come to think of it . . ." He ran inside the production office, yelling into his headset, "Call Nicole!"

"Can I drop you off at home, Mrs. F.?" Mort asked, opening the door to his patrol car. "I've got to get back to headquarters to question this buffoon before he sobers up enough to call in a lawyer."

"It's been a strange afternoon," I said, climbing into Mort's car.

"Did you talk to Sunny?"

"No. I never found her, but I did run across Estelle Fancy rummaging through Vera's jewelry."

"No kidding! Did she steal anything?"

"I hope not, but I can't be certain. I left a note for Terrence Chattergee suggesting he lock the trailer door."

We were about to drive away when I remembered Cecil.

"Do you think Mr. Chattergee will take care of him?" I asked after I had explained the situation. "He can't just be left alone."

"I doubt it," Mort replied. "He flew back to California this morning."

"Oh, no!" I said.

"Want me to stop at the pet store to pick you up some doggie bones, Mrs. F.?" he said, a knowing grin on his face.

"That won't be necessary," I said as I pulled out my cell phone and dialed the number for Jack and Tobé Wilson's kennel and veterinarian center. "Tobé," I said, "this is Jessica. I need a favor."

Chapter Thirteen

When I came downstairs the next morning, Cecil was curled up on the settee in my living room snoring gently. At the sound of my steps, he opened one eye and watched me approach.

"Get down," I said. "I didn't say you could sleep on my furniture. Didn't I make a bed for you on the kitchen floor?"

Cecil arched his back and stretched, sliding his paws forward and digging into the cushion with his claws like a cat. He jumped down delicately and shook his little body as if ridding his fur of water, then pranced into the kitchen without looking back.

I followed after him and watched as he lapped up some water, then stood at the back door looking up at me expectantly. "You're certainly well trained," I said, as I attached his leash and walked with him outside. "But there has to be a better home for you than mine."

The phone was ringing when we returned inside.

"Did I wake you?" Seth asked.

"No. I was outside walking with Cecil."

"Who's Cecil?"

"It's a long story," I said.

"Well, you'll have plenty of time to tell it if you want to accompany me up to Bangor today."

"Why are you going to Bangor?"

"Remember that colleague I told you about? I sent him photos of the entrance and exit wounds I found on the actress."

"Oh, yes. You said you weren't sure which was which."

"Ayuh. That's true. But he thinks he knows. He's a forensic pathologist, a former medical examiner from Chicago, retired now, but consults for those who have tricky questions regarding autopsies. He's spent his career looking at gunshot wounds, and he invited me up to see his lab and review the photos. He said you could come, too, if you like."

"I would like to," I said, "but it's a long ride to Bangor. Can you take off that much time?"

"Already rescheduled my patients. Jed Richardson said he'd fly us up today. You game to go?"

"What time are you leaving?"

"Ten o'clock. We can stop for lunch before we see him."

"I have one errand to run," I said. "I should be able to get a ride out to the airport after that. I'll meet you there."

"Sounds good."

He was about to say good-bye when I added, "If I remember correctly, the last time we were in a small plane, you told me you'd be happy never to have that experience again."

"Ayuh. I'm not a happy flier, but a lot depends on the pilot."

"Meaning?"

"I figure we'll get to Bangor safely with Jed at the controls—and you in the backseat. See you later."

He hung up before he could hear my sputtering at the other end of the line. Clearly Seth didn't trust me as a pilot. I'm a competent pilot—not nearly as experienced as Jed, of course, but careful and with a good feeling for the balance and workings of a small plane. I wasn't about to take offense at my good friend's teasing—he was teasing, wasn't he?—but a little devil on my shoulder said I should arrange with Jed to get the right-hand seat on our way back to Cabot Cove. With dual controls on the plane, Seth would never know who was doing the flying. We'd see what Dr. Hazlitt had to say then.

The errand I needed to run was to our local veterinarian, Jack Wilson. Jack and his wife, Tobé, were long-time friends, and I've written before about Tobé's beloved pig, Kiwi, now deceased, which she used to walk on a leash in town, to the delight of our citizens as well as the summer tourists.

Since it was early enough to squeeze in an appointment before Jack's regular office hours began, I called and he agreed to keep Cecil for the day. I'd been planning to bring Cecil in anyway so Jack could give him a checkup. He was going to test to see if the dog had a microchip. If so, Jack could trace Cecil's health records and make certain his inoculations were up to date.

I didn't have a carrier for Cecil, but he was accustomed to traveling in someone's arms, so he made no objection when I tucked him into my shoulder bag (emptied of its contents, of course) and placed the bag in the basket of my bike. As I pedaled over to Jack and Tobé's office, I crooned to Cecil, much the way I'd seen Estelle Fancy do when she'd lured him out from under the desk on the movie set. Had any of my neighbors seen me talking to my shoulder bag, they surely would have thought that Jessica Fletcher was losing her marbles. Fortunately, my voice lulled Cecil to sleep, and he napped all the way to the vet.

"He looks to be in fairly good condition," Jack said once he'd examined Cecil, "except for his teeth, of course—or lack of teeth, I should say. What do you feed him?"

"I've only fed him a few times. I took a bag of kibble from his late owner's place, and supplemented it with cooked hamburger cut up in small pieces."

"There are pet food formulas for senior dogs, but you can save money if you cook for him. Meat should be the main ingredient, then vegetables and starch. Chihuahuas love potatoes. He won't eat a lot. But he'll need something to chew to exercise the few remaining teeth he has."

"I wasn't planning to keep him very long," I said, dismayed at the idea of a permanent canine houseguest. I've owned many pets during my life, almost all of them adopted from a shelter, but in recent years, with my busy travel schedule, I felt it wouldn't be fair to adopt another animal only to have to board it when I was on the road. "I'm hoping the daughter of his owner will claim him," I told Jack. "I haven't had the chance to talk with her yet."

"Don't worry about him today. We'll take care of him. What time do you expect to be back?"

"I'm not certain. May I call you later?"

"Sure. We close at five, but there's always a tech on duty in the kennel."

It was too far for me to ride my bicycle out to the airport, so I left it in Jack's parking lot and called for a cab to drive me. My plan was to have Seth drop me at the vet's office when we got back from Bangor, assuming it wasn't too late, and I could ride home with Cecil the same way we'd come.

It was still a bit early when I arrived at the airfield. I wasn't due to meet Seth for another hour, but Jed was already conducting his usual preflight check.

"Morning, Jessica," he said, meeting me at the side of the plane. "Nice day for flying."

"Good morning, Jed. Yes, it is."

"We're expecting some scattered clouds. Might be a bit of turbulence over the river on the way in, but otherwise should be a smooth ride."

"Sounds good, Jed."

"Want to log a few hours of flying while we're at it?"

"I'd love to," I said, "but I suspect that Seth wouldn't be comfortable knowing I was at the controls."

"He doesn't have to know," Jed said, winking at me. "We'll let him sit in the copilot seat on the way to Bangor, and then say it's your turn to be up front on the way back."

"I like the way you think," I said, not letting on that those were my plans precisely.

I left Jed to finish his inspection of the plane and walked around to the back of the hangar, intending to drop in on Mitchell Elovitz to see if he knew where Sunny was. There was no way I was going to give Cecil to Estelle Fancy, but my hopes of Chattergee taking over care of the Chihuahua had been dashed when he returned to California. Sunny was my last resort. If she didn't want the dog, I was going to be stuck with him.

I knocked on the door of the green production trailer and listened. When there wasn't a response, I turned the knob and peeked inside. I gasped at the scene before me. No one was in the production office, but someone had been there recently and had left the place in a shambles. Storyboards were strewn all over as if thrown around in a fury. The video monitors had been swept off the desks. The wastebaskets and recycling bins had been upended. The floor was covered with papers. I stepped inside, gingerly making my way toward the back of the trailer, hoping that no person had been a target of the rage that had clearly been behind the trashing.

I heard a loud whistle behind me and whirled around.

"Boy, lady, you must have some temper." In the doorway I'd left open stood the actor Walt Benson, shaking his head.

I put a hand up in defense. "I didn't do this. I just arrived."

"Well, someone was in a bad mood."

"It looks that way," I said, skirting the shattered remains of the video monitors.

"Anyone back there?" Benson asked.

"I don't think so," I said, "but I want to be sure."

When I completed my circuit of the trailer and assured Benson that no bodies were lying about, he came inside, righted two overturned chairs, offered me one, and sat in the other himself. "Doesn't look like the stars are aligned in the right place to resume filming, as our mutual friend Estelle Fancy would say."

"Who would do something like this?" I asked.

"Beats me, but if weird stuff keeps happening, I'm going to put in for hazard pay."

"What 'weird stuff' are you referring to?" I asked. "Are you including Vera's death in that?"

"Yes, indeed! A murder isn't the normal course of events when you're making a film. And I heard some vagrant was wandering around here threatening to shut down production; the guy actually challenged one of the grips to a fistfight. Also, Estelle reported a theft from Vera's trailer. She's not the only one either. Someone broke into hair and makeup and walked off with Audrey's gun. I'm glad I still have mine," he said.

"You carry a gun?" I asked.

"Sure do. It's not safe around here." He heaved a big sigh.

"I think I'd better call the sheriff," I said.

"Are you sure he's not on the lot? He practically lives here."

"I'm not sure," I said, dialing Mort's number on my cell phone.

He didn't answer, but I left a message about the vandalizing and suggested that he come to the production office.

"I'm beginning to think this movie is jinxed," Benson said.

"Aren't you scheduled to start filming again today?"

"So I hear, but there's been no announcement about a leading lady. I'm hoping that's why Chattergee ran out to California. Maybe he'll bring us back a star. This movie needs something to get its juices flowing. Of course, Brannigan will be heartbroken if she doesn't get the part. She's been lobbying hard for it."

"Does she carry a gun, too?" I asked.

He gave a bark of laughter. "Do you mean did she kill Vera to get the part? She's capable of it."

"Good heavens!"

"Just kidding, but we're all cutthroat when it comes to good roles." He picked up one of the storyboards from the floor. "Do you think we should call a couple of PAs to clean this place up?" he asked, leaning the board against a wall.

"I think we should leave everything exactly as it is until the director and the authorities get here. Mitchell Elovitz will know if anything's missing, although burglary doesn't appear to be the motive."

"How can you tell?"

"Whoever did this left valuable electronic equipment," I said. "If they were looking for something to steal, that would have been at the top of their list."

"I hope this won't cause another delay to filming. I'm getting antsy hanging around with nothing to do. And I'm losing my shirt in the nightly poker games."

"That's right. You were playing poker the night Vera Stockdale was shot. Did you hear anything? Did anyone in the game comment on a strange noise?"

"You couldn't have heard anything if an earthquake occurred," he replied. "Elovitz had his stereo set at a deafening volume. That's why I kept stepping out of the game to rest my eardrums."

"Did anyone else step out of the game?"

"Everyone at some point," he replied. "Barry and Elovitz came out to smoke a cigar. Chattergee doesn't let anyone smoke around him."

"Do you mean Eric Barry?"

"Yeah, the first AD."

"I didn't realize he was at the game."

"A number of guys stopped in for a hand or two, then took off. Barry said he had a date and left early."

"What time is early?" I asked.

Benson shrugged. "Around eleven, I guess."

"Do you know who he had a date with?"

"One of the PAs. I heard she gave him an earful for being late."

"Was Terrence Chattergee there the whole time?"

"As far as I know. I was whipped when the game broke up, but he was on California time. It was the shank of the evening for him."

"Did anyone leave the game for an extended period and then return?"

"I see where you're going with this, but these are all good guys, Mrs. Fletcher. I don't see any of them carrying a grudge against Vera, except maybe Chattergee, but he's the one who insisted she be in the film."

There was a knock at the door and one of the production assistants poked his head inside. "Is Jessica Fletcher here?"

"Yes," I said. "I'm here."

"The pilot is looking for you."

"Oh, my goodness," I said, glancing at my watch. "I forgot all about my flight."

"You go ahead," Benson said. "I'll wait for the sheriff."

The production assistant held the door open and extended a hand to help me as I rushed down the stairs. "What happened in here, Mr. Benson?" I heard him ask as I trotted away.

Chapter Fourteen

Jed was standing on the tarmac, tapping his toes, and Seth was already in the front passenger seat of the Cessna when I raced around the side of the hangar and waved frantically. I didn't want them to leave without me.

"I'm so sorry," I said. "I lost track of the time."

"I knew you were here somewhere," Jed said as I climbed into the plane. "Handy having those production assistants around to send on errands. They're all so polite and helpful. I'm not accustomed to that from young people."

"Glad you decided to join us," Seth said as I buckled myself in.

"I got waylaid," I said, "but I'm here now."

Jed taxied to the end of the runway. He looked ahead and to each side, ensuring that there was no one on the ground who might get in the way, peered into the sky checking for air traffic, then pushed the throttle in to rev the engine and we moved forward to start our takeoff. Mentally I followed his every move, watching the instruments on the panel to confirm that we had the full mixture of fuel and that we'd reached the proper airspeed before he pulled back on the yoke and the nose lifted. I eyed the altimeter to see our height off the ground, and the compass to verify our heading. My hands may not have been on the controls, but my mind was flying the plane.

Once we were airborne, I looked down to see a Cabot Cove patrol car, red lights flashing, speeding toward the airport. I felt guilty that I hadn't waited around for Mort or one of his deputies, but Walter Benson could give as good an account as I. He'd come into the production office only moments after me. I didn't know any more than he did.

The roar of the Cessna's engine made conversation between the front seats and the back difficult, so I settled in for the short flight to Bangor, reviewing what I knew about Vera's murder and what remained to be discovered, including the name of the murderer, of course.

The night the movie star was killed, she'd visited her ex-husband to complain that someone had sent her a disturbing note. Terrence Chattergee said he hadn't read it; Estelle Fancy claimed ignorance, too. I wondered if the sender had suggested a meeting, and if the hangar had been the location designated for their tryst. It was a logical place to choose. The production crew knew not to go near a "hot set."

Zee thought he'd heard carpenters hammering that evening but hadn't seen anyone when he went into the hangar to examine his equipment. He said he'd gone back to his trailer at nine thirty. Vera was with Chattergee at nine, before he left for the poker game. Based on Seth's autopsy, the estimated time of death had to have been before two a.m. Could Vera have spied Zee in the hangar and waited for him to leave? Was the person she was meeting already there, hiding in the shadows when she arrived? Did her killer sneak inside knowing the intended victim was waiting? Or had Vera been shot elsewhere and her body transported to the set? And what did that piece of film mean? Had Mort succeeded in getting blowups of the individual frames so that we could discover what movie it had come from?

And now Neil Corday enters the picture, the husband of the real-life judge who'd been murdered. Mitch Elovitz was right about one thing: Corday wanted to halt the production. And Elovitz's suggestion wasn't completely off target: What better way to go about stopping the movie than shooting its star? But how would Corday have known about the set in the hangar? Had he been skulking around the airport unnoticed all this time? And why would he pick out Vera? Was it because she was playing his deceased wife?

So many questions, and so much still to learn.

Jed put down at Bangor International Airport and taxied to the area reserved for general aviation, for private planes. He checked in with operations to arrange for refueling and to update a time to leave. The three of us then grabbed some lunch at the airport's Red Baron Lounge before Seth and I took a cab to the laboratory of Dr. Carlton Smith.

"Carl, so good of you to invite us," Seth said, when

the doctor answered the door of his modest Cape Cod–style house.

Dr. Smith was the personification of roly-poly. A round man with a fringe of gray hair around his bald pate, he wore half-glasses on the end of his nose and bright red suspenders and a belt to hold up trousers that barely buttoned beneath his belly. If he'd had a white beard, he could have easily been mistaken for Santa Claus. As it was, he was clean-shaven and smelled of a heavy dose of spicy aftershave that seemed to trail him like an aromatic cloud.

"Thank you for having us, Dr. Smith," I said when we'd been introduced. "I'm very honored to be here and eager to hear what you have to say about this case."

He waved away the compliment. "Don't even mention it. It's my pleasure, and besides, I've always wanted to meet you, Mrs. Fletcher," he said, holding my hand and peering into my eyes. "And you must call me Carl."

"Thank you, Carl. I'm Jessica."

Seth coughed. "And how is Sarah?" he asked, taking off his cap and hanging it on the clothes tree that stood in the entryway.

"Fine. Fine," Dr. Smith said, dropping my hand and heading down a narrow hall to the back of the house. He stopped abruptly at a closed door and turned to me. "I have to say, my wife will be so disappointed she missed you. She's such a fan of yours, but she's a 'pink lady' at our local hospital, and today's the day she's on gift shop duty. I'm afraid I didn't tell her about you coming until it was too late for her to change her plans."

"That's wonderful of her to do," I said. "I'm sure Seth can tell you how important volunteers are to the running of a hospital."

"That they are," Seth said, coming up behind me.

"Please tell your wife I'm sorry I couldn't meet her," I said. "I'll be happy to send her a book if you think she'd like it."

"She'll be tickled pink," Carl said, then giggled. "Of course that's what she was wearing this morning." He pulled out a ring of keys on a retractable wire attached to his belt and used one key to open the door. "Welcome to my humble lab."

Dr. Smith's laboratory, actually a spare bedroom off the kitchen, did indeed appear humble. It was lined with filing cabinets five drawers high, many of the drawers so stuffed with files that they couldn't be closed. Next to a narrow window was a bookcase filled with what appeared to be boxes of ammunition. On a long table were two microscopes, and next to them a computer monitor with a split screen and a keyboard. A rack on one wall held row upon row of videocassettes, a visual record of autopsies the doctor had performed, he told us, and of those on which he had consulted in the past.

"Do you still refer to these autopsy tapes?" I asked.

"Those old cassettes are too bulky to file," he said. "My wife wants me to get rid of them, but they still come in handy every now and then. Today I keep my videos on DVD or thumb drive," he said, "and just tuck them in the files. Used to try to keep them all on the computer, but after it crashed from the overload, I had an intern come in and index the deaths according to cause, manner, and mode. So I just have to search the index to find the autopsy I want to review. Works out much better that way."

He waddled behind a battered desk that was surprisingly neat considering the state of his files, sank into a creaky wooden chair, and flipped open a purple file folder. "Take a seat, please," he said, waving at a pair of folding chairs that faced the desk. "I made prints of your photos, Seth, so I can show you what I'm thinking."

Seth and I pulled the chairs close to the desk as Dr. Smith spread out the enlarged photos.

"These were not easy wounds to decipher, Seth," he said, pushing one of the pictures forward. "I'm not surprised you had trouble determining which was the entrance wound and which the exit."

"Glad to hear that from an expert," Seth said. "When I mentioned it to Sheriff Metzger, he was miffed that I couldn't give him a definitive answer. Made me question my skills."

"Oh, no, your skills are fine," Carl said. "This would have stumped many of the experts, too."

I could sense Seth relaxing in his seat as if a burden had been lifted from his shoulders. I hadn't known that Mort had been aggravated with Seth's inability to state with certainty which wound was which.

"Entrance and exit wounds made by bullets are usually not so difficult to distinguish," Carl said, taking another picture from his file and placing it on top of the others.

"So you're sure it was a gun that caused them?" Seth asked.

"Oh, absolutely. These have all the characteristics of bullet wounds. Why do you question it?"

"They haven't found the bullet yet," he replied, "much less the gun."

Carl looked over his glasses at Seth. "Don't you worry, my boy. They will." He focused on the photos in front of him again. "As you can see in this image—which isn't one of yours, Seth—this wound is round and pretty neat, with a narrow gray abrasion collar. That's typical of an entrance wound when the bullet pushes the skin inward." He looked up. "You tell me if I'm being too graphic for you, Jessica."

"That's all right," I said. "I appreciate knowing the details."

"Here's the exit wound from the same bullet," he said, pointing to another image. "It's larger than the first one, and there's a ragged edge as the tissue is extruded. That's pretty standard, and most pathologists can make the call."

"Isn't there generally more blood from the exit wound than the entrance one?" Seth asked.

"Usually, yes, but not always," Carl replied. "Many factors can affect the characteristics and alter the appearance of wounds—how far away the shooter was standing, for instance, or how fast the bullet was spinning when it entered the victim's body, or the pathway it made as it traveled through the body, or whether it passed through something else before or after it hit the body."

"Like what?" Seth asked.

"Like a window," Carl replied, "or something hard." He stacked the two photos and put them aside.

"Now, in the case of your victim, the reading is not as clear." He pushed two photos in front of us. "They both look like entrance wounds."

"They do," I said, surprised that they appeared so similar, when the differences had been so apparent in the previous set of photos. "Why?"

"This can happen if you get what we call a 'shored' or reinforced wound."

"I don't think I've ever heard of that before," I said. I looked at Seth. "Have you?"

Seth was frowning down at the picture, but he nodded. "Ayuh," he said slowly. "I do remember that."

"A shored wound simply means that something pressed into the skin and supported it, like a wall, say, or the floor," Carl continued, "so when the bullet exited, there wasn't room for the skin to be pushed out as it normally would be. Whatever it was shores up the skin to give the hole a different appearance, and make an exit wound appear to be an entrance one."

"Oh, dear," I said. "What do we do now?"

"What we do now is decide which is which. Our decision is critical because it can be the difference between a charge of murder one and a determination of self-defense, which some consider a justifiable homicide."

"There was nothing at the crime scene to suggest self-defense," I said. "Wouldn't she have had to be holding a weapon on the shooter for it to be self-defense?"

"I didn't say this was self-defense," Carl said, "only that we need to know which wound is which to rule it out. In this case, I believe she was, indeed, holding on to something."

"Then you *do* think it was self-defense?" Seth asked.

"Not at all," Carl replied. "I think she was holding something up to her chest when she was shot in the back."

Seth and I questioned Dr. Smith for another hour while he pulled out picture after picture to prove his point. "If you still have access to the body, this is what I recommend you do," he told Seth, and proceeded to outline procedures for Cabot Cove's substitute medical examiner to follow in case he ever needed to justify his interpretation of the wounds in court.

With the purple file folder under his arm, Seth gave his old colleague a hug as we bade Dr. Smith good-bye. "Carl, you're a lifesaver."

"Any time, any time," Carl said. "And bring Jessica again. I'll make sure Sarah stays home." To me, he said, "I won't tell her about the book. I'll let it be a happy surprise when she gets it in the mail."

"He suspects I'll forget to send his wife the book," I told Seth in the cab on the way to the airport.

"What makes you say that?"

"Carl is a logical man. He's thinking that if he doesn't say anything, then she won't be disappointed if I don't come through. But if he mentions it, and I forget to keep my word, then she'll be annoyed with him as well as me."

"Then you'd better put that book in the mail pronto."

"I'll pack it up as soon as I get home," I said.

Over our lunch at the airport, I'd told Seth and Jed about Cecil, my temporary pet. Seth had agreed to drive me to Jack Wilson's veterinary office when we returned, but he refused simply to drop me off. "You're gonna be tired after a long day. It'll be dusk by the time we get there. That's not the time to ride your bicycle home with a dog in the basket. Do you even have a light on the bike?"

"Of course," I said. "I have a light, and front and back reflectors."

"But you're not wearing light-colored clothes and you'll be hard to see on the side of the road. Don't argue with me. We can put your bicycle in the trunk and you in the backseat with the dog."

"Why can't I sit in the front seat and hold him?" I asked.

"I don't want to worry about some strange animal jumping out of your arms and getting underfoot while I'm driving."

"He's not strange," I said.

"My car. My rules. You'll sit in the back, and hold on to him with both hands."

"Yes, sir, Dr. Hazlitt," I said with a mock salute.

Which is what we did. I had sat up front with Jed on the way home, and he'd given me some flying time. Seth snoozed through the flight and I didn't have the heart to tease him about my skilled piloting when he'd had such an eventful day.

By the time I unlocked my front door—not easily accomplished with Cecil in one arm—it was nearly dark. I'd invited Seth to stay for a light supper, but he'd declined.

"I want to study these photos while Carl's analysis is fresh in my mind," he'd said.

We agreed instead to meet at Mara's Luncheonette for breakfast.

The message light on my telephone answering machine indicated I'd missed two calls while I was away. I pressed the button to listen. The first was from Mort: *Heard you'd gone to Bangor with Doc Hazlitt, Mrs. F. Any chance you can stop by the station house tomorrow? I have something I want to go over with you.*

The second message was a man's voice, but not one I recognized. *You saw what I can do today, you old biddy. Your house is next if you don't mind your own business. And it won't only be equipment that gets broken. Stay out of it if you want to stay safe.* At the sound of the second voice, Cecil growled, his lips curling back in an aggressive expression. I placed him on the floor and he stood by my side, barking. I leaned down and patted his head. "You're a good protector, Cecil," I said. "Good dog!"

I called Mort's house and left a message with his wife, Maureen, that I would meet him at his office in the morning. Then I removed the tiny tape from the answering machine and put it in a pocket of my shoulder bag. I wanted to play the message for Mort to see if he recognized the voice. I suspected that whoever it was may have used some device to alter the sound, but I couldn't be sure. Was this Neil Corday? Was he the killer? Who else would threaten me?

I wrapped up a book for Dr. Carlton Smith's wife and added the package to my bag. The post office was close by the police station, so I could run both errands after breakfast.

Before getting Cecil settled for the evening, I walked to the front door to ensure that I'd locked it. I double-checked the rear door as well, and all the ground-floor windows, too. I was more annoyed than frightened by the nasty message. I've been the target of threats before, and while most people who leave such messages get perverse satisfaction simply by recording an anonymous warning, there is always the possibility that a felon might be inclined to follow up a threat with action. At least I wouldn't make it easy for someone to break in.

That evening, when I sat in bed reading the new Jaden Terrell thriller, I heard the clicking of Cecil's nails on the stairs. He paused at the entrance to my bedroom, then calmly walked to the bed and looked up at me.

"What do you want?" I asked him.

He placed a paw on the side of my mattress and barked at me.

"C'mon," I said, smiling. "You can do it."

He made a tepid attempt to jump up, then sat on his haunches and barked again.

I leaned down and with one hand lifted him up.

He walked across the covers to the end of the bed and turned in a circle three times before settling down at my feet and closing his eyes. I was tempted to pick him up and march him back down to the kitchen, where I'd made a little dog bed for him. "Start as you mean to go on," my mother used to say. But I had to admit to myself that the message on my answering machine had made me uneasy. I left Cecil where he was, deciding a tiny watchdog was better than no watchdog at all.

Chapter Fifteen

"They're flying in a big star next week to replace Vera Stockdale, but listen to this." Evelyn Phillips, editor of the *Cabot Cove Gazette*, leaned across the table and lowered her voice. "She's going to play the jilted girlfriend. They're giving the part of the judge to Lois Brannigan."

"That should make Lois happy," I said.

"I'm not so sure," Evelyn replied. "I was told they're going to beef up the part of the girlfriend and make the judge into the supporting role."

"Which is what it was to begin with," I said as I smeared cream cheese on my bagel.

"Sounds like more work for you, Jessica," Seth said.

"Maybe we can just use the original script we had before making all the changes that Vera Stockdale demanded," I said.

Mara walked over with a coffeepot in each hand. "More coffee, ladies? Doc? I just made fresh decaf."

"Not for me, Mara," I said. "Thanks anyway."

"You can top me off," Seth said, before putting a forkful of blueberry pancakes in his mouth.

Evelyn shook her head. "I'm wired enough as it is."

"Are you suggesting *my* coffee makes you jittery?" Mara said archly.

"Never," Evelyn replied. "I had two cups at home before I ever got here."

"Well, then, serves you right. I won't have you impugning my coffee."

Evelyn looked up at Mara. " 'Impugning?' Where did you come up with that word?"

Mara laughed. "That nut job ambulance chaser Neil Corday—remember him?—comes in yesterday saying Jessica Fletcher was 'impugning his reputation.' I told him he should shut up and drink his coffee, or take his insults out the door. I wouldn't hear anything bad said about our Jessica."

"Thank you, Mara."

"You're welcome, Jessica."

"Did he leave?" I asked.

"I gave him a to-go cup and he was gone."

"What time was that?"

"Somewhere around eight thirty. We were that busy, I didn't really notice the time."

"Got any more syrup?" Seth asked.

"You still have half a pitcher there."

"More like a quarter," Seth said. "And I've got half a stack to go."

Mara rolled her eyes. "Be right back," she said. She wound her way around the tables toward the kitchen, stopping to fill a few coffee cups along the way.

"Why are you interested in what time he was here?" Evelyn asked.

"Someone left the production office in a mess yesterday," I said. "I was just trying to figure out if Corday had an alibi."

"Do you know when it happened?" Seth asked.

"I really don't," I said. "I'm going to ask Mort about it when I see him later."

"You don't have to," Evelyn said. "We had it in the paper this morning. Nothing was taken, but a lot of stuff was smashed. The director thinks it happened overnight. He forgot to lock the door."

"How did you learn about it?" I asked.

"Police scanner. One of the specials the sheriff brought in to work while the movie company is here took the call. I drove out as soon as I heard the details. Got a great interview with Walter Benson. That is one handsome man. We used his picture on the front page. Didn't you see it?"

"I didn't have time to read the paper before I left this morning," I said. What I didn't say was that when I'd carelessly left the newspaper on a chair in the kitchen, Cecil had clamped his mouth around it and run from the room. By the time I retrieved the paper, after a game of tug-of-war, he'd managed to shred the front page.

Evelyn pulled a copy of the newspaper from her bag. "Here," she said, pointing to Benson's photo. "How did you know about the mess in the production office if you didn't read my article? I thought you were in Bangor yesterday."

"I was," I said, taking the newspaper and biting into

my bagel to stall for time. I didn't want to admit to Evelyn that I'd been the one to call the police to report the damage. Better that she wasn't aware of my involvement. If she knew about it, that would be certain to spur a follow-up piece in the next day's edition, and I didn't need my name in the newspaper. There were already too many people who knew I was associated with the movie company and interested in Vera's murder. And given the nasty message on my answering machine the night before, clearly I'd upset one of them.

Mara came to my rescue. "Don't let on I give you special treatment," she told Seth, placing a full pitcher of syrup on the table in front of him.

"What's the matter, Mara?" Seth said. "You running low on maple syrup?" He poured a generous portion over the rest of his pancakes.

"You may think that's funny, Seth Hazlitt, what with all the forests we have inland," Mara said, fists on her hips, "but the mild winter ruined the maple sugar season, cut way down on the sap. I'm almost out of Grade A medium."

"I'll keep it in mind," Seth said. "Next time I'll order eggs so I won't pose a threat to your syrup supply."

Seth's use of the word "threat" brought my head up. If Evelyn's article hadn't mentioned my call to the police, how did my nasty caller know I'd seen the mayhem he'd created?

"I'll take my check, Mara," I said, blotting my mouth with my napkin and gathering up my things.

"You want me to wrap that up?" she said, eyeing my half-eaten breakfast.

"No, thanks," I said, looking at my watch. "I have an appointment I have to keep." I smiled at everyone. "Please excuse me. Seth, I'll call you later. Bye, Evelyn. Bye, Mara."

"Tell the sheriff I'll be by after breakfast," Seth said.

Evelyn looked from me to Seth. "Is there something you're not telling me, Dr. Hazlitt?" she said, pulling out her pad and pen.

Seth took another forkful of pancakes, pointed to his full mouth, and shook his head. I couldn't chance looking back as I made a hasty exit from the luncheonette.

At the police station, I held the door for two new deputies carrying out orange traffic cones. The officer at the front desk was chewing the eraser of a pencil as he leaned over a paper.

I waved as I walked by.

"Morning, Mrs. Fletcher."

"Morning, Edgar."

"What's a seven-letter word for 'puzzle'?" Edgar asked.

" 'Mystery,' " I replied.

"Gorry! That fits."

Mort was on the phone. "No, we don't have any new developments on the movie star's murder," I heard him say. "Yes, I've got my entire staff working on it day and night." He pointed to the chair in front of his desk and I took it. "I know, but these things take time. There are a couple of hundred people over at the airport. The killer could be any one of them." He rolled his eyes and moved his fingers together and apart to mime the talky caller. "You'll have to ask the producer about that. They don't tell me their plans."

"Do you want some coffee?" I mouthed, pointing to his empty mug.

He nodded.

I went to the coffeepot in the staff lounge and filled Mort's mug, adding two packets of sugar and a generous splash of milk. I made my way back to his desk and set the mug down.

"I'd love a cup, too," Edgar called out.

I laughed. "You're not on the phone."

He picked up the receiver and pretended to take a call. "Now I am."

"Get your own," Mort said, hanging up his phone. "We've got business here. Come on, Mrs. F. Let's find somewhere we can talk." He picked up his mug and a manila envelope and led me outside to a picnic table by the side of the building.

"I need the fresh air," he said apologetically. "Besides, I think someone has bugged the station house."

"You're kidding," I said.

"Yeah. I don't know how, but information gets out. It's like there are spies everywhere. Do you see anyone up that tree?" he said, squinting at a red maple.

I looked into the branches of the tree. "Not unless you count that squirrel," I said. "Who were those officers I saw leaving the station?"

"I called on the state's incident management unit. They sent us some special police. Between the movie and the murder, there was just too much for me and my small staff to handle. I could spend the day on the phone with the press alone." He took a gulp of his coffee.

"I thought there seemed to be more police around lately," I said.

"Thanks for the call about the vandalism in the production trailer, by the way. I couldn't get out there until the afternoon, but one of the specials investigated."

"So Evelyn informed me. Thank *you* for not telling her I called it in."

He smiled.

"By the way, Walter Benson told me yesterday that he carries a gun. And I forgot to mention that the makeup lady has misplaced hers. I told her to call you. Did she?"

Mort shook his head, disgusted. "Can you believe them?" he said. "It's like the Wild West out there. How the heck am I supposed to conduct an investigation when everyone's armed and there's no bullet for comparison?"

"Have you heard back from the bureau?" I asked.

"They returned the chair. Said they were able to pull up multiple fingerprints on the top and sides and found type O blood on the back of the seat, but no bullets."

"That's too bad," I said. "What are you going to do with it?"

"We cleaned it off and sent it back to the movie company. I have no other use for it. Can't believe the bullet wasn't in the chair."

"We'll find it," I said. "It's got to be somewhere."

Mort pressed his lips together and gave a soft snort. "I hope you're right," he said. "So tell me, how was Bangor? The doc called me with the news. Can you give me any details?"

"Seth said he'd stop by this morning. I'd rather he give you the report directly. I may not get everything technically correct."

"Makes you think, doesn't it?"

"It does. I keep wondering what she might have done to make someone shoot her in the back."

"She may not have done anything," he said. "Her murderer may just have wanted the satisfaction of shooting someone famous."

"You mean like the young man who killed John Lennon?"

"Yeah. Or the ones who take potshots at presidents. There isn't always a logical explanation."

"But those people *want* to get caught," I said. "They won't get famous otherwise. Our killer is staying in the dark, hiding in the bushes."

"Well, we'd better flush the perp out soon," Mort said. "I want these people to finish filming here and go home. I've had enough of Hollywood fame to last me a lifetime. Oh, speaking of movies—I almost forgot; I've got something for you," he said, handing me the manila envelope.

"And I've got something for you, too," I said, digging in my bag for the answering machine tape.

"What's this?" he asked when I handed it to him.

"Someone isn't happy with me. I'm hoping you may recognize the voice. I'll need the tape back. It's the only one I have."

He put it in his breast pocket. "We'll listen to it together before you leave."

"What's in here?" I asked, shaking the envelope.

"Look inside."

I opened the flap and pulled out a sheaf of papers with blurry color images.

"It's from the film we found around Stockdale's

neck," he said. "My neighbor, the science teacher, used his overhead projector to enlarge the film. He took those pictures of the images with his cell phone and e-mailed them to me."

I sifted through the pages. It was a love scene showing Vera in the arms of an actor. They were on a beach. I could make out palm trees in the background, but not much else.

"Recognize what movie it's from?" Mort asked.

"No. I have no idea."

"Think Elovitz might know?"

"It's possible, but there's not a lot here to go on," I said. "I don't even know who the actor is."

"Me either. I showed them to Maureen, too. She loves old romantic movies. Makes me watch *Sleepless in Seattle* every time it's on cable TV."

I smiled. "I like that one, too."

"I liked it the first time I saw it, but after the fifth, it began to drag a bit."

"You're a good husband, Mort."

He turned red. "Yeah. That's what Maureen says."

"Can I keep these?" I asked, holding up the papers.

"Those are your copies. I have a set in the file. If you can help me identify the film, I'd appreciate it."

"I'll certainly try. Of course, once we know what movie it's from, we still have to figure out why the killer tied it around Vera's neck."

Mort held up his hand. "One mystery at a time, please."

Chapter Sixteen

There was a line of people when I arrived at the post office, and both windows were staffed. I took my place at the end to await my turn. Before I'd left his office, Mort had listened to my answering machine tape and made a copy for himself, but he didn't recognize the voice of the caller. "Just make sure you lock up your house, Mrs. F. None of this small-town open-door policy like they had out at the airport."

"Given what happened to Vera Stockdale, I think the production people are probably locking their trailers now," I'd said.

"Yeah, well, nothing like a murder to make you aware of your vulnerability," he'd replied.

I was lost in my own thoughts when Lee, our postmistress, called out, "Next."

The lady behind me gave me a little shove.

"Oh, sorry," I said, moving forward to the counter.

"How are you, Jessica?"

"Just fine, Lee. Yourself?"

"Terrific! Debbie and I got to be extras in a scene the movie people shot at Loretta's Beauty Shop. Right, Deb?"

"Loretta's shop looks gorgeous," Debbie said from the next window over.

"How do you want this package to go, Jessica?"

"First class will be fine, Lee. It's a book."

"Then we'll send it media mail and save you a few pennies." Lee weighed the package and took out a panel of stamps. "Yes, ma'am, let me tell you something," she said, taking my money. "I thought it was going to be exciting, but it was mostly boring."

"That often happens," I said. "There's a lot of waiting around."

"You said it!" Debbie put in. "But waiting around with Walter Benson made it all worthwhile. I couldn't keep my eyes off him."

"He's a looker, all right. You're all set," Lee said to me. "Here's your change and your receipt."

I turned to leave just as Eve Simpson swept into the post office wearing a feather boa over her suit jacket.

"Jessica, there you are. I've been looking all over town for you."

"Hello, Eve. How are you?"

"How am I? I am *merveilleuse, extraordinaire*—oh, what is the French word for 'fabulous'?—and it's all thanks to you." She raised her arms dramatically.

I didn't dare look around. I knew all eyes were trained on us. "Thanks to me? What did I do?"

"You got me a part in the movie! A speaking part! I have lines!" Eve sang out each sentence as if she were onstage. "And it's all thanks to you. I knew the casting director would give me a role once you gave her the word. And she did."

The woman who had been behind me in line rushed over. "You know the casting director, Mrs. Fletcher? I'm so sorry I pushed you. I'm Eloise Hanford. My Penelope just had the starring role in our school's spring play. Can you get her an audition?"

"I've only just met the casting director," I replied. "Besides, I really didn't get Eve her role. She did it all herself."

"Don't be modest. You were the best help ever," Eve said.

"Jessica, Jessica," another woman called out.

"Have we met?" I asked.

"I studied singing when I was in middle school. I'd love to be in the movie. Are there any singing parts?"

"Hello, Jessica. Harvey Wincombe here. I can do a great imitation of a bull moose in heat. Want to hear?" He tented his fingers together and pressed them over his nose, making a groaning noise very much like a moose.

Before I knew it, I was surrounded by people beseeching me to put them in the film.

"Jessica Fletcher? If you've got influence, I've got the perfect person for you to cast—my nephew Jerry. And I wouldn't mind being an extra."

"Eve!" I called out. "You started this. Get me out of it."

"Ladies and gentlemen," Eve declaimed. Her voice was loud enough to carry across town. "I will take the names of everyone who wants a part. Just line up here, please." She had her day planner and pen in hand. "Just give me your name and phone number, and I'll write it down for Mrs. Fletcher. Here's my card. If you need any help with real estate in Cabot Cove, Eve Simpson is the one to call. Thank you, Eloise Hanford. Who's next?"

I slipped out the door while Eve was taking names.

Chapter Seventeen

Relieved to escape the post office unscathed, I decided to return home to walk Cecil before I went on any more errands. I wasn't sure how often a dog should be walked. It had been quite a number of years since I'd owned a pet. And I hoped he hadn't made another mess, as he'd done with the morning newspaper.

As I neared my house, I spotted someone sitting on the front steps. It was Sunny.

"Hi, Mrs. Fletcher," she said, waving. She stood, dusted off the seat of her jeans, and walked down to meet me at the gate.

"Your timing couldn't be more perfect," I said. "You're just the person I want to see."

"That's great because I wanted to see you, too. I came to ask a favor."

"Well, come on in," I said, parking my bike on the path. "Would you like some lunch?"

"I had a late breakfast, but I'm always up for a mug of tea. And a cookie, if you have any left."

"I think we can scrounge up one or two."

At the sound of my key in the front door lock, Cecil started barking.

"Who's that?" Sunny asked.

"I think he'll be a familiar face," I said, opening the door.

"Cecil!" Sunny cried, kneeling down.

The little dog jumped into her arms and licked her nose.

Sunny buried her face in his fur. "Oh, Cecil, I forgot all about you. But what are you doing here? I thought Ms. Fancy had you." She looked up at me as she put the dog down on the floor. "How did you get him, Mrs. Fletcher?"

"Let's just say Ms. Fancy didn't fancy keeping Cecil," I said, closing the door and locking it firmly behind us.

"And you gave Cecil a home. That was very kind of you."

"But only a temporary home," I said, frowning at her.

"Don't you like him?"

"It's not a matter or liking or not liking. I travel too much to take on a pet. It wouldn't be fair to either of us."

"Oh, too bad," she said, following me into the kitchen. "I can't keep him. When I'm not working, I'm in school. They don't allow pets in my building."

"Oh, dear. I was hoping you'd want him. What about your father?" I asked as I filled the kettle at the kitchen sink and put it on the stove.

Sunny rolled her eyes. "He'd never take Cecil. He wasn't a fan of Vera's dogs to begin with, but can you imagine such a big guy walking such a little dog?" She laughed at the picture. "No, there's no way he'd take him."

I excused myself to go to the answering machine, sliding in the tape I'd played for Mort. If people had tried to leave me a message that morning, they would have been frustrated. When I returned to the kitchen, Sunny had already taken out the milk and sugar and placed two mugs and napkins on the table.

When we were settled with our tea, I said, "I tried to find you the other day. Did you go to California with your father?"

"I did. He wanted to have me along while he made arrangements for my mother's burial. She doesn't have any other relatives—at least none that she was in touch with—and I wouldn't have the first idea what to do."

"I'm so sorry for your loss," I said. "I hadn't known that she was your mother."

"I know. I should have told you, but . . ." She picked up her spoon and stirred her tea.

"I understand," I said, touching her arm.

She sighed. "I thought if anyone knew, they would treat me differently. I didn't even go visit her in her trailer. We kept our distance."

"Was she unhappy about that?"

"Just the opposite. I wasn't allowed to work on her set and I had to swear I wouldn't acknowledge her. At the time, I thought she just didn't want anyone to know she had a twenty-one-year-old daughter. She always lied about her age."

"And now do you think there was a different reason?"

"I don't know," she said, setting the spoon aside but keeping her gaze on the tea. "Maybe she didn't want me on the set because I'd be too much of a distraction. We weren't close. I'd been away too long. By the time I came home from boarding school the summer before college, it was like living with a stranger." Sunny raised her bewildered eyes to mine. "I imagine it was for her, too. Don't you think so?"

"Is this the first time that's occurred to you?"

"Ever since her death, I've been thinking a lot about her—and my relationship with her—but I couldn't discuss it with anyone, not even my father. Even now, I haven't told anyone else at the production company who she was to me. Ms. Fancy knows, of course, but the only others who know are Mitch and the first AD. He's the one all the PAs report to."

"Would that be Eric Barry?"

"That's right." She gave me a soft smile.

"Someone said he's your boyfriend."

"Oh, no," she said, her smile disappearing and her eyes flying up to the ceiling. "A production company is worse than a small town for rumors, isn't it?"

"Then Eric isn't your boyfriend?"

"Well, he might want to be, but I don't really have a boyfriend. I hope he's not spreading it around that we're a couple."

"I thought he was a little old for you," I said, sipping my tea.

"He's not too old for me," she was quick to say. "I like older guys."

Like Zee, I thought, but said, "Just not Eric."

"We might hang out every now and then. It's easy to

be with him since he's the only one who knows my true identity. But that's exactly why I would always wonder if he was interested in me or in gaining access to my father." She picked up the spoon again and stirred her tea thoughtfully. "Anyway, he's not really my type."

"I must have misunderstood," I said. "I'd heard you were angry with him for showing up late for a date—"

"A date? Oh, I know what you're referring to. Eric said he wanted to go over the next day's schedule with me, and then he makes me wait around until midnight while he plays poker with his cronies. I may be a lowly PA, but I do not appreciate being abused that way."

"Where were you waiting for him all that time?"

"I was with the other PAs in the catering tent for a while. But when the van came to drive everyone back to the houses they were staying at in town, I got left behind to wait for Eric."

"Were you all alone?"

"That's what made me so mad. I'm sitting there counting the stars and he's whooping it up with the boys. And when he finally shows up, he reeks of beer— and not only that, but he said he didn't have any schedule to go over. He just wanted to see me." Sunny's nostrils flared at the remembered offense. "If people are talking about it, I guess I shouldn't have yelled at him," she said, breaking a cookie in half and putting it on her plate.

"Any other PA would've gotten fired for that, wouldn't they?"

"Probably." She picked up the cookie, then looked up at me in horror. "Oh, my gosh, that's the night Vera was killed, wasn't it? I was just sitting around looking for the

Big Dipper while someone took out a gun and killed her. If I'd known where she was . . ." She trailed off.

"But you didn't know."

"Maybe I could have stopped it. Maybe if I was with her, the person wouldn't have dared to shoot her."

"Or maybe you would have been shot, too," I said. "Nothing good can come of thinking about what might have been. You have to accept what is and move forward."

Sunny took a deep breath. "My father said the same thing. He said she had little room in her life for other people, including us. Her career was all-consuming, even though she almost lost it when I came along." She took another bite of the cookie and sat back in her seat.

I knew there was something she was holding in, but I didn't know what it was. I gave her time to think.

"Mrs. Fletcher? I want to tell you something, but I'm asking you not to tell anyone else."

"If it has to do with your mother's murder, I can't promise not to discuss it with the sheriff."

"You can tell him, but please, don't say anything to anyone in the production company."

"All right. That sounds fair."

Sunny straightened in her seat. She cleared her throat and looked at me, her eyes pleading for understanding. "I was in the hangar where my mother was killed before her body was discovered and I didn't know it."

I nodded, but didn't say that Zee had already given the sheriff that information, and that it was the reason I'd been looking for her.

"Isn't that awful?" she said, glancing away. "I was right there and I didn't sense anything. I had no intuition, no feeling that anything was wrong. It was just another day."

"Are you suggesting that if your relationship had been closer, you would have known she was dead?" I asked.

"Well, wouldn't I have? Other people talk about knowing the instant they've lost someone they loved. You read about it all the time. They're aware of the spirit leaving; some even say they get a final message. I was aware of nothing. I certainly didn't get a message." She paused, then said, her voice small, "Does that mean I didn't love her?"

"It means nothing of the kind, young lady," I said sharply. "It means that there wasn't anything obviously amiss, nothing that could have alerted you to the situation."

Sunny's eyes opened wide.

"But if you want to take it as some indicator of your relationship," I said, softening my tone, "perhaps her spirit was protecting you, keeping you from making such a horrible discovery yourself, and keeping your memories of her as she was in life, not death."

Sunny let go of the breath she'd been holding. "Do you really think so?"

"What I really think is that it's important not to hold grudges or focus on regrets, especially when someone has died. Your mother loved you in the only way she knew how, and you returned her love the same way. Now, what were you doing in the hangar that day?"

Sunny blinked. "Zee and I were packing up his camera mount in the case."

"Why were you with Zee?"

"I was just asking him some questions about what he does. I like him. I know he's pretty old for me," she said, hastily adding, "but he's not any older than Eric Barry. Zee is . . . I don't know. He reminds me a bit of my father. He's very quiet, but he's always aware of everything and everyone around him. I tease him because his nickname means 'sea' in Dutch and German. Zee sees everything."

"That's interesting," I said.

Sunny laughed. "That's what people say when they don't know *what* to say."

I smiled. "Sometimes," I said. "Now, what was that favor you said you had to ask me?"

"That's right!" Sunny paused, collecting her thoughts. "I don't know how to ask you this exactly."

"Straight out is usually the best way."

"May I come live in your spare room again? I promise not to bend your ear anymore."

"Is that all?" I said. "From the way you were fidgeting and fussing, I thought this must be serious. Of course, you may stay in my guest room. And you're welcome to bend my ear anytime."

"Thanks so much, Mrs. Fletcher. The production company will pay my rent."

I started to say something, but Sunny put up her hand to stop me.

"They do that for everyone. It's in the budget."

"Okay. Do you need a ride back to the airport to pick up your things?"

She blushed. "I left my bag at the back door. I was hoping you'd say yes, but I didn't want to appear like I took you for granted."

"Well, then, you put your things away while I straighten up here. No arguments. However, I do have one requirement if you're going to stay with me again."

I'd caught her halfway out of her chair. "What's that?" she asked, sinking back into the seat.

"When you're here, you're to be responsible for Cecil. I know you work late and I'll care for him when you're working. But once you get home, you walk him and feed him in the morning before you leave."

"I think that's a pretty fair deal," she said, grinning.

Chapter Eighteen

"Jessica, how nice of you to stop in," Jacob Borden said.

After a quick lunch, I left Sunny at the house attaching Cecil's leash, and went downtown to the office of Cabot Cove's esteemed judge. But he wasn't the one I wanted to see. I was planning to show the photos Mort had given me, the ones taken from the strip of film, to Jacob's wife, Lorraine. She was a fan of old movies in general and of Vera Stockdale's movies in particular. When I'd spoken with her at Mara's she'd said she'd seen every one of the star's films.

"Hello, Jacob. I should have called ahead. I was hoping to catch Lorraine. Is she working with you today?"

"Not at the moment. She's off to a meeting, not sure which one. I can never keep track."

"She's a busy lady. I'll call again and—"

"Actually," he said, "I expect her back soon. And I'd like your opinion on something, if you have the time."

"I always have time for you, Jacob. What's on your mind?"

"Come on in. I was just going over the trial transcript of the Harris case. You modeled a great deal of your book on it."

My laugh was rueful. "Given what's been going on recently with the motion picture, I'm not sure I ever should have written that book."

"I'm glad you did. I really enjoyed it, especially since the case raised a lot of unresolved issues. Let's talk about it."

I followed him to his office and for a moment it felt as though I was back in the hangar on the "hot set." But this was Jacob Borden's real office, not the replica created for the movie.

"Coffee, tea? Only take a jiffy. I was about to make a cup for myself."

"I've just had some, but you go ahead."

"Be back in a minute."

In his absence, I gazed around the office, delighted by his collection of humorous figurines of lawyers and judges and impressed with the extensive law library he maintained. Judge Borden was known for having an encyclopedic knowledge of case law, and he often impressed lawyers arguing before him with his erudite manner and rock-solid legal grounding. He ran an orderly, no-nonsense courtroom, but was famous for breaking the tension of a trial with witty asides.

"I'm drinking decaf these days," he said when he returned with his cup of tea. "Lorraine says I talk too fast when I'm on the full-strength stuff."

"It must be working. You seem very calm to me," I

said, sitting in one of two visitor chairs. "So, what's prompted you to go back and revisit the Harris case?"

"That seems to be all that anyone is talking about these days," he said, taking his seat in the maroon wing chair. "Ever since the arrival of the film crew—and especially since the murder of Vera Stockdale—the Harris case has been relived all over town. I knew Ruth Harris. When she was gunned down walking her dog, I naturally thought of that custody case she'd ruled on, where the husband threatened to kill her in front of the whole court. He was the first person the police zeroed in on."

"But they ruled him out."

"That's right. And then they focused on Ruth's husband."

"You *have* heard that Neil Corday is back in town."

"I happened to see him downtown just yesterday. He's taken a long fall since his days as an attorney in Cabot Cove. Almost didn't recognize him—he looked like a derelict. He had a promising career once, until he went off the deep end and got involved with the wrong people. I hate to see any attorney disbarred, but it was justified in his case."

"He certainly has been acting strangely since returning," I said. "He attacked me."

Borden bolted forward in his chair, a shocked expression on his face. "Attacked you? Physically?"

"Yes. I'd been at the airport talking with people involved with the film production. I was leaving when he ran at me and pushed me down. He towered over me, raised his fists, and started ranting about my book, how I'd ruined his life. It was disconcerting, to say the least. Fortunately, Sheriff Metzger came upon the scene and intervened, handcuffed Mr. Corday, and had him taken to police headquarters. He was quite drunk at the time."

"That doesn't excuse his behavior," Jacob said. "I can imagine how upsetting it must have been for you. You say that Sheriff Metzger arrested him? He obviously didn't remain in custody very long."

"I chose not to press charges," I said. "Mort kept him a few hours and then released him. He's become quite a thorn in the side of the director and others involved with the filming."

Jacob sat back, formed a tent with his fingers beneath his chin, and said, "In your book, you left open the possibility that the wrong person might have been convicted of killing the judge. Did I read that correctly?"

"You did," I said. "I wrote it that way because I'd always suspected that Jenny Kipp was wrongfully convicted. Since I was writing a novel, not a true-crime account, I could present the facts any way I wanted. In the actual case, the evidence against her seemed to me to be circumstantial. I thought she was innocent. The jury obviously didn't agree with me. I attended Ms. Kipp's sentencing hearing. Judge Hammersmith gave her the maximum penalty."

Borden smiled, the sort of smile one displays when a pleasant thought has struck. "Judge Hammersmith," he said. "Martin was aptly named. His sentences were always tough. He and I were good friends. We didn't always see eye to eye on many matters, but he was a good and fair judge. It was quite a shock when he suffered a heart attack while presiding over a trial and died on the bench." A sad smile this time. "I suppose it's called dying with your boots on. He was too young to die, just sixty-one."

"I didn't know him well," I said. "You asked about my book leaving room for speculation about Jenny Kipp's conviction. I remember talking with you a few months after the trial. You expressed your own doubts. Why?"

"Certain factors, some of which never became public." He pointed to a foot-high pile of papers and files on his desk. "The trial transcript," he said, "and some material that never made it into the testimony."

He had my attention.

He shuffled through the pile, came up with a folder, and handed it to me. The label on the tab read INTERVIEW: TIFFANY PARKER.

"Tiffany Parker," I said a few times. "She was the other woman romantically involved with Neil Corday."

"Yes, she was. Of course, you know how rumors of that sort get started around town, and pretty soon everyone takes it as fact. It's like politicians repeating a lie over and over until people begin to believe it. Anyway, in this circumstance, what was a rumor turned out indeed to be a fact. The report you're holding was prepared by a private investigator that Jenny Kipp's court-appointed attorney hired. He got a lot of flak for that, spending taxpayer money to defend someone who most people believed was guilty. At any rate, the investigator interviewed Tiffany Parker at length, and she was surprisingly candid about her affair with Corday. According to what she told this investigator, she and Corday had been having an affair for six months leading up to his wife being shot."

"Mr. Corday certainly got around," I offered. "Jenny Kipp, Tiffany Parker, and probably others. He obviously possessed some sort of magnetism that attracted certain women despite his being married to Judge Harris."

"Well, he was a handsome guy with a thriving law practice—until he began to consider himself above the law, got involved in a slew of shady financial dealings, and tried to bribe his way out of trouble. I remember when he got a snoot on—this was after Jenny Kipp's trial—and lambasted everyone who'd believed that he'd killed Ruth. Made an absolute fool of himself. I wasn't the only one who was glad to see him close up his practice and leave town." Jacob's phone rang and he leaned forward to see the identity of the caller. "Do you mind if I take this?" he asked.

"Not at all."

While Jacob talked on the phone, I idly thumbed through the private investigator's notes. One paragraph stopped me:

Ms. Parker claims that the victim's husband, Neil Corday, told her on more than one occasion that he wanted to get rid of his wife so that he could marry her. On one occasion he even said that it wouldn't be long before she was dead and he'd be free. Ms. Parker said that when she confronted Corday about her rival for his affections, Jenny Kipp, he told her not to worry—that once his wife was out of the way, he would "take care of her," meaning Kipp. That conversation took place just days before the murder of Judge Harris.

I sat back and tried to force a recollection of what I remembered about the Kipp trial, from reviewing the transcript, and from what I'd read in the *Cabot Cove Gazette*, which had published a special section while the trial was taking place.

Tiffany Parker had testified as a prosecution witness at Jenny Kipp's murder trial. Jenny, after finding out that Corday had also been romantically involved with Tiffany, confronted the pair with a weapon that turned out to have been the gun used to kill Corday's wife. That was damaging evidence against Jenny, and many thought it was the pivotal point in the trial that led to her conviction and prison sentence.

"That was Lorraine," Jacob said, breaking my train of thought. "She's on the way home. Did you look through the file? Interesting, isn't it? You can take it home if you want, but I'd like it back when you're finished with it."

"Thank you," I said. "I would like to read it more carefully. These notes made by the investigator were never introduced during the trial, were they?"

"No, they weren't, Jessica. It was ironic, because even though Tiffany Parker had testified as a prosecution witness, Jenny Kipp's attorney wanted to call her again as a defense witness to testify on Jenny's behalf. After all, what she'd related to the investigator about Corday and his statements about his wife would have helped Jenny's cause. Don't you agree?"

"I certainly do."

"But Tiffany surprised everyone by denying that she'd ever said those things, and threatening to deny it again if she were put on the stand. The defense decided to try an end run around her by asking to enter the investigator's notes into the record, but the prosecutor,

Oscar Whittle, vehemently objected. That led to a lengthy bench conference with Judge Hammersmith, who upheld Whittle's objection."

"Too bad," I said. "Had the investigator used a tape recorder, Tiffany wouldn't have been able to deny that she'd said those things about Corday."

"Correct. I think the private investigator learned a tough lesson there."

"Any idea what caused Parker to recant her statements?" I asked.

Jacob's cocked head and raised eyebrows answered my question.

"She was bought off," I said flatly.

"A fair assumption, Jessica. Of course, it's always possible that Ms. Parker had a sudden bout of amnesia, but we both know that's unlikely. No, I think it fair to at least contemplate that she was paid to change her story—or not to tell it."

"By Neil Corday," I said.

"He had the most to lose if Jenny Kipp was found not guilty of the killing. If that's what happened, an innocent woman is sitting in prison."

I shivered at the thought. Among many things that send chills up my spine are people who are behind bars for crimes they didn't commit. It must be unbearable to wake up each morning in a tiny cell knowing that you don't deserve to be there.

"I haven't seen or heard of Tiffany Parker in a long time, Jacob. Did Corday ever marry her?"

"Never did."

"Do you know anything about her whereabouts these days?"

"I personally don't, but Lorraine might. She's bumped into her from time to time while working with her antipoverty group over in Cross Acres."

Cross Acres was a hardscrabble area on the outskirts of Cabot Cove. It had fallen on hard times with the closing of a plant that had provided most of the jobs there.

"She lives in Cross Acres?" I asked.

"According to Lorraine." He looked up at the sound of the front door opening. "You can ask her yourself, Jessica. The lady of the house has arrived."

"Jessica! What a nice surprise!" Lorraine said, bustling into her husband's office, her arms full of shopping bags.

Jacob rose from his seat to accept a quick peck on the cheek from his wife. "Jessica actually came to see you, dear," he said. "I was just the icing on the cake."

"Let me just drop these in the kitchen," she said to me. "Then I can give you a proper greeting. Anyone want tea or coffee?"

"I already offered," Jacob called to her back as she left the room. "I'm well trained," he said to me.

Lorraine was back a moment later, a smile on her face. "Now that my arms are empty, let me give you a hug," she said to me.

"You look like you had a good afternoon," I said when I sat down and she collapsed in the chair next to mine.

"Charles was having a sale on shoes and it was a mob scene," she said. "But I fought my way to the counter and came up with these." She held out both legs, showing off a new pair of alligator flats. "They're not real, of course. 'No alligator was harmed in the making of these shoes,'" she intoned, sounding like a narrator on a National Geographic special.

"A shoe sale!" Jacob said. "I told Jessica you were at a meeting."

"I was at a meeting. The sale was after the meeting," Lorraine said patiently. She looked at me. "I'm teaching a quilting class at the senior center. It's ironic, really. There are some women there who are far more experienced quilters than I am, but they're not good at explaining to others what they do. Ellen Purdy was supposed to teach the class, but she's too busy. So I was elected."

"You're a wonderful quilter and I'll bet you're an equally wonderful teacher," I said.

"The nicest thing is we're making small quilts to donate to the hospital. It's a worthwhile project and the ladies don't get too competitive about their work when they know it's going to be given away."

I laughed. "A laudable goal."

"A necessary one," she said, smiling. "I know Jacob must have entertained you with his legal stories, but he said you came to see me."

I reached for my bag and withdrew the manila envelope Mort had given me. "I have some photographs I'd like you to look at."

Lorraine's gaze flitted to Jacob and back to me. She shrugged. "Where were they taken?"

"That's what I need you to tell me," I said, handing her the papers. "I know you're a fan of old movies. These are frames from a movie in which Vera Stockdale was featured. I'm hoping you'll recognize what the film is."

"This is the strangest request you've ever made, Jessica," Lorraine said, sifting through the images. "But I do love Vera Stockdale films, and if I'm not mistaken, that's Robert Manheim," she said, pointing to the man holding Vera in his arms.

"How come I never heard of him?" Jacob said, coming around his desk to peer over his wife's shoulder.

"He died very young. He was killed in a jeep accident after the movie came out. It was in all the papers, lots of pictures of Vera mourning her costar. In a way, his death made her more famous. He was forgotten pretty quickly, but she went on to make a lot more films, as we all know." Lorraine handed the photos back to me. "It's too bad she didn't have a chance to make her comeback. I was really looking forward to seeing her again. Was she still beautiful?"

"Very beautiful," I said, slipping the photos back in the envelope. "Do you remember the name of this film?"

"I almost do. Give me a minute," she said, scowling and looking from Jacob to me. She shook her head. "These senior moments make me think I'm losing it."

"No danger there," said her husband. "You're always sharp as a tack."

"That's it! Thank you, Jacob."

"What did I say?"

Lorraine smiled at me. "The name of the movie is *Danger Comes Calling*. I think it might even have been her first film, but you can look that up online. Is that a help?"

"A big help," I said, standing. "Thank you. I'd better run. I want to stop at the library to see if they have a copy of this film."

"You can borrow mine," Lorraine said, walking me to the door. "I'm pretty sure I have it on DVD at home. I'll have Jacob drop if off tonight. Is that soon enough?"

"It's perfect."

"You can probably play it on your computer if you don't have one of those fancy machines that take all the different formats."

"I knew you were the right person to come to," I said, giving her a hug. "I should have the production company put you on the credits as the consultant to the script consultant."

"Oh, that would be fun, but only if they underline my name and put stars around it. Those credits roll so fast you never have time to read them."

Chapter Nineteen

Lorraine was as good as her word, and that evening Jacob dropped off their copy of *Danger Comes Calling*. Thankfully Sunny was working late. I didn't want to have to explain to her why I was watching her mother's first big picture. She didn't know about the piece of film the killer had tied around Vera's neck and I hoped it would remain a secret.

I slipped the disc into my computer and opened a media program to run it. Since the computer was my video player, I took notes on a lined legal pad while I watched and tried to figure out why the film had been important to Vera's murderer. It was a three-handkerchief melodrama, a star-crossed romance in which the lovers parted tearfully at the end.

Apart from the camera work, which focused fondly on the beautiful faces of its stars, I could see nothing in the story to arouse the fury of a viewer, unless Vera had been stalked by a rabid fan who was jealous of her movie lover. Mort and I had asked Chattergee if Vera had ever complained about a stalker, but he had dismissed the idea, citing her many years away from the screen. Still, I couldn't rule it out entirely. People with a fixation on a movie star often are mentally ill. Such an illness might not resolve over time.

According to the Internet Movie Database Web site, the movie was Vera's first starring role. She'd had smaller parts in a few pictures before, but that changed when she met Terrence Chattergee. Not her husband at the time, he was the producer of *Danger Comes Calling*. I remembered that Estelle Fancy had taken credit for getting Vera the part. I wondered if her involvement was confined to a reading of the stars and the portents they implied, or if she had somehow played a more active role.

I made the mistake of taking the folder that Judge Borden had loaned me upstairs to read in bed after the movie. Consequently, I spent a sleepless night wrestling with the mystery of Vera's murder and the probable miscarriage of justice in the conviction of Judge Harris's alleged killer. Two murders, years apart, but a murderer—or two—still on the loose.

The next morning, I debated whether to take a trip out to Cross Acres and attempt to make contact with Tiffany Parker. I decided that more research was in order first, although it would be informal research and perhaps not the most reliable. I headed downtown to Mara's Luncheonette on the assumption that its proprietor has a finger on the pulse of pretty much everything and everybody in Cabot Cove.

Mara was sitting alone in a booth when I entered,

shoes off, hair damp from having handled the breakfast crowd, sipping a Coke, and finally getting around to reading that day's *Cabot Cove Gazette*.

"Mind if I interrupt your much-needed rest?" I asked.

She laughed. "If you were a few other characters in this town, Jessica, I'd tell you to get lost. But it's always good to see you. Something to eat, drink?"

"Nothing, thank you," I said, sliding onto the bench opposite hers. "I have a question about a *character* from the town."

Her eyes widened. "Is there a scandal brewing?" she asked, obviously hoping that there was. "I bet it has to do with the murder of that actress out at the airport."

"Actually, it doesn't, Mara. Do you remember a woman named Tiffany Parker? She—"

"Of course I remember her. She was one of Neil Corday's hotties. Didn't I tell you he was in here the other day, looking and acting like the swine he is?"

"Yes, you did."

"If you ask me, Corday was the one who knocked off his wife. It would be just like him. Judge Harris was a sweetheart. How she ever ended up married to that man is beyond me. He used to parade his girlfriends around in public. Was in here once with Parker. Jenny Kipp, too. It's too bad about *her*; she got a life sentence. But I suppose it's better than how his wife ended up."

I let Mara vent her feelings about Corday and his women before saying, "I've been told that Tiffany Parker moved out of town and is now living in Cross Acres. Do you ever see her?"

"Me? No. She was never a regular customer. Besides,

I don't get much business from folks over there." Mara looked around to make sure no one was listening, but her only customer was Barnaby Longshoot and he was across the room, hunched over a cup of coffee, paging through an issue of *Maine Boats, Homes & Harbors* that someone had left behind. Nevertheless, she leaned forward and lowered her voice. "You know, when she was living in town and chasing anyone who wore pants, she picked up quite a reputation."

"I never really knew her," I said. "How did she earn a living?"

Mara snorted. "Earn? Well, I don't know if that's how you'd term it. She had a liking for men with money, especially married ones. Corday was only one of her sugar daddies. There were plenty more. She left town a few times to hook up with men from other places, sort of a traveling 'companion,' but she always ended up back here with a closet full of expensive clothes and enough money to pay her rent. I understand she bought a house in Cross Acres—they're cheaper out there—probably with money she got from her sugar daddies." She leaned closer. "Rumor has it she's lost her looks and has a bad prescription drug habit."

"I'm sorry to hear it," I said.

"We reap what we sow. What's your interest in her?"

"I've been thinking a lot about the questions raised by my book and whether they should also be in the movie. So far, the script has remained faithful to the book; in the book I left the reader with the possibility that the character based upon Jenny Kipp was innocent."

"So you think Tiffany Parker killed Judge Harris?"

"No! Not at all."

"Then you agree with me that Corday did it. I knew it!"

"Mara, please don't jump to conclusions. I'm not pointing a finger at anyone. All I'm saying is that I wasn't convinced Jenny Kipp was guilty. But a jury of twelve good men and women listened carefully, weighed the evidence, and came to a different verdict."

"Yeah, but did they hear *all* the evidence."

"What do you mean?"

"You know, don't you, that the prosecutor, Oscar Whittle, and Corday were drinking buddies? I always thought Whittle went after Jenny to help his friend out."

"You aren't suggesting that—"

Mara held up her hands in defense. "I'm not suggesting anything, Jessica. All I know is that when Whittle left town to join that la-di-da law firm in Boston, Corday followed. Now he's back, as obnoxious as ever."

"Hey, Mara, can I get some more coffee?" Barnaby called from across the room.

"Help yourself, Barnaby," Mara replied. "You know where the pot is." She sat back in her seat. "So, what's the latest scuttlebutt on the murder of the diva?"

"I don't have any," I replied.

"Come on, Jessica. I gave you good stuff on Tiffany Parker. Can't you give me a tidbit on Vera Stockdale?"

"I only know that they've started filming again."

Mara waved her hand. "Old news," she said, a disgusted look on her face.

"Hey, Mara, you're out of milk," Barnaby called, shaking an empty carton at her.

"Oh, for goodness' sake," Mara said, slipping out of

the booth to go take care of Barnaby, giving me my opportunity for escape.

"Thanks, Mara," I called as I headed for the door. "I have to go."

"Don't think you're off the hook, Jessica Fletcher. You owe me some gossip."

"Maybe next time," I said. "Bye."

I have to admit that I listen in at the Cabot Cove gossip mills—Mara's Luncheonette, Sassi's Bakery, and the post office—when I'm looking for information—not that I always believe what I hear. Gossip is often based on a kernel of truth, but that kernel can be stretched out, embellished, and turned into something completely untrue as it moves from mouth to ear. It's the game of Telephone all over again. I take what I hear with the proverbial grain of salt. And I try not to pass it along. It's really not fair to gossip. I'd rather let those involved tell their own story. But sometimes it's helpful to know what people are saying about someone to figure out how to approach them. Or perhaps I'm just making excuses for my nosiness.

Now that I'd found myself immersed in *two* murders—the slaying of Judge Ruth Harris and the killing of Vera Stockdale—it was enough to muddle my brain and make me wonder whether I should have taken a long vacation while the film was being shot in Cabot Cove. Too late for that now.

I looked up Tiffany Parker's number and called her on my cell phone.

"Hello?"

"Ms. Parker?"

"Yes."

"This is Jessica Fletcher. I don't believe we've ever met, but I was speaking with someone recently who mentioned you."

"What is this about?" she asked in a heavy voice.

I knew that to mention Neil Corday and his wife's murder early in the conversation might prompt her to hang up on me, but there was no way around it.

"I'm not sure if you're aware that a Hollywood production company is here in Cabot Cove filming a motion picture. It's based upon a book I wrote, *A Deadly Decision*, a fictionalized account of the murder of Judge Ruth Harris. Did you ever hear of it?"

"Oh, sure, Jessica Fletcher, the mystery writer. I read your book. You called me to ask me *that*?"

"No. Actually, I'm calling because I had the opportunity to review some of the transcript from Jenny Kipp's court case, as well as a report written by a private investigator who interviewed you before the trial."

In the silence that ensued I heard her light a cigarette and draw deeply on it. I also heard what sounded like a child's voice in the background.

"Ms. Parker?"

"Yeah, I'm here. Look, I really don't want to talk about that."

"I can understand, but—well, a woman who may be innocent is languishing in prison for a crime I don't think she committed. I probably wouldn't have even thought of contacting you except that Neil Corday, the murder victim's husband, is back in Cabot Cove and—"

"He is?"

"Yes. He arrived a few days ago and has been causing trouble with the film crew. He also attacked me."

"He's back?" she said, her voice taking on an angry tone. "Where did he come from?"

"I don't know, Ms. Parker. I was hoping you could tell me more."

"He went to Boston with that crud Oscar Whittle."

"Yes, I've been told that Corday and Whittle were friends, and that Corday followed Whittle to Boston."

"He didn't stay there long. I don't know where he went after that."

"No?"

"That's where he was the last time I talked to him, the last time I saw a cent in child support. And he owes me big-time."

It was my turn to fall silent while gathering my thoughts. "I wasn't aware that you had a child with him," I said. Apparently Mara wasn't aware of it either or she'd certainly have mentioned it.

Her laugh had the edge of a knife. "Oh, yes, the kid is his. I don't care what he says."

"And he was paying you child support?"

"For about a minute and a half. He said he wasn't the father, and I knew I'd never be able to fight him about it in court. He's a lawyer. All those guys stick together. He sent me money for the hospital and the doctors, and a few bucks after that. Then poof, he disappeared. Not a red cent more. Neil Corday is one slimy guy, Mrs. Fletcher. The lowest of the low." Another cigarette was lit.

"Ms. Parker," I said, "would you allow me to visit you?"

"What for?"

"I'd just like to talk to you about the interview that

you gave a private detective, and why you recanted what'd you'd told him."

"What, and plop myself in legal trouble? I've got a young daughter who doesn't need her mommy behind bars. Corday may have given me the down payment for this house we live in, but I work two jobs to pay the mortgage and put food on the table."

"I appreciate that," I said. "It's just that there's a woman already behind bars, Jenny Kipp, who I don't believe belongs there. If what you told the private investigator is true, Neil Corday might well be the one who put her there. Look, all I ask is that we sit down and discuss this further. I'm not a lawyer, but it seems to me that someone who comes forward to right a wrong should be praised, not punished. If you'd like, I'll confer with someone with knowledge of the law before we get together."

"So Mr. Neil Corday is back in town, huh?" she said.

"As I was saying, Ms. Parker, I can—"

"Yeah, you do that, Mrs. Fletcher. And then I'll decide if I want to talk to you." She lit another cigarette, started laughing, coughed, and said, "Thanks for calling."

The line went dead.

I called Jacob Borden and caught him just as he was about to leave his office for a speaking engagement. I told him of my conversation with Tiffany Parker. "Would she be in legal jeopardy if she came forward and swore that what she'd originally told the investigator was the truth, that Corday had told her on more than one occasion that he wanted to get rid of his wife, that on another occasion he said his wife would be dead soon?"

"I'd like to give it some more thought, Jessica," Borden said, "but my initial reaction is that if she did that, the new DA would be more than willing to grant her immunity. Besides, the statements she made weren't in court and under oath. I'll get back to you with my definitive answer tomorrow."

"Thanks, Jacob."

"No, thank *you*, Jessica. There's nothing more that this judge wants to see than justice being done."

Chapter Twenty

An hour later, as I was in the process of preparing dinner for myself, the phone rang.

"Hello, Jessica. Jacob Borden here. Good time to talk?"

"Hello, Jacob. Yes, perfect timing. I just made a casserole for myself and put it in the oven. It won't start to burn for twenty minutes."

He chuckled. "I'll set my timer," he said. "Jessica, I've done some serious thinking about what you told me about Tiffany Parker, and the possibility that she's willing to offer testimony that might cause the Jenny Kipp case to be reopened."

"I appreciate your looking into this."

"I took a look at case law regarding someone giving false information to authorities, as Ms. Parker did with the defense attorney when she recanted what she told the private investigator."

"And?"

"It's murky. On the one hand, by withdrawing her

statement, she played a significant, if unwitting, role in seeing that Jenny Kipp was convicted of Judge Harris's murder. Although the investigator didn't have legal authority as, say, one of the lawyers in the case would have had—and she wasn't under oath—it still represents having provided false evidence in a felony case. The law doesn't look favorably on people who do that."

"For good reason."

"However, I called Joe Scott in the DA's office. Interestingly enough, he told me that the Kipp case has always bothered him. He wasn't the prosecutor in her trial—it was Oscar Whittle—but he's looked at the transcript from time to time. He didn't mince words, Jessica. He felt that Whittle bent over backward to thwart the defense's case, and that Judge Hammersmith went along with it."

"Oooh," I said, "that sounds ominous."

"Nothing like that. I might not have ruled the way Judge Hammersmith did, but that's beside the point. The defense wanted to offer what Ms. Parker had originally told the investigator—namely, that Corday had said he wanted to get rid of his wife, and that Ms. Kipp wouldn't be a problem anymore once his wife was dead. But Whittle objected strenuously that it represented hearsay and Judge Hammersmith upheld that objection."

"Did you tell Mr. Scott that Ms. Parker might now be willing to come forward and admit that her original statement to the private investigator was the truth?"

"Yes, I did."

"How did he react?"

"Positively. He told me that if she would do that, and was willing to testify to the fact, he'd be willing to go to court and ask that the case be retried. He was confident that she would be given immunity in return for her testimony."

"That's good to hear, Jacob. I'd like to get back in touch with Tiffany Parker and pass along what you've told me."

"That sounds fine, Jessica. I should mention that Joe Scott was not a fan of either Oscar Whittle or Neil Corday. He had some rather nasty things to say about them."

"I'll keep that in mind," I said. "Many thanks, Jacob, for taking the time to look into this."

"As I said, judges like to see justice done, especially when someone is serving time for a crime she might not have committed. Let me know what Ms. Parker says."

I'd no sooner hung up when the phone rang.

"Mrs. Fletcher? This is Tiffany Parker."

"Yes, Ms. Parker. I was about to call you."

"You told me that creep Corday was in town? Is he still around?"

"I assume he is, although I haven't seen him in the past few days."

"Well, I'd like to tell my story—my *real* story—to see that he gets what's coming to him, but only if there's no downside for me. I don't want to end up in jail making sure he gets his."

Her vindictiveness toward Neil Corday was a little off-putting. It had been my experience that people with a deep-seated hatred for someone didn't necessarily make the most reliable of witnesses, since their accusations were likely fueled by their anger. But the fact that she'd made statements implicating Corday at an earlier time lent credence to what she would have to say today. At least that was how I saw it.

"I'd suggest that I come to see you," I said, "but I don't drive and—"

She laughed. "You don't drive?"

"I'm afraid not. But I could—"

"I'm off tomorrow. I'll come to you," she said. "I *do* drive."

"That would be fine."

"What about my chances of being in hot water legally?"

I explained how I'd received assurances that if she testified, and told the truth, she would be granted immunity. When she didn't respond, I added, "I can ask the legal expert I spoke with if he would be willing to meet with you, if that would put your mind at ease."

"Yeah, I want to hear what he has to say. Corday's tricky. He's hurt me enough; I don't want to give him an opportunity to slip in some legal mumbo jumbo that lands me where *he* should be—in jail."

"I'm certain that you don't have to worry about that, Ms. Parker," I said. "But I will try to arrange for you to meet with Judge Borden."

"A judge?"

"Yes, a very good friend and a wonderful man and jurist. When would be a good time for you to come?"

"Tomorrow morning?"

"That would be fine. I can't guarantee that he'll be available tomorrow, but I'll certainly ask."

"Okay," she said. I could almost see her rubbing her hands in glee as she said, "I only wish I could see Corday's face when he finds out what I'm doing."

I had nothing to say in response, and after I gave her directions to my house, we ended the call.

Lorraine answered when I called Jacob Borden at home. He came on the phone, and I told him of my conversation with Tiffany Parker and asked whether he would be willing to meet with her the following day.

"Happy to," was his reply. "I'm free for lunch if that works for you and Ms. Parker."

"I'm not sure that going out to lunch is the best idea," I offered. "Could we meet at your office at, say, twelve thirty? I'll bring sandwiches."

"Sounds good to me," he said. "See you then."

My casserole did, in fact, burn, but it was salvageable. I ate it in fits and starts because my phone kept ringing.

Sheriff Mort Metzger called to complain that the film crew had backed a truck into Monte Cogan's car and bashed in the rear fender.

"You know Cogan, Mrs. F. He was threatening to sue everyone, including Mayor Shevlin, for allowing the crew to come to town."

"He's a hothead, Mort, but I'm certain he'll change his mind. By the way, Lorraine Borden came up with the name of the movie the strip of film is from," I said.

"Cogan wasn't the only problem," Mort said, continuing his diatribe. "A truck delivering food supplies to Peppino's had to park two blocks away because of roped-off streets and refused to haul the supplies that distance. I took an earful from the restaurant owner."

"Mort, did you hear me? The movie is called *Danger Comes Calling*. It was Vera Stockdale's first starring role."

"He demanded that I open the street on which the restaurant is located. I can't do that unilaterally. The mayor gave the production company a permit to close the street temporarily."

"Well, did you talk to Elovitz?" I asked, giving up on telling Mort about the movie for now.

"He told me 'no way' in no uncertain terms. I'm telling you, that twerp thinks he's king of the world."

"They're only here for a limited time, Mort . . ."

"I have another call, Mrs. F. Have a good night."

Evelyn Phillips of the *Cabot Cove Gazette* called next to ask whether I'd heard a rumor that Lois Brannigan, the actress who'd replaced Vera Stockdale in the role of the Judge Harris character, was suspected of murdering the diva in order to get the part. I denied ever hearing any such thing, and Evelyn hung up, obviously disappointed.

And before I managed to get to the dishes, there were four other calls, all of which I ended as quickly—and politely—as possible. One was from a friend, photographer Richard Koser, who knew Neil Corday from when he practiced law in Cabot Cove, and he reported that he'd seen him early in the evening at the bar of a restaurant where he and his wife, Mary Jane, were having dinner. "He looked drunk as a skunk," he reported, "and was raving about how Jessica Fletcher was a pain in his—"

"I get the picture, Richard."

"Just letting you know he was bandying your name around, Jessica."

Once in bed, I put together my thoughts on the upcoming day, the arrival of Tiffany Parker and our planned visit with Judge Borden. The hard shell that she wrapped herself in was obviously a defense mechanism against the hurt she'd experienced in her life. Her reputation for using men to get what she wanted certainly was a negative one, especially since it included married men like Neil Corday. In a sense, her decision—to come forward now—represented revenge, but also possibly a stab at atonement for the manipulative life she'd led . . . at least I hoped so.

Life is a series of choices. Hopefully we choose a path in a mostly positive direction, but sometimes we let ourselves be led astray. The murder mystery novels I write always include a character who takes the latter path, and suffers the consequences. Life! What a miraculous, complicated thing it is for everyone.

I was up early, anticipating Tiffany Parker's arrival. The van had already picked up Sunny, who, as promised, had walked and fed Cecil before she left for work. I was reading the paper when I heard a car with a loud engine pull up in the driveway—it obviously needed a muffler replacement. I opened the door and waved, scooping up Cecil before he scampered out to greet my visitor.

Tiffany Parker climbed out of her car and hesitantly patted her hair. She seemed unsure whether to come to me, but she decided to head my way eventually, and we shook hands on my front step.

"Somehow I didn't picture you with a little dog," she said, giving Cecil a pat on the head.

"He's just a temporary visitor," I said, hoping it was

true. "I wondered whether you'd bring your daughter with you," I said as I led her into the house.

"I thought about it, but—you know kids—they get antsy when there aren't toys around. I have a neighbor who babysits when I go to work. She has her. Some days it costs me as much for the sitter as I make."

I'd prepared a carafe of coffee and had laid out a platter of small powdered doughnuts I'd picked up the day before from Sassi's Bakery. "Help yourself," I said.

She took a chair at my kitchen table, put two doughnuts on her plate, and ate one before I had a chance to pour coffee into her cup. "These are good," she said as she started on her second.

I joined her at the table. She was a tall woman, attractive if you discounted what could be described only as wear and tear on her long, slender face. She was thin, her arms sinewy. She had attempted to tame her thick hair by using a rubber band to pull it back into a chignon, but several locks were poking out, giving the bun a spiky look. Heavily applied makeup emphasized pretty blue eyes, but was not able to conceal the lines and ruddiness in her complexion. After finishing her third doughnut, she said, "So, where's Corday?"

"I don't know," I said, "but I did hear that he was in a local restaurant last night, quite inebriated, according to the person who saw him."

"Good," she said. "I can't wait to see the creep squirm." She grabbed two more doughnuts for her plate, and I began to wonder when she'd last had a good meal.

We drove to Judge Borden's office in Tiffany's car, an older tan Chevy with a great deal of rust on its body and a faulty muffler that made the car sound as though it was being driven by a teenager enamored of the noise. If I had hoped to keep my association with Tiffany quiet in order not to alert Corday to our acquaintance, riding in her car was going to make it difficult.

The upholstery was torn in multiple spots, and she had to toss a pile of items into the rear seat to make room for me in front. I asked that we stop at a deli a few doors down from the judge's office, where I bought sandwiches—egg salad, which I knew was one of Jacob's favorites, and, at Tiffany's request, roast beef, plus soft drinks. Jacob's wife, Lorraine, welcomed us and we settled in Jacob's office. He walked in a few minutes later, greeted Tiffany, and without wasting any time said, "So, tell me about what Neil Corday told you concerning his wife's murder."

Tiffany was overtly nervous about speaking with a judge, and her false starts mirrored it. But Jacob was smooth and skillful in the way he drew her out, and after forty-five minutes the whole story had been told.

"You're very courageous to come forward like this," he said.

"But what do we do now?" I asked.

Jacob laughed. "I suggest we enjoy our sandwiches. Lorraine set the table in the kitchen, if that's all right with you. When we're finished, I'll call Joe Scott in the DA's office and recommend that he arrange for Ms. Parker to go over there and give a formal statement."

"I won't be in trouble?" she asked.

"No, you won't be in trouble," Borden said. "But you should be represented by a lawyer, who can negotiate the immunity arrangement in exchange for your testimony."

"Well, that pops it," Tiffany said. "I can't afford a lawyer."

"Joe will have a public defender available for you."

The tension that had hung over us now abated, and we broke for lunch. When Jacob left to make his call, Lorraine refused to let us help clean up and shooed us out of the kitchen. We returned to Jacob's office. Needing a stretch, I strolled around the room, taking in the wall-to-wall, ceiling-to-floor bookcases that dominated the room.

"Those books contain centuries of law," Jacob commented when he finished his call.

"Have you read them all?" Tiffany asked from where she sat.

"I wish I could say I have," Jacob said. As he did, he reached up and pulled down one of the volumes, *The Nature of the Judicial Process.* "I often turn to this particular book, not so much for legal guidance but because it's so beautifully written and is filled with wisdom." He smiled and pressed the book to his chest. "Thank goodness for Benjamin Cardozo," he said.

I let out an involuntary gasp.

"Are you all right?" he asked.

"Yes. I'm sorry," I said. "I just thought of something."

Chapter Twenty-one

"I don't know, Mrs. F. There's gotta be a thousand books on that set."

"Probably more like three or four hundred, but I agree it's a lot of books to look through."

Tiffany had dropped me at the sheriff's office and I'd waited more than an hour for Mort to return. Jacob's law library had given me an idea, and I was eager to share it with him.

"My guys said they checked every one of them."

"They probably checked the spines looking for bullet holes," I said.

"Right! And there were none. So how could the bullet get in a book if it didn't go through the spine?"

"When Seth and I went to see Dr. Smith, the forensic pathologist, he said that Vera must have been pressed up against something for the exit wound to be shaped the way it was. I think she may have had her arms around a book. It could have been one of the law books from the shelves on the set. Or it could be that book on acting that she always carried around. I don't remember seeing it in her trailer. If that's the case, the bullet would have entered the front or back of the book, but not the spine, which is maybe why it wasn't found."

"That's a pretty big *if*, Mrs. F. You want me to drive all the way out to the airport on a hunch? I can't do it today. I just got back in the office. I have too much to do."

"I understand, Mort, and I appreciate all the time you give me, but Estelle Fancy suggested that Vera liked to walk around a set to get a feeling for her role."

"So you think she was absorbing the atmosphere by sitting in the judge's chair and looking through a law book?"

"It's possible, except, she must have been standing when she was shot through the back. The State Bureau of Identification didn't find a bullet or bullet hole in the chair."

"It sounds pretty far-fetched to me."

"But if I'm right—and if we find the book—you'll have an important piece of evidence."

"And if you're wrong, I'll have wasted several hours I could have used tackling the mound of paperwork I have on my desk. Plus, Maureen is making one of her more reliable dishes tonight and I don't want to be late for dinner."

"What is she cooking?"

"I'm not sure what it's called, but it's some kind of corkscrew-shaped noodle with eggplant and tomato sauce. The last time we had it, it was so good, I didn't believe she'd made it. Now that she knows I like it, she's been making it more often."

"That's wonderful," I said.

"Tomorrow," Mort said. "We'll go tomorrow. Anything else on your mind?"

"One or two things, if you have the time."

"Go ahead," he said, sighing.

I knew Mort was losing patience, but I decided if I didn't fill him in on everything that was going on, he'd be annoyed when he eventually found out. "You know that fellow who attacked me out at the airport, the one you arrested?"

"Corday?"

"Yes, Neil Corday."

"He had a lawyer at the station by the time I got back there, Mrs. F. He was still three sheets to the wind, but I had to release him. Sorry about that."

"No need to apologize. I didn't raise his name for that. But I had a long discussion with Jacob Borden yesterday, and I saw Jacob again today."

"Are you in trouble, Mrs. F.?"

I laughed. "Not that I know of. I had stopped in to show Lorraine the photos from the strip of film to see if she recognized the movie."

"Did she?"

"Yes. It was from *Danger Comes Calling*, Vera Stockdale's first starring role. Maureen would love it. But if the killer was leaving a message, for the life of me I couldn't figure out what it was."

"Should I watch it, too?"

"I'm sure Lorraine and Jacob would lend you their copy if you want to see it."

"Maybe another time. What else?"

"While I was waiting for Lorraine, Jacob shared a

very interesting file with me." I gave Mort details about Tiffany Parker's interview with the private detective, and told him about my efforts to have her come forward. "Parker's testimony could possibly exonerate the woman jailed for the killing of Judge Harris. At least, it could be reason enough to call for a new trial," I said.

"You're dealing in a lot of long shots, Mrs. F.," Mort said. "I don't think I'd want to go to the racetrack with you."

"I know, but they're important bets, Mort. I'm hoping that Tiffany Parker can save Jenny Kipp from a lifetime behind bars."

"But that would mean that you're pointing a finger at Corday as the killer. Do you think he's just going to stand by while you try to get him arrested? You'd better tread carefully around that character. I don't want to find you gunned down while walking that little dog you ended up with. If he got away with it once, he might try it again."

"I'll be careful," I assured him.

It was late afternoon by the time I returned home. Cecil was scratching frantically at the back door when I walked in. I attached his leash and we took a stroll around the neighborhood, my mind occupied with the events of the past few days and with what Mort and I might find at the airport tomorrow. When we returned from our walk, I was surprised to see Sunny. She'd come home earlier than I'd expected, and she'd brought Eric Barry with her.

"Hi, Mrs. Fletcher," Sunny said, her face pale. "You know Eric, don't you?"

"Yes, of course," I said, shaking his hand. "Eric escorted Sheriff Metzger and me around to interview people the day we found your mother." My gaze moved from one to the other. They were clearly worried, and I wondered what had upset them. I focused on Sunny. "Are you all right?" I asked.

"I'm not sick or anything," she said. "We came to show you something." She looked at her watch nervously. "We have to get back, but I told Eric that we had to show it to you. It's too important to wait until later."

"What do you have to show me?"

"This." She dug into the pocket of her jeans, pulled out a crumpled piece of paper, and set it on the table. She ran her hand across it, trying to smooth out the wrinkles. Then she stepped back. "Eric found it," she said.

"I thought she had a right to see it. I knew it would be upsetting, but I couldn't keep it to myself."

"You did the right thing," Sunny said to him. "I'm strong. I can take it." She turned to me. "We think it's an important clue."

"A clue?"

She swallowed hard. "Yes. To my mother's murder."

The writing on the yellow sheet of paper was in black pencil, the letters straight up and down, the strokes strong and dark as if the author had dashed off the note in anger. It said:

> You gave me up for money, you pathetic excuse for a mother.
> You dumped me on a poor family in Mexico and walked away.

Did you think I wouldn't find out who you were?

You owe me. And you'll pay.

"Where did you find this?" I asked.

"Eric found it in the garbage," Sunny said, shooting him a glance.

He coughed to clear his throat. "Actually, I was taking out the garbage from our trailer," he said, "and I tripped. When I was putting the trash back in the pail, this fell out. It's on yellow paper, the same kind we use for interoffice memos. I thought maybe it was instructions or something that I'd missed, so I read it. As soon as I saw it, I thought it might have to do with Ms. Stockdale's murder."

"And so you told Sunny about it," I said.

"I thought she ought to know. I would want to know, if it was my mother."

"Do you know who wrote this?"

"It looks like Zee's writing to me," he said. "Besides, who else would put something in our garbage?"

"Do you know if he was adopted as an infant by a Mexican family?" I asked.

He looked uncomfortable. "I don't. He never talks about his personal life. But he has a Spanish name."

Sunny had been hopping from one foot to the other. "Do you know what this means, Mrs. Fletcher?" she said.

"I wouldn't jump to conclusions," I said. "But I do think it's something we should share with the sheriff."

"No. You don't understand," she said, tears starting.

"If Zee killed Vera because she gave him up as a baby, then Zee is . . ."

"Zee is her brother," Eric finished for her.

"First, we don't know that Zee wrote this note," I said. "Second, even if he *is* its author, he threw it away. He may have regretted writing it. Third, even if he gave it to Vera, it doesn't prove that Zee is the one who killed her. All this note does is give Sheriff Metzger a reason to question him again."

"I always thought he was an oddball," Eric said to Sunny. "I told you not to hang around him."

"He's not an oddball. He's just quiet, introspective, like my father. I knew we had something in common, but I don't believe he's violent. Zee wouldn't kill anybody."

"Well, someone killed her," Eric said. "And here's a motive." He looked at me. "You don't know of any other motive, do you?"

"That still doesn't make your interpretation the correct one," I said.

"Maybe we should take this to your father," Eric said, sweeping the note off my kitchen table.

"Maybe we should take this to the sheriff," I said, plucking it out of his hands. I opened the drawer where I kept aluminum foil and plastic bags, slipped the note into a baggie, and tucked it in my shoulder bag. "There are already far too many fingerprints on this," I said. "I hope the sheriff's lab will be able to sort them out."

"We have to get back," Eric said, shooting Sunny a meaningful look. "I'll be missed."

"Okay," she said. "Thanks for taking time off to drive me."

"You can stay here if you want," he said. "I can make excuses for you."

"You don't need to make excuses for me. I'm all right. I'll go back to work." She turned and gave me a quick hug. "I know you'll do the right thing with the message. I'm only praying it doesn't mean what we think it does."

But I was afraid it did.

When they left, I went to my office and looked up a number I hadn't used for a long time. Then I dialed it.

The operator answered in Spanish.

"I'd like to speak with Chief Javier Rivera," I said, attempting to use the little Spanish I knew. It was only polite; I was calling Mexico after all. "Please tell him it's Jessica Fletcher calling."

Moments later, he came on the line. "Señora Fletcher," the police chief said. "This is a surprise. It has been a long time since you were in San Miguel de Allende."

"Yes, it has. But I always remembered your kindness and cooperation when I was there last. I hope your family is well."

"They are. My son is pitching for our local baseball team. And how are your friends Señor Buckley and his lovely wife?" he asked, referring to my publisher Vaughan Buckley and his wife, Olga.

I had met Chief Rivera when visiting the Buckleys' vacation home in Mexico. During my time there, Vaughan had been the victim of a kidnapping.

"Do you have a new mystery for me to solve?" he asked.

I could hear the smile in his voice. "Actually, I do," I replied. "I'm hoping you can find out information about the birth of an American child in Mexico."

"I will need a little more detail than that," he said.

I gave him the year of the birth and the possible names of the mother and father. "Whatever details you can add would be very helpful," I said.

"I'll see what I can find out, *mi amiga*."

Chapter Twenty-two

Sunny got back around midnight. I heard her tiptoe to her room, trying not to wake me. But she needn't have gone to the trouble. I was in bed, but I was wide-awake, and that wasn't going to change. I spent a sleepless night throwing off and pulling up the covers, rolling from side to side, and punching my pillow.

Now the slice of film from *Danger Comes Calling* began to make sense. Was the note in my bag downstairs the one that Chattergee said had upset the star? If Zee thought Vera had given him up for adoption in order to star in the movie, any resentment he harbored would be understandable. *Danger Comes Calling* was Vera's first starring role, the part she'd almost lost forever when Chattergee's wife insisted that he fire her, and the role she'd been reinstated in several months later when the producer's wife filed for divorce. Audrey, the makeup lady, had said Vera had hidden out in Mexico during that time. Perhaps Vera hadn't been getting over her heartbreak, as the movie magazines of the time had speculated. Perhaps she'd gone to Mexico to have a baby away from prying eyes. Had Zee been born in Mexico? The time frame fit. I was hoping the chief of police in San Miguel de Allende could use his influence to confirm the details.

Eric seemed eager to pin the crime on Zee. *His* motive was clear: jealousy. Eric had left the poker game at eleven, but he hadn't met Sunny until midnight. Where had he been during that hour? Jealousy was not unknown to Lois Brannigan either. How convenient that she'd taken over the role Vera had held, the one she'd wanted all along. And look at Estelle Fancy. She'd spoken of Vera's Gemini personality—fickle and impulsive—but was she Vera's friend, enemy, or a bit of both? And our executive producer, Terrence Chattergee, was in the middle of it all. His relationship with his former wife was volatile. All these years later, they'd still been battling.

The particulars of Vera's murder melded with thoughts of the late judge Ruth Harris and her wayward husband, the women with whom he'd cheated on her, especially the one currently behind bars, a possible case of justice perverted. The characters I'd written about, and those I'd recently met, invaded my dreams and occupied my waking thoughts. I was so restless that Cecil jumped down from the bed and curled up on the easy chair where I'd abandoned the book I was trying to read before bed.

I slept later than I usually do, and in the morning, groggy and irritable, I came downstairs to find a note on the kitchen table from Sunny, telling me that she was off to work, that Cecil was walked and fed, and thanking me for passing along the new evidence to Sheriff Metzger.

I spent an hour sipping a cup of tea and paging through my Spanish-English dictionary, trying to make sense of the issues that had interrupted my sleep. Finally I gave up and called Mort's office.

"Sheriff Metzger is at a meeting with the special police detail, Mrs. Fletcher," the desk officer told me. "He should be back after lunch."

"Thanks, Edgar," I said. "Would you please ask him to call me when he's free?"

"Will do."

I debated climbing back into bed for a much-needed nap, but decided a wake-up shower would probably be as effective. I had just returned downstairs, dressed and refreshed, when the bell rang. I opened the door to Eve Simpson.

"*Bonjour*, Jessica. I hope you don't mind my barging in like this," she said. She looked down and squealed when she saw Cecil looking up at her, his head cocked at an angle. "When did you get this adorable little dog?" she said, swooping down and lifting the Chihuahua into her arms.

He rewarded her with a lick on her chin.

"Come in, Eve. What can I do for you?"

"Oh, isn't he the sweetest thing!" she exclaimed, carrying Cecil into my kitchen. "A cup of coffee would be divine, and a snack if you have anything on hand. I'm famished."

"I'm sure I can come up with something," I said, trying not to let my earlier grumpiness creep back into my demeanor.

While I put on a pot of coffee and looked to see if I had any leftover powdered doughnuts from my meeting with Tiffany Parker, Eve played with Cecil, cooing at him and laughing when he danced at her feet.

"So, where did this cutie-pie come from?" she asked.

"Cecil was Vera Stockdale's dog," I said.

"The movie star?"

I nodded. "There was no one to care for him, so I'm filling in as a temporary parent until her family decides what should be done with him."

"Ooh, you poor thing," Eve said, addressing Cecil. She looked at me. "You really should keep him yourself. Just think! He's famous! A movie star's dog. He would be a wonderful comfort for you."

"Perhaps," I said, wondering why Eve thought I needed comforting. "But I travel too much to keep a pet. I told Vera's daughter that. I'm hoping she'll make some arrangement for him." I realized as soon as it was out of my mouth that Eve didn't know that Sunny was Vera's daughter. My tired brain had betrayed me. I wished I could take back the words, but it was too late now. If Eve picked up on my slip, Sunny's secret wouldn't be a secret for long. Eve loved nothing more than passing along a delicious morsel of gossip. I mentally crossed my fingers, hoping Eve wouldn't ask who Vera's daughter was. Quickly, I set a plate with two doughnuts in front of her, went back to the stove to pour our coffee, and brought the mugs to the table.

Eve had already eaten a doughnut. "These are from

Charlene Sassi's bakery, aren't they?" she said, breaking the second doughnut in half and feeding a crumb to Cecil. "I can always tell."

"They are," I said. I took a sip of coffee and sighed into the cup. "May I ask what brought you here this morning, Eve?"

"Well, I'm a bit embarrassed to tell you," she replied.

I waited, knowing the story would come out anyway.

"I know you won't believe this after all the trouble I went to, Jessica, but I'm afraid I have to bow out of your movie."

My brows rose almost of their own accord. Eve had spent weeks plotting how to get into the movie and now she was backing out?

"What happened?" I asked.

"I'm just too busy," she said. "I spent an entire day at Loretta's Beauty Shop—it looks terrific, by the way—while the movie people shot a scene. I just can't waste my time like that. I have clients who need me, I have houses to sell, and business to conduct. You wouldn't believe how many calls I got from the people whose names I took at the post office. Anyway, the first AD said the scene would have to be reshot, something about skewed continuity, and I told him to find another girl."

"And he was all right with that?"

"Well, he nearly pitched a fit, but the director said it was okay; it was just fodder for the editor or something like that. *C'est la guerre.* My fifteen minutes of fame will have to come another time."

The telephone rang. I excused myself to answer it,

crossing my fingers that it was Mort to tell me when he would pick me up to go to the airport. But I couldn't hear the voice on the other end of the line. "Who is this, please?"

"Can you hear me now?"

It was Hamilton Twomby. I'd been expecting to receive a call from him.

"Jessica, we have some screenwriting to do."

"When would you like to get together?"

"I have to be on the set this afternoon. They're filming the scene with Brannigan as the judge. What a headache. Now that Lois is the new Vera, she's picking up Vera's old habits and making demands about the script."

"Oh, that's too bad."

"Can you meet me at the set? We can work during the breaks."

"I was hoping to come out to the airport today," I said. "I'll look for you when I get there."

"I'd better be off, Jessica. You don't mind, do you?" Eve said when I hung up the phone. She lifted Cecil and gave him a kiss on the top of his head. "*You* are just adorable. I wish you were mine," she said, putting him down.

So do I, I thought.

"Sorry to eat and run," she said to me. "I found a great place for Rhonda Chen away from the airport. I'm helping her move in."

I waited impatiently to hear from Mort, occupying myself by reading the e-mail I'd neglected for the past few days, looking up Vera Stockdale's career online, and dawdling over lunch. At last the phone rang, and

I thought it might be Sheriff Metzger. Instead, it was Chief Rivera calling from Mexico.

"A good time?" he said.

"A very good time," I replied.

"Well," he said, "I was able to come up with the information that you were seeking. It was almost exactly as you told me."

"Almost?" I said, ready to write on a yellow legal pad on my desk. "I'm listening."

A few minutes later we ended the call. "I can't thank you enough," I said to Chief Rivera as I glanced out the window to see Mort in his patrol car pulling up in front of my house.

"It was my pleasure, señora," Chief Rivera said. "You will have to let me know the results of your investigation. I hope I have solved your mystery."

"You've made an important contribution," I said. "I'll let you know how it turns out. My regards to your wife and son."

I didn't even get a chance to think about what I'd just learned before the phone rang again.

Tiffany Parker's voice was breathless. "Mrs. Fletcher, he's here."

"Who's there?"

"Neil. Neil Corday. He's pounding on the door and trying to break in."

"Don't open the door," I said. "Did you call the police?"

"No. I'm afraid they won't believe me. I'm scared. He's drunk and he said he's gonna get even."

"I'll be there as soon as I can."

I opened the door just as Mort raised his fist to

knock. "Come on," I said, rushing outside. "We have to hurry."

"What's up now?"

"We have to get out to Tiffany Parker's house in Cross Acres. Neil Corday is threatening her life."

Chapter Twenty-three

"She sounded desperate," I told Mort as we drove from my house to Cross Acres.

"What'd she say again?"

"She said that Corday had arrived at her house, drunk and in a rage. Somehow he must have gotten wind that she'd given the private investigator damaging information about him and revealed the comments he'd made before Jenny Kipp was charged with his wife's murder."

"I talked to Joe Scott in the DA's office just before I picked you up. Looks like he's about to petition the court to reopen the Harris case."

"Not good news for Neil Corday," I said. "If Corday did shoot his wife, he'll be desperate to keep Tiffany from testifying against him. He's obviously unstable, Mort."

"We're spread a little thin these days, but I'm going to call in for extra help." He radioed headquarters and reported our destination. "Make sure we get another squad car over there."

"What I can't figure out is why he dared to return to Cabot Cove. When I first called Tiffany, she wasn't keen on changing her statements to the investigator. But when I told her that Corday had returned to town, her whole manner changed. I don't think I told you that he fathered a child with her."

Mort swerved to avoid a bicyclist busy reading a text message on his cell phone and not paying attention to where he was going. "Should give him a ticket for texting while driving," Mort growled.

"Does the no-texting law apply to bicycles?" I asked.

"It should. Ms. Parker didn't say whether Corday was armed?"

"No, but it's safe to assume if he's threatening her life, he may have some weapon," I said. "She said he was drunk. I fear for her *and* her child."

Mort turned off the highway and headed down a narrow two-lane road leading toward Cross Acres.

"Do you ever hear anything about Jenny Kipp?" I asked.

"Last I heard, a legal aid lawyer had filed a motion to reopen the case. She didn't have anything to base it on, but now—"

"Now she will—if nothing happens to Tiffany Parker. Can you go faster, Mort?"

"Not if you want to live to get there, Mrs. F."

"Sorry to be a backseat driver," I said.

"I don't like front-seat drivers, either," he said as he turned on the siren and the flashing red lights on the roof of the squad car and increased his speed a little. A few slower drivers pulled off to the side of the road to allow us to pass.

The road narrowed even more as it entered the unincorporated village of Cross Acres, a strip of gas stations, a few timeworn restaurants, a launderette, and a shuttered Woolworth's in the middle of a small shopping center.

"Cross Acres has certainly fallen on hard times," I commented, although I didn't need a visual confirmation. The problems of the village were pretty well known to everyone in Cabot Cove. Our mayor, Jim Shevlin, had spearheaded a drive with the Maine Development Agency to allocate funds to help rebuild it, an unsuccessful effort to date.

Mort had entered the address I had for Tiffany into the vehicle's GPS system. According to the map display we were a few turns from her house. He switched off the siren and flashing lights and slowed down.

"What do you intend to do?" I asked in a whisper, although it was unnecessary.

"Confront Corday."

"But what if he *is* armed?"

Mort ignored my concern and said, "I'll go to the door, Mrs. F. You stay by the car unless I motion for you to join me."

"All right," I said, "but be careful. If he has a gun— and we know he's deranged, and drunk—there's no telling how he'll respond to seeing you."

Tiffany's house was a small one-story dwelling at the end of the street. A healthy growth of grass and weeds in the tiny front lawn, and peeling yellow paint on the house itself, testified to its neglect. A late-model white car was parked in the short driveway, and Mort looked at the license plate. "Rental car," he muttered. It blocked a second car, the one in which Tiffany had driven me to Judge Borden's office. Mort pulled up, parking his car across the end of the driveway, effectively keeping either of the other cars from leaving. He'd taken off his Stetson during the trip, but now put it on, took a breath, got out, and approached the front door, his right hand resting on the weapon in the holster on his hip. He'd told me to stay with the car, which didn't mean I had to remain inside it. I got out and gently pressed the passenger door shut to avoid making a noise that might startle him.

He was almost to the door when a female shriek from inside the house pierced the air. Mort didn't hesitate, nor did I. My fight-or-flight reaction kicked into gear and I ran toward the house as Mort flung open the door, his weapon drawn. I came up behind and looked past him to where Corday had Tiffany pinned to a couch, with one hand on her throat. His other arm was raised in the air, a gun in his hand, poised to strike her in the head.

"Drop that gun!" Mort commanded.

Corday looked up, fury in his eyes. "You!" he roared at me. "Didn't I warn you to stay out of this?"

"I don't take well to anonymous telephone threats," I said. "I see you've thrown Tiffany's belongings around in the same way you trashed the production office."

Corday's lip curled. "I knew your buddy the sheriff would tell you about that."

"Actually, it was the other way 'round," Mort said,

still holding his gun on the lawyer. "She told me about it. Now let me see you drop your weapon. Don't be stupid! Drop the gun and let her go."

Corday's angry eyes moved from Tiffany to me and back again. He seemed conflicted on whether to heed Mort's warning or not. In that moment of indecision, a child's cry was heard from another room in the house.

"My baby," Tiffany wailed as she struggled to get out from under his grip.

I had to say something to break the impasse. My speaking up may have been inappropriate, but it was instinctive. "Mr. Corday," I said, "please let her go. There's a small child who needs her. Don't complicate your situation. Please, release her so she can go to her child."

"You heard Mrs. Fletcher," Mort said. "I'm running out of patience. I'll shoot you, Corday, if you don't drop that gun immediately and let Ms. Parker up."

To my relief, Corday released his grip on Tiffany's neck, got to his feet, and glared at us. He still held the weapon, although now the barrel was pointed in our direction.

Tension clogged the air in the small room. Tiffany slowly pulled herself up to a sitting position and massaged her neck where his fingers had restrained her. The child cried again. I glanced at Mort, who still pointed his revolver at Corday. At that moment I was certain that both men would pull the trigger, but then Tiffany's small daughter appeared, sobbing, crying, "Mommy. Mommy." Tiffany bolted from the couch and scooped up her child.

Her sudden movement distracted Corday, and Mort

took advantage of it to charge him. He brought his own weapon down hard on Corday's wrist, sending the weapon he'd been holding skittering across the floor, where it stopped at my feet. Mort wrestled Corday to the floor and held him there, a knee on his chest, his revolver held against Corday's temple. I picked up Corday's gun. I hated the feel of it in my hand and looked for somewhere to deposit it. But I had second thoughts and continued to hold it to ensure that Corday wasn't able to retrieve it.

Corday let out a moan and ceased being combative. He allowed Mort to turn him over and place handcuffs on his wrists behind his back.

"What can I do?" I asked.

"Nothing, Mrs. F.," Mort said as the sound of sirens outside reached us. He shook his head. "Better late than never."

Tiffany's daughter was now cuddled in her mother's arms. Her crying had stopped as Tiffany stroked her hair and whispered that everything was going to be all right. The sheriff allowed Corday to sit against the couch.

"That was a pretty dumb thing you did," Mort told him.

Corday snarled, "You don't know what you're talking about." He jerked his head toward Tiffany. "She's a liar, a dirty liar. What are you gonna do, believe some hophead?" He turned to Tiffany. "Tell 'em, Tiffany, about all the pills I got you, how I took good care of you, paid to have the kid delivered, even gave you money to put down on this house. Tell 'em, Tiffany. Go on, tell 'em!" He was shouting now.

"Pipe down," Mort said.

"Maybe it would be better if she didn't stay in this room," I said to Tiffany, indicating her daughter.

"Good idea, Ms. Parker," Mort said.

When Tiffany left the room, I realized that I was still holding Corday's gun. I opened my shoulder bag and dropped it inside.

Two deputies knocked on the doorframe and crowded into the small front room. Tiffany returned alone moments later as Mort instructed the officers to take custody of the prisoner.

"Well, look at you, the hotshot lawyer," she taunted Corday as the deputies pulled him to his feet. "Why I ever got involved with you is beyond me."

"Just keep your mouth shut," he said.

She laughed. "Like hell I will, and that's where you belong. In hell."

He struggled to break free, threatening to kill her if she didn't shut up, but the deputies held him fast.

"Maybe you'd best go tend to your little girl," Mort suggested to her. "You'll have your chance to tell a jury what he did."

Tiffany looked disappointed that she couldn't continue to berate Corday, but she heeded Mort's advice. She left the room again, returning with her child as the deputies muscled Corday toward the door.

"Book him on assault, intent to kill, and possession of an unlicensed weapon. I'll think of some more charges when I get back."

We watched the deputies lead Corday from the house and settle him in the backseat of their vehicle just as a second squad car arrived.

"You okay?" Mort asked Tiffany.

"Sure," she said, touching her skin where the pressure of Corday's fingers had left red marks. "I loved seeing him squirm."

I wished that she wasn't taking such obvious glee in her former lover's predicament. She would need to tone down her hatred of him when dealing with the district attorney's office, and especially during any testimony she would be called upon to give. Juries—and judges—don't take well to displays of revenge.

The second set of deputies entered the house and Mort instructed them to take Tiffany's statement.

It felt good, even liberating, to walk outside. Mort checked the car that Corday had driven and found the rental agreement. "I'll call the rental agency when we get back and tell them to come get the car."

I looked back at the house as Mort started the engine. Through the window I could see Tiffany talking to the deputies. Then she turned and looked outside, hands on her hips and what looked like a satisfied grin on her face.

"Not the most likable of women," Mort commented as we headed back into town.

"I know what you mean," I said. "She elected to become involved with Corday, a married man, and she took what she could from him."

"She's lucky we have him in custody now. He's a dangerous man."

"What's important is that Judge Harris's real killer be brought to justice and that Jenny Kipp taste freedom again."

"I hope it works out that way."

Mort was quiet on the way back to town. "What are you thinking?" I asked.

"I'm thinking about those movie people and how glad I'll be when they're done and gone. They make more noise than a taxi driver in a traffic jam."

I hesitated before saying, "I called you this morning, not to talk about Tiffany Parker and Neil Corday, but to say we need to get out to the airport as soon as possible. May we go now?"

"Gee, Mrs. F.," he said. "Don't I get a break?"

"It's important, Mort."

With a heavy sigh, he took the next turn toward the airport.

"May I make a suggestion?" I said, knowing I was treading on thin ice.

"What now?"

"Do you have any more deputies you can call in?"

"Why?"

"Because if things go the way I think they will, it might be time to arrest Vera Stockdale's killer."

Chapter Twenty-four

It was getting dark when Mort pulled into a parking space behind the hangar that housed the interior set where Vera's body had been discovered. We got out of the car to find two young crew members functioning as sentries outside the door. A red bulb had been inserted in the overhead lamp and was illuminated, a signal not to come inside.

"Sorry, folks. They're shooting right now. We can't let you in."

Mort pointed to his badge and said, "We're here on official business."

There was a feverish whispered discussion between the pair, but the answer was the same.

"We can't open the door right now," one of them said.

"If we interrupt the scene, we'll be fired," his companion added.

"How long do you expect them to be filming?" I asked.

They looked at each other and shrugged.

"I'll give it five minutes," Mort told them, "and then I'm going in with or without your permission." He walked back to the car and leaned against the door. I joined him there. He withdrew his cell phone and dialed a number. "Hon? I'm out at the airport with Mrs. F. Yeah, there's always a new development. No, don't wait for me to eat dinner. I don't know how long I'll be. Maybe an hour or two, maybe more. Can you put it in the fridge? I can heat it up when I get home. Sure. Me, too."

I gave Mort the note Sunny and Eric had brought to the house.

"When did you get this?" he asked.

"Last night," I said and explained the circumstances.

"So you think Zee did it?" he asked.

"If he wrote that note it's certainly incriminating. He's admitted being at the set the evening Vera was killed."

"Yeah, I checked with the carpenters he mentioned hearing. They never saw him, and they said they were out the door by eight."

"So no one can verify his whereabouts before, during, or after the time she was killed."

"He's a pretty cool customer," Mort said. "If what you say is true, he kills Ms. Stockdale, calmly goes back to his trailer, and even brings Sunny to the scene of the crime the next morning. Does he know she's Vera's daughter?"

"Apart from her father, only three people in the production company are supposed to know of her relationship—Mitchell Elovitz, Estelle Fancy, and Eric Barry."

Mort chuckled. "You know the saying: 'Three people can be counted on to keep a secret if two of them are dead.' You can't count on three people to keep a secret."

"You're right, of course. Zee rooms with Eric Barry. Eric strikes me as the kind of man who would boast of knowing Terrence Chattergee's daughter, especially since he's jealous of Zee and suspects him of flirting with Sunny."

"But if he thinks Zee is her brother, why be jealous?"

"He just learned that yesterday."

"If Zee did kill Vera, why do you think he chose this time to do it?"

"I don't have an answer for that, Mort. I can only speculate. He's had a lot of years to build up resentment of his birth mother. The motive is there. As for the timing, maybe this was the first opportunity that presented itself. The director said Zee was especially excited about working with her."

Mort nodded and checked his watch. "Yeah, the motive and opportunity are there, but there isn't much more to go on." He counted on his fingers. "We've got no gun. We've got no bullet. No fingerprints. No witnesses. I can arrest a man on suspicion, but any decent attorney will get him off. We've got no proof."

"Maybe we can entice him into making an incriminating statement," I said.

"How, Mrs. F.?"

"I'll think of something."

"I hope you do. Otherwise this will be a colossal waste of time. Are you sure we should even be here?"

"Oh, yes. If Zee is the murderer, his emotions will be running high since he's at the scene of the crime again, watching another actress, Lois Brannigan, sitting in the same chair in which Vera Stockdale died and taking over her role. I'm counting on him being off balance."

"He strikes me as a pretty self-assured young man," Mort said.

"We'll just have to see how he reacts."

Another Cabot Cove marked police car pulled up next to Mort's, its window rolled down. "What's up, Sheriff?" one of the deputies in the car asked.

"Not sure I know," Mort answered. "You," he said, pointing to one of the deputies, "go around to the back and watch the doors. Make sure no one leaves." He pointed to the other deputy. "You, just hang loose till I tell you it's okay to cut out or come in. Got your walkie-talkies?" he asked, patting his own, affixed to his shoulder.

"Yes, sir."

"And if anyone comes out of *this* door," I added, "don't let him or her leave."

The deputies looked quizzically at their boss.

"Just do like the lady says," he said. He squinted at his watch. "I think we've given those bozos enough time." He pushed himself off the car and walked toward the young men standing guard.

I followed.

"Okay, boys, I'm going in, like it or not."

"Please, Sheriff, we don't want to get in trouble. It'll only be a little while longer."

"How the heck will you even know when there's a pause in filming?" Mort asked.

One pointed to the red bulb. "When they stop, they turn off the light."

"Let's give it a few more minutes," I said to Mort. "We have time."

"You have time, Mrs. F. Me? I don't have time." He pulled off his Stetson, stomped back to the car, got in, and drove it to within a few feet of the door. Before exiting the vehicle he pressed the button that set off the siren.

A piercing wail filled the air, followed by a kind of *whoop-whoop*, then another rising, blaring note so loud I had to cover my ears.

The light over the entrance went out, and a moment later the door was flung open. A red-faced, breathless Eric Barry yelled over the racket of the siren. Fortunately, we couldn't hear what he was saying.

Mort shut off the alarms, held up his ID, and marched up to Eric. "Police business," he said. He turned to me, a satisfied smile on his lips. "Come on, Mrs. F. I think they just decided to take a break in the filming."

Chapter Twenty-five

"What in heck is going on?" Mitchell Elovitz shouted, coming up to us when we were halfway around the back of the set.

"Sorry to interrupt," Mort said, "but I need to talk to your people."

"Great! Talk to them when we're done filming for the day."

"Nope," Mort said. "I want to talk to them while they're all together—like now."

Elovitz looked to me. "Can't you talk some sense into him, Mrs. Fletcher? With everything that's happened, we're running way behind schedule. Lost minutes cost big bucks."

"I understand," I said, "but solving Vera Stockdale's murder is more important than losing a few hours of filming."

Lois Brannigan came up behind Elovitz. She was in full makeup and wore a black judge's robe, her costume for the scene being shot on the office set. "Why is this happening?" she demanded, a hand on a hip, anger in her eyes. "I had my lines down perfectly. Now you've broken my concentration."

"The sheriff here wants to *talk* to us," Elovitz said sarcastically.

"What is *she* doing here?" Brannigan asked, pointing at me.

"Mrs. Fletcher is the reason I'm here," Mort said, "and she'll be asking some questions of her own. Now, if you'll please excuse us, I don't enjoy standing in the dark arguing with you." With that, he strode past Elovitz, Brannigan, and Barry and onto the set, with me at his heels.

Thirty crew people milled about the hangar, on and off the set. The cameraman, Jason Griffin, was perched on top of a crane operated by Zee, the camera lens pointed down on the scene. The script girl, Nicole Domash, was busy taking still photographs.

Elovitz announced that there would be a break in the filming. "We're going to take ten in a few minutes," he said. "The sheriff and Mrs. Fletcher have something to say to all of us. It's a lousy time to do it, but I don't have any choice." He looked at Mort. "You'll have to wait a minute or two. Is that a big deal?"

"I'll give you five," Mort said, looking at his watch.

"This is going to be fun," I heard the actor Walt Benson say, as he walked back to take a canvas chair with his name stenciled on it.

Elovitz, seated in his director's chair, a New England Patriots' cap set backward on his head, focused on a shrouded monitor and yelled out instructions. "Audrey, I got some reflections off stray hairs on Lois. Can you spray her down? Karla, her hem is sagging. Fix it. Get me a light on the dog when we resume. Where's the wrangler?"

Hamilton Twomby lumbered over, waving the script in the air. "Thank goodness you're here. Miss Brannigan wants some lines changed," he said.

"You don't need me to change a few lines," I said. "Besides, this is not a good time."

"What *is* a good time?" He lowered his voice. "Look, we're not going to do much, but we have to make it look like we're accommodating her. Elovitz said to give it a good show. We just have to placate her. A tweak here and there should do it."

"Not right now," I said firmly. "We have some other business to attend to first." I wasn't going to allow our murder investigation to play second fiddle to rewriting the scene.

While the rest of the crew looked on, Lois took her place on the set and waited while Audrey sprayed her hair and ducked up and down in front of the actress, trying to spot the stray hairs. Meanwhile, Karla used her teeth to tear off a piece of gaffer's tape and pressed it to the underside of the hem on Lois's robe. When they were finished, Lois sat down in the wing chair at the desk. Zee moved away from the crane, leaving the cameraman up in the air, and settled on a black case next to the canvas cart that bore his initial. Behind him, partially in the shadows, Estelle Fancy shook her head, setting off the tinkling of her long earrings. Arms folded across her chest, she wore a stern expression on her face. Other crew members milled around the hangar, talking or laughing.

"Quiet on the set," Elovitz yelled.

All conversation stopped.

The director made a show of looking at his expensive watch. "Okay, Sheriff, you have the floor."

"Sorry to barge in like this," Mort announced, "but Mrs. Fletcher and I have some questions for you."

A few technicians headed for the door, Sunny among them. I hadn't noticed her when I first came in.

"Whoa," Mort said. "I don't want anybody leaving until we're done. Got that?"

Zee stood and started to walk in a direction opposite from the door, toward the large, dimly lit empty portion of the hangar.

"Hey, Zee," Mort yelled. "Get back here."

Zee turned and glared at Mort, but did as he'd been told and resumed his seat on the equipment case.

"All right, everybody, listen up," Elovitz shouted. "The sooner the sheriff and Mrs. Fletcher say what's on their minds, the sooner we can get back to work. Nicole, you've got all the shots you need to maintain continuity?"

"Yes."

"Good. I want hair and makeup ready to touch up Lois again when we resume filming." He turned to me and Mort. "Go ahead," he said, not attempting to mask his annoyance.

I'd taken the opportunity to leave Mort's side and to peruse the shelves of books that defined one side of the set. They were typical of law books, all perfectly uniform, each one looking like the next, their spines identical. But one caught my eye just as Mort said, "You're up, Mrs. F."

I turned to face the thirty members of the cast and crew. To say I was uncomfortable addressing them would be an understatement. Many of them had come to the fringe of the set, but the principals I was interested in hung back. I looked for Zee and saw that he had moved to a place out of the glare of the lighting that illuminated the set. Mitchell Elovitz sat in his director's chair, Nicole Domash perched on her stool, beside him. I also checked to see where Eric Barry was. He stood next to Sunny and Estelle Fancy. Why was Estelle here? Was she Lois's astrologer now?

"First of all," I said, "I apologize for having interrupted your filming. I know that the murder of Ms. Stockdale has been difficult for all of you, and having to change the cast in the midst of filming must be especially daunting. Sheriff Metzger and his people have been working day and night to bring the killer to justice, and I know that most of you applaud that."

"*Most* of us?" someone asked. "We *all* want to see that happen."

"Yes, *most* of you," I repeated. "Obviously, the person who killed Vera would just as soon see the murder remain unsolved."

"Are you saying that one of us on this set did the dirty deed? Snuffed out her life?" Elovitz asked, with a less than subtle tinge of sarcasm, from where he sat in his director's chair.

"That's exactly what I'm saying," I said.

An uneasy buzz of whispers ran through the crowd.

"It would be convenient if Vera had been killed by someone not involved with this production," I said in a loud voice to quiet them. "But, unfortunately, that's not the case. One of you in this close-knit family of professionals fired the shot that took her life."

I saw Sunny put her hand over her mouth to stifle a gasp. From the shadows, her father, Terrence Chattergee, emerged. He put his arm around his daughter's shoulder, drawing her into his side.

"I'm well aware that Ms. Stockdale could be difficult, and that there are many in this room who did not think kindly of her. But one of you carried your hatred for her to an extreme."

There was nervous shuffling of feet, and mumbled questions and comments.

"I wonder if I could ask one of you young men to do me a favor?" I said to some techs standing together. One stepped forward.

"I admire the way the designer duplicated a real judge's office on this set," I said, "right down to this wall of law books. I know that police looked at the spines of the books when searching for the bullet that killed Ms. Stockdale and found nothing. But there's one book that particularly catches my attention. Would you be good enough to pull it down for me?"

"Which one?" the young man asked.

"That one on the top shelf," I said, pointing. "See? Its color and height are slightly different from the others."

He grabbed a small stepladder and placed it close to the shelves, climbed up, reached for the book in question, and handed it down to me.

"Thank you," I said. I read the book's title from its front cover: "*Famous Actors' Famous Monologues*." Then I continued. "Many of you know that Vera Stockdale treasured this particular book and carried it with her wherever she went. There were those of you who scoffed at her for doing so, considered it an affectation. But to her this volume contained precious material that both inspired and instructed. She cradled it when she carried it, pressed it against her chest as though it were a child." I paused to allow what I'd said to sink in. I continued: "Unfortunately, its beautiful cover has been marred by this bullet hole."

That announcement elicited gasps, then excited chatter.

I held up the book for all to see, then turned to Mort, opening the book to a page where the bullet protruded from the leaves.

Mort drew a pair of latex gloves from his pocket and put them on. He pulled the bullet that had killed Vera Stockdale from the book and dropped it in a plastic bag. "Good work, Mrs. F.," he murmured to me.

"Thanks," I said as I closed the book and handed it to him. "You have your bullet, Mort. All you need now is the gun that fired it—and the person who pulled the trigger."

Sunny stepped away from her father and edged closer to the front of the set. "How did the book get up there, if she was holding it when she was shot?" she asked.

"The killer put it there," I replied, "after Vera either fell or was lifted into the wing chair." I turned to face Lois, who sat in the chair.

She jumped up. "I didn't realize this was the same chair," she said. She walked swiftly off the set to stand next to Elovitz. "It wasn't me. I wasn't anywhere near the set that night." She shivered.

"Go on, Mrs. Fletcher," Sunny urged. "How did you figure it out?"

"Although Vera was discovered sitting here on this set, the fact that the bullet wasn't lodged somewhere in the chair indicated that she must have been standing when she was shot. But if that was the case, it was odd that no bullet was found."

"Couldn't her body have been moved?" Elovitz called out.

"The sheriff considered that," I said, "but the laboratory technicians and medical examiner who inspected her clothing couldn't find anything to suggest that her body had been anywhere else before we stumbled upon it."

"But how did you figure out where the bullet was?"

"I've been grappling with that ever since the day we found her body. Where could the bullet have gone? It wasn't until Dr. Hazlitt and I visited a friend of his, a leading forensic specialist, that the answer came to me. It's now clear what happened. Whoever killed Vera Stockdale shot her while she stood next to the chair. She either fell into it or was placed there by her killer, who took the book that had stopped the bullet and put it on the shelf among all the others with the hope that it would not be found."

"That's pretty clever," Elovitz said.

"I agree with you," I said.

"Seems to me that it's Mrs. Fletcher who's the clever one," Mort said, "finding what no one else could."

"Hear, hear," Terrence Chattergee said, stepping forward and applauding. "But finding the bullet doesn't translate into knowing who killed Vera."

"You're absolutely right, Mr. Chattergee," I said. I turned to Audrey, the hair and makeup stylist, and Karla, the wardrobe mistress, who stood together behind where Elovitz sat. "Audrey," I said, "you told me when I visited you in your trailer that the handgun you're licensed to carry was missing."

"That's right," she said, "only it isn't missing anymore. I found it this morning right where I usually kept it, in the drawer. I must have missed it the last time I looked." She laughed. "You know how they say that men have 'refrigerator blindness,' never finding things in the fridge. I guess I have drawer blindness. It was there all the time."

"Or maybe it wasn't," I said. "Maybe whoever took it, and used it to shoot Vera, put it back."

"You think that it was my gun that killed Ms. Stockdale?" Audrey said.

"I'd say that it's a good possibility. How many people have been in your trailer in the past few weeks?"

"Geesh," she said, looking around. "About a dozen, I guess, but I was always there."

"Always?"

"Yes. Except for the time Zee came to hang my equipment rack. He chased us out of the trailer, said it was going to be dusty and noisy."

"And after Zee—Ernest Zalagarda, to be more formal—had visited your trailer was when you found the gun was missing?" I checked Zee for a reaction. There wasn't any. He sat stoically on the equipment case, eyes locked on me, his mouth set in a hard, straight line.

Audrey said to Zee, "Is she right? Did you take my gun?"

There was an edge to his voice as he replied, "Why ask me? This old snoop seems to have all the answers."

Mort used his walkie-talkie to call in one of the deputies. He motioned to Audrey to approach. "You don't have the gun with you, do you?"

"No!" she said. "I'd never take it on the set."

"Please accompany my deputy back to your trailer and give him the gun. We need to test it for fingerprints and match it against the bullet we just found."

"Sure, but I hate to miss the rest of this show."

"You can come back afterward. The deputy will let you in."

Mort whispered something to the deputy, who then escorted Audrey out.

I addressed Chattergee. "I see that you're no longer hiding your relationship with Sunny."

"I thought it was time to acknowledge that Sunita is my daughter," he said.

Benson began to laugh. "Daughter? I thought she was your little piece on the side."

"And Vera Stockdale was her mother," Chattergee added.

Benson's laugh turned into a cough and his face turned red.

"I'm glad that it's now in the open," Chattergee said, ignoring the actor. "I love having my only child back in my life, and the tragedy is that Vera, dear Vera, isn't alive to share in the moment."

"I know that Sunny is equally happy to be close to her father again," I said. "But Sunny isn't your only child. Years ago, before she was born, there was another child, born in Mexico. Am I right, Zee?"

"You seem to have all the answers."

"Vera had been given the starring role in *Danger Comes Calling*, but your wife at the time, Mr. Chattergee, suspected you of having an affair with the new star and demanded that she be dropped from the picture."

"She was wrong, of course. She always was, but I caved in that time and fired my star," he said with a dismissive chuckle. "You must read the gossip pages, Mrs. Fletcher. That entire phase of Vera's career has been thoroughly covered in the trade press."

"'Thoroughly covered,'" I repeated. "I don't recall there being much written about where she'd stayed in Mexico, and what she did there."

"And for good reason," he countered. "She went to Mexico to escape the harsh glare of the tabloids, and was quite successful in keeping her activities in Mexico private. What's that got to do with Vera's murder? Yes. I dropped her from the production. So what?"

"You dropped her from the production," I said, "until you divorced your wife. Then you reinstated Vera in the role."

Chattergee sighed deeply. He walked with deliberate slowness to where Mitchell Elovitz sat, placed his hand on the director's shoulder, smiled, and said, "Unless you have something to say that directly focuses on Vera's murder, I humbly ask that we be allowed to do what we do, namely continue with our work on this film version of your book. I can't imagine that your fine sheriff needs to see his precious time wasted with Hollywood gossip."

"You know, Mrs. F.," Mort said, "maybe we should—"

I held up my hand in a gesture to buy a few more minutes from Mort. "All right," I said, "let's focus on your wife's tragic murder. Let's—let's name who her killer is."

A hush fell over the room.

I whispered to Mort, "Maybe you should ask your deputies to join us here in the hangar."

"You think so?" he said.

"Yes, I think it's a good idea."

"All of you know that Vera Stockdale died on this set," I said to the crowd. "What none of you knows, except those of us who found her—and the killer, of course—is that a length of film had been wrapped around her neck. It was a scene from her first big picture, *Danger Comes Calling*."

I pulled out a copy of the note that had been written to Vera, and that Sunny and Eric Barry had brought to me. "This threatening note was written to Vera Stockdale," I said, holding it up for all to see. "I won't bother reading it. It was found in the trash in the trailer of Ernest Zalagarda, better known to all of you as Zee. It isn't an accident that his last name has a Mexican origin. Zee was born in Mexico because his mother didn't want a child to get in the way of her career. Isn't that right, Zee?"

"You think you know everything, don't you?" he said, jumping up from his seat. "I've been waiting to get even all my life, waiting for the perfect opportunity to arise. I knew who she was. My *abuela* told me I was the son of a star. Some star! She dumped me like a bag of trash. I tried talking to her, tried to get her to tell me why she left me behind, but she wouldn't respond. She told me to forget the past; it was unimportant. Unimportant! To who? Not to me! She denied being my mother, turned her back on me. I told her she would never turn her back on me again. I yelled for her to turn around. I wanted her to see my face, to acknowledge that her son had come to kill her. But she wouldn't face me."

"So you shot her in the back," I said.

"She deserved it. She was a b—"

"Shut up!" Chattergee shouted. "You don't know what you're talking about."

Zee turned to face him. "What are you afraid of, *Dad*? Having a bad reputation with your Hollywood friends? I should have shot you, too, for what you did—sending her away to Mexico to hide the evidence of your illicit affair. Hollywood big shots, the famous actress and the handsome, successful producer." He spit on the floor of the set, which caused everyone to gasp. "That's what I think of you, *Dad*." He put a nasty emphasis on the word. "If I still had the gun, I'd take you out, too." His laugh was sardonic.

Sunny, who'd begun to cry, said, "You're my brother."

"You can come visit me in jail like a loving sister, you know, bring me cookies and maybe a hacksaw."

"Take him in," Mort ordered his deputies.

The deputies flanked Zee, pulled his arms behind his back, and cuffed him.

"Just a minute," I said. "I want to say something to Zee."

"Go ahead, Mrs. F."

I looked at the dark-haired man, who bore such a strong resemblance to his father and his sister. "I'm sorry for you, Zee. Instead of coming forward and claiming your place with your natural family, you have been nurturing your anger all these years, letting it build up and curdle your soul. But the irony is, Vera was right."

"What are you talking about?" Zee ground out.

"She wasn't your mother. She was sent to Mexico to help out a friend, someone who had been having an affair with Mr. Chattergee. His wife at the time assumed it was Vera—and so did you—but it wasn't Vera Stockdale. You murdered the wrong woman, Zee."

"What are you saying?" Elovitz asked.

"I'm talking about Zee wanting revenge on the woman who abandoned him at birth in Mexico," I said. "The reality is that Vera Stockdale wasn't his mother."

"I've heard enough," Chattergee said. "This little meeting is over. Get him out of here and let us get back to making a movie."

"I don't blame you for wanting this to be over, Mr. Chattergee," I said. "The truth is often not pleasant to hear. You are Zee's father, but Vera was not his mother. Isn't that right, Estelle?"

All eyes went to where Estelle Fancy stood in the shadows. She looked confused, unsure of what to say or do. "I . . . I had no idea that's why she was killed. I thought she must have been cruel to someone as she always was to me. But I owed her, and she never let me forget it." Slowly, she crossed the set and stood before Zee. "I'm so, so sorry," she whispered. "I didn't know it was you. You were born when Saturn and Mars were at their zenith, a position for souls that are destined to suffer." She shook her head. "I knew it was wrong to leave you alone to face your fate. But I never forgot the baby I gave up. I'm so sorry."

The deputies escorted Zee from the hangar. Terrence Chattergee and Sunny took Estelle into their arms to comfort her.

Mort said to me, "You did it again, Mrs. F."

"I'm just glad it's over," I said, feeling my energy drain from me.

"I got it!" the cameraman, Jason Griffin, called out from his perch on the crane behind the camera. "I was rolling the whole time, got every second of it. It's better than the script."

Chapter Twenty-six

By the time Sheriff Metzger dropped me at home, I felt as though I'd run two consecutive marathons. Despite my exhaustion, I walked Cecil and put down a bowl of food. The little guy wasn't interested in how tired I was.

I went into my home office. There were a number of messages on my answering machine, including three from Evelyn Phillips. I decided they could wait until I had time to call back. I made the same decision for almost all my other calls, but I did return the one from Seth Hazlitt.

"Seth, it's Jessica."

"I hear that you've had quite a day."

"Who did you hear that from?"

"A patient, whose name I'm sure you're familiar with."

When Seth didn't offer the name, I asked, "Do you want me to have to guess who this patient is? I'm really not up to playing guessing games, Seth."

"No, I suppose you're not, considering what you've just gone through. Does the name Walter Benson ring a bell?"

I'd been standing while making the call. Now I collapsed in a chair. "Benson? The actor? A patient?"

"Yes. He arrived on my doorstep, driven by someone working on your movie. Nothing serious—tightness in the chest, that's all. A tranquilizer and a good night's sleep and he'll be fine. He was quite upset. He told me that you and our good sheriff had solved the murder of Vera Stockdale. He's a nice chap, obviously full of himself. But I suppose all handsome leading men share that trait. So tell me, Jessica. Is it true?"

"No, it's not true. I didn't solve anything. The killer confessed. What happened was that—" I paused, unable to bring myself to continue. "Seth, can we have this discussion at another time, say tomorrow? It was a busy day. Not only was Vera Stockdale's murder solved, but Mort and I were—it doesn't matter. Tomorrow?"

"Breakfast at Mara's?"

"No, not somewhere public. Come here, say at ten?"

"From the way you sound, I'd say you won't be up to making a decent breakfast. My house at ten. I'll send a cab to pick you up at a quarter to."

"Thank you, Seth. I'll see you in the morning."

I sprawled on the couch in my office and fell fast asleep, accompanied by Cecil, who curled up on a large, soft pillow I'd put on the floor for him. I was awakened an hour later by the sound of Sunny using her key in the front door and closing it behind her. Cecil barked. I got up and went to the kitchen, where my houseguest stood looking out the window over my garden.

"Hello," I said, startling her.

"Oh, hi, Mrs. Fletcher. I hope it's okay that I'm here."

"Why wouldn't it be, Sunny? This is your home, at least for the time being."

"I just wanted to come and thank you."

"No thanks are necessary," I said.

"They are," she said. "And if my mother were alive, I know she'd say the same thing. It's funny. I don't know much about her, but in my heart, I'm convinced I'm right. I just . . . I can't believe that my father would have done that, had a son with Ms. Fancy and then abandon him."

I resisted the temptation to become philosophical and excuse her father's behavior as being part of the human condition; obviously he was a man with flaws and foibles. But I wasn't in that frame of mind, and instead I said, "Many people suffered from your father's decision, Sunny. He allowed someone else to take responsibility for his actions. I don't know how Zee's grandmother came by her information, but she was proud of his origins. Zee, on the other hand, resented his abandonment mightily and allowed it to fester for all these years. It's tragic on many levels, for him, for your mother, of course, and for Ms. Fancy, too. Lots of people were hurt, including you."

"I was happy when my father acknowledged that I was his daughter. I looked forward to building a relationship with him. But now—"

"Don't decide anything like that yet," I said. "It will take a while for you to process what has happened."

"I feel so bad for Zee. I always wanted a brother." She said it in a low, drawn-out, breathy voice that testified to her disbelief that he was, in fact, her sibling. "He'll never be free, will he?"

"His fate will be in the hands of the justice system and a jury."

She sighed, then said with renewed conviction, "At least I know who my real family is now."

"I'm glad that you can take away something positive from all this," I said. "Are you planning to stay in this evening?"

"No. My father asked me to have dinner with him. I said I would."

"A good decision, Sunny. Let him explain himself. Talking is the best way to help you understand each other. Is he picking you up?"

"He's outside, waiting in the car."

Clearly, Terrence Chattergee did not want to see me. I walked Sunny to the door and she gave me a kiss on the cheek like a daughter kissing a mother on her way to meet a date.

The phone continued to ring throughout the early evening. I monitored the calls on the answering machine and chose not to pick up. One was from Eve Simpson, who said that if I was serious about not keeping Cecil, she would love to have him. That message on the machine made me smile. Along with everything else, I'd worried about the little dog's eventual fate.

After giving Cecil a final walk for the night, I succumbed to my fatigue, mental and physical, and fell into bed for what turned out to be a very deep and welcome sleep.

*   *   *

The taxi dropped me off at Seth's house at ten on the nose. He was in the kitchen whipping up French toast and frying slices of Canadian bacon.

"Smells good," I said.

"Ayuh, that it does. I was down at Mara's earlier. Hope you don't mind."

"You've already been to Mara's for breakfast?"

"Just a light one, Jessica. I wanted to hear what the rumor mill had to say about your day yesterday before I heard it from the horse's mouth, you might say."

"I feel as though I should whinny."

"No need for that. Looks like you've trumped yourself."

"Meaning what?"

"Meaning that you've solved your share of murders in the past, but never two in one day. Congratulations!"

I shook my head.

"They say at Mara's that Vera Stockdale's son killed her. Always hate tales of matricide."

"They have it slightly wrong, Seth. Yes, he did kill Vera, but she wasn't his mother. Ms. Stockdale's astrologer is his mother."

"Nobody mentioned that. They were also talking about how you personally wrestled Neil Corday to the ground, disarmed him, and—"

"Seth," I said, holding up a hand. "Stop right there. This is like that game of Telephone where eventually the truth becomes distorted. Finish up cooking and I'll tell you what *really* happened."

After I'd related to my dear friend an accurate description of events at Tiffany Parker's house and at the hangar, he asked, "How did you know that this young fella, Zee whatever his name is, was the actress's killer?"

"He was the only one with a clear opportunity. We knew he was on the scene at the right time. He admitted that himself. But that's all we had, and he knew it. What we lacked was a motive. We knew there was a threatening note. Chattergee had said Vera was upset by it. But no one could find it. When Eric Barry came up with the note, it became clear—Zee wrote it to the woman he thought was his mother."

"A case of mistaken identity," Seth said, shaking his head.

"Sad but true. He'd been stoking his anger by watching her first big movie. He even carried it around with him; Mort's deputies found it under the bed in his trailer. He was just waiting for an opportunity to get revenge; and Vera gave it to him. He confronted her while she was taking a private moment to absorb the atmosphere on the set. Vera, instead of setting him straight with the truth, made the tragic mistake of dismissing his concern. He'd planned the murder for years, even given himself a name to reinforce his mission. Zalagarda is Spanish for 'ambush,' and that's what he did. He ambushed Vera."

"But she wasn't his mother."

"He didn't know that. And while I suspected that might be the case, I didn't know it for certain either until I had the callback from my friend in Mexico, the chief of police in San Miguel de Allende. At first I'd assumed, as Zee had, that Vera had given birth to a baby in Mexico after she was dismissed from the film.

But the ladies in the hair and makeup trailer said Chattergee was a real ladies' man. And Estelle Fancy kept a picture of him in her trailer with his arms around both her and Vera. I thought it was possible that Estelle had as strong a link to Chattergee as Vera. At his request, it was she who convinced Vera to take the role. When I confronted her trying to take Vera's jewelry, she slipped and said Vera once told her she could have Chattergee *back*. If she could have him *back*, they must have been a couple at one time. She also said that Vera Stockdale had only done one favor for her in the actress's life."

"What was that?"

"It had to be when Terrence Chattergee—and he was the father of the baby—sent Vera to accompany Fancy to Mexico to have the baby. Chattergee didn't want the world to know that he'd cheated on his wife and had impregnated his lover, and Fancy wanted nothing to do with raising a child out of wedlock."

"So you figured it all out."

"With a lot of help. I may have had my suspicions, but it was Chief Rivera's willingness to dig into records from long ago that confirmed the startling news that it was the astrologer, not the actress, who bore a son in Mexico. So you see, Seth, others provided me the material that allowed me to put it together."

"Must have shocked some people in that hangar when you laid it out."

"I guess so, especially Walter Benson, who suffered chest pains. Glad he'll be all right."

"And what about Corday? I sort of liked the vision of you wrestling him down and getting his gun away from him the way folks at Mara's describe it."

I couldn't help but laugh. "Mort was the one who disarmed him, Seth. All I did was set things in motion by convincing Tiffany Parker to testify honestly about what Corday had said about getting rid of his wife, and setting Jenny Kipp up for the fall. Jacob Borden was a huge help. My hope is that the DA will reopen the Judge Harris murder case based upon Tiffany's testimony."

"Corday was never an honest, decent man," Seth said. "He was a real scoundrel in every sense of the word." He shook his head. "Those people live in a different world than we do, Jessica, different goals, different morals, different rules."

"You find people with skewed views in every walk of life, Seth. Thankfully they represent only a very small minority."

"Ayuh, that's right, Jessica. Fortunately, they're few and far between here in Cabot Cove. Eat your French toast. It's getting cold."

Chapter Twenty-seven

Four Months Later

The film crew completed filming and left town, which allowed Mort Metzger to stop taking antacids by the fistful and get back to his regular policing duties. I'm invited to the premiere of the film when it's released, scheduled to be in eight months. I haven't decided yet whether I'll go. I may wait for the DVD version to come out and watch it with my friends in the comfort of my own home.

To my surprise, Eric Barry sent me a disc on which the entire episode in the hangar, filmed by the cameraman, was captured. I watched it once and never told anyone about it. It's stashed in a box filled with miscellaneous CDs and DVDs, and I have no intention of ever watching it again.

Naturally, the aftermath of that day on the set inside the hangar was consumed by legal goings-on. The district attorney, Joe Scott, reopened the Ruth Harris case, on the basis of Tiffany Parker's potential testimony. Corday was held on suspicion of premeditated murder; his trial is slated to begin three months hence. Jacob Borden was scheduled to preside over the trial but recused himself because he'd been involved with me in developing Tiffany Parker as a witness. He did, however, preside over preliminary legal proceedings involving Zee Zalagarda's arraignment. Zee's court-appointed attorney made a motion for a change of venue, and Judge Borden granted it. His trial, also scheduled to begin in three months, will be held in Portland, Maine's largest city, where the attorney felt his client would benefit from the larger, more diverse population of potential jurors. Corday also asked for a venue change, claiming that his poor reputation in Cabot Cove would taint the jury pool. His request was denied.

While the justice system's wheels slowly turned, everyday life resumed in the town I love so much. Eve Simpson adopted Cecil and was seen everywhere with the Chihuahua nestled in her oversized handbag as she showed houses to prospective buyers. "This little dog belonged to the great actress Vera Stockdale," she would say. "I was supposed to be in the film with her but tragedy struck and—well, you know how she was murdered in cold blood. You'll love the house I'm about to show you."

Loretta Spiegel was thrilled with the way her salon looked when the film company was finished with it. After numerous people had complimented her taste, she'd decided to keep the black-and-white decorating scheme. "Everyone and her sister is doing seafoam these days," she said. "It's already old hat." At the grand reopening she hosted, Loretta confided in me that all her customers want to be seen in the same beauty parlor that will be featured in the upcoming movie. Business was booming.

Evelyn Phillips had a field day reporting in the *Gazette* on everything that had occurred. I gave her one long interview but refused her repeated requests for more. I'd done a fairly good job of relegating Vera Stockdale's murder, and Neil Corday's arrest, to a secure mental lockbox of events in my life that I preferred to forget.

The impact the entire episode had on me became evident one day while I was in my home office making notes about the next novel I was under contract to write. My phone rang.

"Hello?"

"Jessica Fletcher?"

"Yes."

"This is Waylan Geist. I'm a producer in Hollywood. I'm calling because I've just finished reading one of your older murder mysteries, *The Clamshell Murders*. I love it! Absolutely love it! I want to obtain an option for the screen rights. It would make a terrific movie, especially if it was shot right where you set it, in that quaint little town of yours, Cabot Cove."

"Oh," I said, "I'm so sorry, but the film rights for that book have already been bought."

"What a shame. Who owns the film rights?"

"You wouldn't know that person. It's an old friend of mine who lives in Maine. Thank you for your call and your interest."

The call ended and I suffered a moment of guilt for having stretched the truth. *The Clamshell Murders* had never been optioned or bought for a motion picture. I was the "old friend" who owned the film rights, and as far as I was concerned, the book would never be made into a film—especially if it meant Cabot Cove would have to become a movie set again.

James William Edward Grant, seventh Earl of Norrance,
and
Marielle Grant, Countess of Norrance,
request the honour of your presence
at their
New Year's Eve Ball
Castorbrook Castle
Chipping Minster
Gloucestershire

"Great old pile, what, lass?" George murmured to me as we both leaned forward in our seats to capture the view of the twin towers of Castorbook Castle through the windshield.

I patted my shoulder bag, which held the precious invitation, and shivered in excitement. I'd been to many wonderful places, but this would be my first New Year's Eve ball in a castle.

"Built in the eighteenth century, in the style known as Gothic," our driver called over his shoulder. "It bears a resemblance to the Palace of Westminster, doncha' think?" He was referring to the building where the houses of Parliament meet in London.

"A smaller, less ornate version," I agreed, "minus Big Ben."

"If you put a giant clockface in one o' them towers, it'd come pretty close." The driver crested the hill, leaving behind the avenue of plane trees. He turned left, taking a route around a large pond, the surface of which mirrored in the shimmering water the banks of rhododendrons along the shore and reflected the tips of the towers.

"Looks like we won't be getting in any ice-skating," George said to me.

"Good thing, since I didn't bring my skates."

"Too early in the winter for that," called out the driver, who had been eavesdropping on our conversation the entire two hours from London. "Don't get snow out here before January—most years, anyway. You'll find a bit o' frost about in the mornin'. Might see a flake or two before the New Year, if yer lucky. Been raining on and off—why I suggested we start out when we did. Don't fancy driving these hills in a storm."

"Thanks, Ralph," George said as the car pulled to a stop in front of the impressive entrance, where a series of arches, flanked by evergreens festooned in red ribbons, led to an interior courtyard.

"Happy to oblige, George. I'll be at the cousin's in Stow on the Wold a few days, if you change yer mind and decide you don't want to miss the fireworks on the Thames." Ralph handed him a card on which he'd written a phone number.

George tucked it in his vest pocket. "I'll keep it in mind."

While the men retrieved our luggage from the space next to the driver's seat, I tugged on the hem of my tweed jacket, smoothed away the travel wrinkles of my skirt, and inhaled the sharp country air. No one was out front to greet us, but perhaps they hadn't seen the car coming or heard the crunch of the tires on the gray gravel. We'd arrived a little earlier than expected.

Ralph had taken the afternoon off from his usual duties as a London cabby to drive us to the Cotswolds, where we would welcome in the New Year as guests of Lord and Lady Norrance, friends of my British publisher, which was how I'd landed on the invitation list.

Ralph cocked his head at the building as he wrestled my rolling suitcase to the ground. "Yer host, Lord Norrance—you call 'im by his title, Jessica—is seventh generation," he said. "Opens the place up to the public every summer—many of the great houses do now, you know—and does the occasional wedding or some such. Not a bad setting to launch a new life together, what? Wish I coulda done that for my daughter Allie and 'er beau, but 'er mum says 'Save yer pennies. A pretty picture won't keep 'em warm in winter.' Too practical by half, that one."

"She was very wise," I said, taking the handle of my bag from him.

"Ralph's a dreamer," George said. "That's part of his charm. But you'd have empty pockets, old chap, if it weren't for your wife, Kay." George clapped Ralph on the shoulder as the driver closed the hackney's door.

"True, and don't I know it."

A former bobby, Ralph had retired due to injuries sustained during a crackdown on gangs by the Metropolitan Police—the drug pusher was caught, but Ralph's knee was a casualty of the operation. Opting out of a desk job, he'd exchanged a life pursuing criminals for one escorting tourists, although many of his customers turned out to be his previous law enforcement colleagues. My companion, Chief Inspector George Sutherland, was one of them.

*   *   *

George Sutherland and I had met years earlier during a trip I'd taken to England to be the weekend guest of Marjorie Ainsworth, the reigning grande dame of British mystery writers. Marjorie had become old and feeble and was confined to a wheelchair, and I'd felt this might be the last time I would see her alive. Despite her advanced age and failing health, she'd recently completed what was being touted as her finest literary effort, *Gin & Daggers*, although there was growing controversy over whether she'd had the help of a ghostwriter.

Yet none of that mattered to me. Simply being able to spend a weekend with this wonderful and wise woman, whose books set a high bar for any of us other writers of crime fiction, was a joy to contemplate. However, I wasn't the only guest that weekend at her imposing manor house outside London. A number of others had gathered, which made for spirited conversation, some of it occasionally contentious. Because she fatigued easily, Marjorie had retired to her bedroom the first night of my stay, after having played the generous and welcoming hostess.

At three o'clock that morning, I was awakened by a sound coming from the direction of her bedroom. Was it a weak female voice crying for help? I got out of bed and went to find out. Marjorie's bedroom door was ajar. I stepped inside and approached her bed. What I saw horrified me. Marjorie Ainsworth was sprawled on her back, a dagger protruding from her chest like a graveyard marker.

Because of her fame, the investigation wasn't left in the hands of the local constable. Scotland Yard was called in, and Chief Inspector George Sutherland arrived to spearhead the inquiry. Not only was he charming, he was undeniably handsome, six feet four, impeccably dressed, and with eyes that were at once probing and kind. We ended up working together to bring Marjorie's murderer to justice, and in the process we developed what might be called a mutual infatuation. Over the years, it became obvious that our attraction to each other went beyond solving murders, and we wondered whether one day we would give life to our romantic inclinations. It hadn't happened, at least not yet, and our time spent together was limited. That was why I'd leaped at the chance to spend New Year's Eve with George at Castorbrook Castle.

"I'm Scotland Yard's favorite cabbie," Ralph had informed me when George introduced us. "Unofficially, of course. Had to bone up on Yard history when I was in training. Couldn't let those nobs in their fancy offices know more'n me."

London cabbies are required to go through an intensely challenging program, learning the history of three hundred twenty places of interest as well as how to find all the streets in the city, a process that can take years. Those in training—"Knowledge boys" and more recently "Knowledge girls"—often make multiple attempts at passing the test, as many newly minted lawyers do in taking American state bar exams. Ralph had passed on his second try, a source of great pride.

"Don't lose that number, now." Ralph started up the engine. "Ta, George. Ta, Jessica. See you next year!"

We waved Ralph off.

"Mrs. Fletcher, Mr. Sutherland, my sincerest apologies."

George and I turned to see a gentleman in a tuxedo hastening toward us, followed by a rough-looking man lumbering behind him. The second man was brushing his hands against the sides of his heavy trousers, raising small clouds of dirt with each pass.

"I'm Nigel Gordon, butler to Lord and Lady Norrance. We were only just alerted to your arrival. You weren't due for another two hours." He looked at his watch. "Angus will take your luggage up for you." He indicated the man behind him. "Please, follow me. The family will soon sit down for tea. Would you care to join them straightaway? Or would you prefer to freshen up before the introductions?"

"I'd prefer to freshen up," I said.

Nigel hurried us across the interior courtyard and into the entry hall, a vast marble space with fifteen-foot-high columns joined by pointed archways and flanking a half dozen closed doors and one open one. I barely had time to notice the intricate carving between the arches, the huge, holiday-themed floral arrangement standing on an oak table, the medieval statues, the velvet-covered benches, and the elaborate Oriental rug underfoot before the butler ushered us through the open door and to the base of a broad staircase, where a redheaded woman wearing a large watch on a chain around her neck awaited us.

"This is our housekeeper, Mrs. Powter, who'll show you to your rooms," Nigel said.

"We do have a lift, if you find the stairs wearing," Mrs. Powter said, eyeing us up and down.

"Actually, I'd welcome the stairs right now." I smiled, but she remained impassive.

"Could do with a bit of up-and-down after the long sit," George added.

"When you're ready, Mrs. Powter will show you to the drawing room, where the family is gathered," Nigel said, giving us a quick nod. "Please excuse me. I shall see you shortly."

He was gone before we could thank him properly, and he was not the only member of the household in a rush. Mrs. Powter set a brisk pace trotting up the steps. The staircase curved around to the second-floor landing before continuing on up. George and I were afraid to stop and catch our breath for fear of losing sight of our escort. Mrs. Powter was halfway down the hall when we reached the third floor.

"I hope these will be satisfactory." She stepped back from the open doors to adjoining rooms.

I walked into the first room. "Oh, this is lovely."

It was a sun-filled square with a four-poster bed, the gold-and-filigree canopy of which almost touched the ceiling fifteen feet above our heads. The walls above the paneled wainscoting were covered in blue silk. A pair of what might be ancestral portraits stared down at the bed and across to the window, which overlooked a garden two floors below.

"Very nice," George said. "I see Angus has already been here." He tapped the top of my suitcase, which had been laid on a bench at the foot of the bed.

"He must have taken the elevator," I said.

"No doubt. Or else he's in training for the hundred-meter sprint."

"I wonder if your room is as nice."

"Let's go see."

Mrs. Powter was still on guard in the hall. "Will you need assistance unpacking?"

"I think we can manage by ourselves," I said.

She looked at her watch. "I'll be back to collect you at half past three. Will that be sufficient time?"

"We'll be ready and waiting." I resisted the urge to salute.

She walked briskly to the end of the hall, opened a door to what was probably the back stairs—or perhaps the elevator—and disappeared through it.

"Seems we've put them out by arriving early," George said.

"We're not *that* early, are we?"

He made a show of looking at his watch. "We're not due here for one hour, thirty-five minutes, and . . . ten seconds, give or take a second."

"Oh, dear. Is it just as rude to be early as it is to be late?"

"Nothing of the kind. Besides, you'd think people who are capable of putting on a New Year's Eve ball would have all the details worked out by now."

"I suspect that if I had a hundred people coming to my home for a party, I'd feel pressured, too."

"You, my lass, would take it all in stride. Now, let's take a peek at my living quarters in Castorbrook Castle. How do they compare to yours?"

"Pretty much the same," I said, entering his room, "although your ancestral portraits appear to be sixteenth century, while mine are of a later vintage."

"How do you figure that?"

"These gentlemen are wearing ruffs." I gestured at the stiff, ruffled collars under the double chins of the aristocrats depicted in the paintings. "Mine are wearing cravats."

"I bow to your superior knowledge of historical neckwear and to your powers of observation."

"I happen to be reading a book on the Renaissance now. The author spends a lot of ink on clothing, jewelry, and hairstyles."

"See how handy it came in?"

I laughed. "I think I'd better go unpack before Mrs. Powter returns with our marching orders."

"And I'll do the same. Shall I knock on your door at twenty-five past, just to be safe?"

"I'd appreciate that."

I unpacked my bag as quickly as possible, shaking out a blue dress I planned to wear down to tea, and hanging up the rest of my clothes in a tall armoire. Buildings of Castorbrook Castle's vintage don't have closets unless the owners have added them in a modernization.

A door fitted into the paneling opened into an old-fashioned bathroom with a claw-foot tub. I washed my hands and face at the pedestal sink and used a linen towel that was folded atop a small round table next to it, before changing into my dress. I wrapped a plaid shawl around my shoulders—the Sutherland tartan, a gift from George—in anticipation of the chilly rooms for which English manor houses are infamous, and tucked a pair of reading glasses into my dress pocket.

Ready in no time, I turned in a circle, examining the contents of my room. In addition to the canopy bed and armoire, there were a single nightstand with a candle-stick lamp, a small desk and chair, a marble fireplace with a coal basket inside, and, under the tall window, a built-in seat with an upholstered cushion. I crossed to the window, leaned on the cushion, and looked out at the view of the countryside's rolling hills and the gath-ering clouds in the distance. Cows were grazing on what was left of the grass in one pasture. The spire of an ancient stone church poked into the wintry blue sky from a valley beyond. Below me was a garden; the high stone walls enclosing it matched the limestone blocks of the house. I tried to picture where the walled garden was located in relation to the house, as we hadn't had time to get our bearings before Nigel had whisked us inside.

The garden had several gravel paths that ran along the back and sides, with concrete benches on which to rest and enjoy the views. The paths crisscrossed in the middle, leaving triangular beds in the center. Flowers, withered from the cold, waved on their brown stems, the only spot of green a few holly bushes. Specimen trees and what I believed were bare rosebushes filled the beds at the far corners, but I couldn't identify any of the other plants from this distance.

A fragment of color closer to the building caught my eye, and I pressed my forehead to the glass to see what it was. It was not a plant but a patch of purple fabric. Perhaps the gardener had dropped a cloth on the ground while he was working. Would that have been Angus? I knelt on the window seat and unlatched the window. A cold breeze reminded me that it was winter, but, holding onto the casement, I bent forward. The wind ruffled my hair and the purple fabric below billowed, floating off to the side, revealing a leg and a dark shoe. They weren't moving.

"Oh, dear."

I raced to George's door and knocked urgently.

"Is Mrs. Powter here already?" George said, buttoning his vest and reaching for the jacket he'd left on the bed.

"No. Come look. Someone is hurt in the garden!" I opened George's window and directed him to look down.

"That swath of purple cloth?"

"Yes, and it's covering a leg and foot. I saw them when the wind blew the cloth aside. If she tried to call for help, no one would have been able to hear her with all the windows closed. She must have injured herself in a fall and is unable to get up."

"We'd better go downstairs and investigate."

"Should we leave a note for Mrs. Powter?"

"No time. She'll have to find us later on."

We dashed down the hall to the door we'd seen Mrs. Powter open and found both the back staircase and the closed brass gate of the elevator.

"I'll take the stairs," George said. "Do you want to wait for the lift?"

"No, I'll follow you. You go ahead."

If I'd known I'd be running down the stairs, I would have chosen better shoes, but I managed to keep George in my sight as we descended several flights spiraling around the elevator shaft. We stopped on what we assumed was the ground floor.

"Which way?" he asked.

"I'm not sure."

"You take that hall. I'll try this one," he said. "If I don't find the garden, I'll look for someone to help. Call out if you find her."

George took off, looking into rooms on either side of the corridor. I went in the opposite direction, following the stone floor, glad of the shawl in the frigid air. At the end of the hall was a heavy curtain. I pulled it to one side to discover an opening that led into a large greenhouse, its tall potted plants blotting out the dimming afternoon light. The leaves of a tropical plant just inside quaked when I stepped into the room, allowing some of the cool air to follow me. On the wall to my right was a heavy glass-paneled door that led to the enclosed garden.

I held back the curtain. "George! Down here," I called. I opened the door, but it was very heavy. I looked around and noticed some wet dirt tracks on the floor. The plant was on a rolling stand. Clearly it had been moved before to hold the door open. I did the same thing and stepped into the walled garden. A woman was lying in a puddle just beyond the door. She wore only her purple dress and brown shoes; without a sweater or jacket, her attire was no match for the wintry day. I knelt next to her, pushing her blond hair aside to feel for a pulse on her neck. I couldn't find one. I lifted her wrist to try again and was surprised to find red stains on her fingers. I wondered briefly if she was a fan of pistachio nuts. When I was a child, mine were often dyed that color, the nuts leaving my fingers and lips cherry red.

But there was no dye on this lady's lips, and from the gray color of her complexion, I guessed that she'd been dead for a while. How awful to die alone, without the comfort of friends and family around you. I shivered and pulled my shawl closer as the icy air and brutal wind reminded me not to linger. I decided I'd better go find George before there were two bodies in the garden.

I heard a bang and turned. The door had slammed shut behind me. I went to it, pulling and then pushing on the brass handle. It was locked. I peered through the glass to see whether someone was inside. No one. "What do I do now?" I muttered, annoyed that I hadn't checked to make certain that the wheels of the plant stand were positioned correctly to keep it from sliding away.

I rapped on the glass with my knuckles, but they made barely any sound. I took off my right shoe and used the heel to knock on the door again. "Hello!" I shouted. "I'm locked out here. Help! Someone help!" There was no answer, only the muffled sound of a dog barking somewhere.

I stepped back and looked up at the side of the building. All the windows were shut, which meant Mrs. Powter must have discovered that we were missing and closed the ones in our rooms, probably grumbling about inconsiderate guests.

A gust of wind caught my dress, just as it had the one of the poor dead woman on the ground. My skirt flew up, flattening against my chest. I shuddered as I pushed down the billowing material. I wondered whether I should cover the victim with my shawl, but it would do her lifeless body little good and leave me without a shield against the elements.

I walked to the outer path by the stone wall, climbed onto a concrete bench, and waved, hoping someone might notice me from one of the myriad windows that overlooked the garden. There were lights on in a few of the rooms. I could see people walking back and forth, but no one stopped to peer outside. In fact, someone drew a heavy drape across a window, undoubtedly making the interior warmer by blocking the drafts. It was bitterly cold on the periphery of the garden, and water from an earlier rain had seeped into my shoes. Even my arm-waving exertions did little to warm me up.

I climbed down and looked across to the glass door. Several yards to its left, wedged between a bush and an ornamental stone column, was another door, a wooden one, which I hadn't noticed earlier. I hurried over. Stepping into a flower bed to get to what I hoped was an exit, I yanked on the handle. The door flew back to reveal a shallow closet, its shelves packed with flower pots, garden tools, seed packets, boxes of Mole-Rid, bottles of insecticide, and bags of aluminum sulfate and lime. Even in the unlikely event I could have squeezed inside the closet, it wouldn't have offered much protection.

Well, George will find me soon, I thought as I retreated to the glass door. *He must be nearby.* I continued knocking on the panels with my shoe and at regular intervals shouting into the wind. Minutes went by with no George. The sky darkened and the temperature dropped. The trees and bushes took on eerie shapes in the gloom. Had he gotten lost? It was not outside the realm of possibility, given the size of Castorbrook Castle. Could he have become disoriented and taken off in a direction away from where I waited? And if the staff was in the kitchen or readying the ballroom, they might not hear him call, just as they hadn't heard me when I pounded my shoe on the door. I pictured George wandering the hallways, unable to find anyone to help.

Stop it, Jessica. He knows to look for you.

My teeth chattering, I switched shoes, taking off my left one and pushing my frozen right foot into the damp leather pump, and resumed banging on the door. My arm was tired, my feet hurt, and the shawl was little protection against the currents of air swirling fiercely around the enclosed garden.

A bolt of lightning illuminated the charcoal sky, followed by a clap of thunder. I huddled against the door, but it provided little shelter. I sank down, shoe in hand, and leaned against the glass, too tired to keep hitting the panes. I felt a drop of water on my head and pulled the shawl over my hair. I drew up my knees, making myself as small as possible, but it was little defense.

Then the door opened behind me. I fell backward across the sill just as the rain began pelting down.

"Jessica, are you all right?" George said, lifting me up. "I'm so sorry. I never came upon anyone to ask for help. This place is huge. I got terribly turned around and had trouble finding my way back, until just now."

"Th-thank g-goodness you're here," I said, my teeth chattering.

George closed the door to the garden and groped along the wall until he found a light switch, bringing the indoor jungle to life. Graceful plants and exotic flowers bloomed in the warm, moist air, making it quite a contrast to the climate I'd just escaped.

He wrapped his arms around me. "You're safe now. How do you feel?"

"I'm cold and miserable, George, but I'm a lot better off than that lady out there."